A

Nicole stood transfixed at the sight of Ben. Her breath caught in her throat and an odd feeling erupted in the pit of her stomach. Ben was different tonight – masterful, not shy or awkward. Without his shirt on he seemed even larger and more powerful. His wet hair glistened and there was a sheen on his bare chest, wide shoulders and mighty arms. His build was that of someone who pumped iron, but she knew he didn't. It was the manual work of the farm that kept him in peak condition. When he turned toward her, she couldn't avoid the package at his crotch.

Other Books by the Author

Masque of Passion
Country Matters
The Ties that Bind
Earthy Delights
All the Trimmings
Heat of the Moment

Always the Bridegroom
Tesni Morgan

BLACK LACE

Black Lace books contain sexual fantasies.
In real life, always practise safe sex.

First published in 2003 by
Black Lace
Thames Wharf Studios
Rainville Road
London W6 9HA

Design by Smith & Gilmour, London
Printed and bound by Mackays of Chatham PLC

ISBN 0 352 33855 5

In memory of Hank, my husband,
lover and soul-mate,
31 May 1951–27 October 2002

1

Everything always looks smaller when I get back from a trip, thought Jody, as she dumped her travel bag in the hallway and headed for the kitchen. Her rambling Victorian house was an egg box in comparison to some of the homes she'd just visited in upstate New York; the palatial mansions of the Long Island set who had hired her to add zest to their gardens. 'Landscape architecture' they called it in their florid, overstated way. Her clients were fabulously wealthy, with the confidence that comes from being immensely privileged. They had encouraged her to sit by luxurious pools, soaking up the sun and sipping long cool drinks – including the eponymous Long Island Iced Tea, no less.

But one thing they didn't know in the good old US of A was how to make a halfway decent cup of tea. She had tried to explain to Paula, her American agent with whom she had stayed in Brooklyn, saying, 'You must have a rolling boil. Water from the hot tap just won't do.' But it didn't seem to sink in. Coffee they were OK with, but a long-standing Italian community had stood them in good stead for that, and these days most New York homes sported sophisticated coffee-making equipment. Foods from a multitude of different eating houses were only a phone call away and the city abounded with a variety of cultural cuisine. But still no good tea. Jody liked the New York lifestyle, but only in short bursts. I'm getting set in my ways, she mused, as she switched on the kettle – a bronze, old-fashioned looking thing that had replaced the sleek forest-green one with matching toaster. She found her favourite mug – dark blue and Libra-oriented – it was all very reassuring.

The sentimental side of her remembered that it only needed Alec there to complete the feeling of all being right with the world. No one had met her at Heathrow this time around, and this was another reminder that she was now alone. Alec had moved out just before she went away. She reflected on why, ruefully reconstructing the scene that would have unfolded. He would have been overjoyed at first, unable to do too much for her. They would have had amazing sex, both starving after the separation. Then it would begin – the probing questions – his jealousy and insecurity.

Nah! she concluded and put him out of her mind. It's better like this. Sex? I do as well with my vibrator – faithful travelling companion that accompanies me abroad with no hassle, no peevishness, no pique and sulking, just ready to oblige whenever I switch on. But, all right, it's no use pretending. There is a part of me that wants to get laid. I'd like to feel a man's weight on me again.

She didn't mean to go down that road, and carried her cup into the hall, putting it down on the side table and letting her fingers idle over the phone. It would be so easy to ring Alec. Within half an hour, traffic permitting, they could be enjoying bed-rolling sex. Instead she sifted through the pile of mail Katrina had stacked up for her, mostly addressed to Jody Hamilton – not even Miss and certainly not Mrs.

Where was Katrina anyway – her live-in companion, confidante, friend of the bosom and keeper of the keys? Off on the town? Screwing some stunning bloke? Maybe even working, or called away on a project? She was a whiz kid at research, and had been head-hunted by various TV production companies. Jody missed her. She was easy on the eye and ear, charming, funny and understanding when it came to relationships – beginning, ongoing or suffering the death throes.

The mail was mostly junk, but there was a card from her mother. 'When are you coming down? The weather is gorgeous. I'm riding a lot (got a stunning new groom) and swimming (remember Shaun?) and taking part in a show at the village hall. I miss you. We haven't had a good chat for yonks.'

Why not? Jody reflected. Get away from the rat race for a while. She was more weary than she realised. It was all very well being lionised, with hostesses falling all over themselves to invite her to their parties, and radio and television companies clamouring to have her on their programmes, but the price was exhaustion. All she wanted to do now was crawl into bed and sleep.

'Hi there! You're home!' carolled Katrina as she opened the front door and stalked into the hall, all long legs and slender elegance. 'How was America? Did you shag anyone? This is Bobby, by the way,' and she waved a hand towards the young man who had followed her.

He was a muscular piece of rough trade who owed much to working out. An inch or so taller than Katrina, as fair as she was dark – his bronzed skin was lightly furred, his bleached-blond locks gelled into spikes. His hands were the size of shovels and, from his stance, Jody could see he oozed casual confidence. He wore deliberately baggy, very low-slung jeans that skimmed his tempting backside and promised a package behind his zipper. His sinewy bare arms protruded from an acrylic mock-goatskin waistcoat with a fake fur lining and leather ties that almost, but not quite, pulled it together over his wide chest. It was one of those retro hippy garments that had been all the rage the previous winter. Goodness knows where he found that. It looked suspiciously like something of Katrina's.

'America was fine,' Jody answered, dragging her eyes from Bobby's crotch. 'But there was nothing remotely shag-worthy.'

'You poor thing. Bobby's been staying here with me, helping guard your property,' Katrina said with a grin, as smug as a cat that's been at the cream. Jody had seen that look many times before. Katrina, not to put too fine a point on it, was a tart.

'Is my studio all right?'

'I've opened the windows a tad every day. It's been hot here. A freak April. We've been sunning ourselves in the garden, haven't we, Bobby? Had a flesh-fest. You should see me. I've got a tan, and a mark where my thong was.' She squirmed round, lifted her T-shirt, pushed her jogging pants down at the waist and stuck out her bottom.

'Show me later,' Jody said, then added casually, 'Seen anything of Alec?'

'Nope. Not a whisker. You two no longer a couple?'

'You've got it in one.'

'Thought I couldn't see any of his stuff about. What went wrong?'

'Have you got a year? Personally, I don't want to talk about it.'

'Oh, dear. Love sucks, doesn't it?'

'I'm not sure I was in love with him.'

'There there,' and Katrina put her arms round Jody from behind. She leaned back against her, inhaling her aromatic body spray. 'Shall we three go on the pull tonight? Well, not Bobby and me, we're an item, but you look as if you could do with some fun.'

'You'll take me to bars and expect a result? You know that's not my scene.'

'Give it a try,' Katrina urged. 'Maybe it's time you found yourself a new stud.'

'And maybe I need an early night,' Jody said dourly, catching a glimpse of herself in the mirror. 'Jesus! Will you look at those lines? I swear to God, I didn't have them when I left.'

'Yes, you did, but were so keen to get to the Big Apple that you didn't even notice. You look great, Jody, no more than twenty-one. How old are you?'

'That's a rude question,' she retorted huffily, leaning closer to the glass and raking through her highlighted bob in search of grey hairs. She didn't find a single one. 'OK. I suppose you'll have to know on my birthday, but that's not till October. I shall be twenty-seven then. Isn't that a bummer?'

'You're a mere baby,' Katrina said consolingly, then turned to Bobby and ordered imperiously, 'Go watch the telly, there's a love. I'm doing reflexology on Jody. Away with you.'

'There's nothing nicer than one's own bed,' Jody said, stripping off when they reached her room. She pulled on her comfortable, faded, shabby towelling robe that she found hanging behind the door. 'Are you sure you want to do this now?'

'Lie down and relax. You know it makes sense.'

Katrina placed Jody's feet on a pillow, then settled at the end of the bed and started. Jody could feel herself drifting. Katrina's skilful fingers rubbed in aromatherapy oils and massaged the sole of her left foot, kneading and stroking, working between her toes, finding pressure points that corresponded to parts of her body that were out of alignment. She had slipped a meditation tape into the player and the dreamy music added to Jody's sense of well being. The feelings in her foot were amazing, each toe sensitive to her touch. She would have fancied her had she swung the other way. As it was her toes were responding as if being manipulated by a man, each one turning into an erogenous zone. Electric charges shot up to her clitoris and nipples.

Katrina moved to her other foot, carefully covering the treated one with a towel to keep it warm. By now, Jody was almost gone – the adrenaline buzz of New York – the totally exhilarating stress level – the flight home, all combining to send her to sleep. She was vaguely aware of Katrina stopping the treatment and tucking the duvet round her, then she dropped into a well of deep, dreamless oblivion.

A phone was ringing. A landline, not a mobile. Jody groped for the receiver on the nightstand. 'Hello,' she croaked groggily, not sure where she was or how she had got there.

'Welcome home,' said an instantly recognisable voice, a mixture of county set, boarding school and her own particular brand of huskiness.

'Miriam.'

'That's me. How you doing?'

'Jet-lagged. I was asleep. Where are you?'

'In Heronswood, the centre of the universe. You know, that hick town where you were born.'

More awake now, Jody fumbled for her bag and found her cigarettes and lighter. She was going to try patches, but had put it off till after the trip. 'So, what's new?' she asked, dragging the pillows behind her and resting back, blue smoke coiling towards the lacy canopy of her brass four-poster.

'Nicole's getting married.'

'She is? Who to?'

'Name of Gregory Crawford. New kid on the block. Where have you been, kiddo? Didn't you know this? I would have thought you'd have caught up with the goss at Christmas.'

'I didn't go home. Spent it with Alec's parents in an attempt to make it work,' Jody said, getting flashes of a suburban semi-detached with all the traditional Yuletide trimmings, and Alec's mother, hot and flushed from so much cooking, falling all over herself in her eagerness to have them signed, sealed and delivered to the altar.

'Did it?' Miriam asked.

'No. It was the final nail in the coffin.'

'Sorry. He seemed a nice man.' Miriam's sympathy made Jody want to cry, till her friend added brightly, 'That's OK. We can be the Three Musketeers again, you and me and Nicole. Maybe not her. She's gone overboard about Greg.'

'Is he fit?'

'Oh, yes, he's fit all right. A tall, dark and handsome soliciter. Suave, too, into politics in a big way. Fancies himself as a Member of Parliament.'

'Can you see Nicole at Number 10? I thought she was into horses and that surly, Heathcliff-lookalike farmer. What's his name? Ben Templeton?'

'All that changed as soon as she met Greg at a garden party. I've never seen a girl so lovestruck. It's pathetic.'

'I take it you don't like him much.'

'Not much. But that's just me. You may find him as desirable as she does. Come on down and take a look. Unless you've got anything more exciting on offer. You can meet him and his friend; a rugger type called Piers. He has political ambitions, too, but I've got plans for him and he doesn't even know it.'

Miriam's voice took on a deeper note and Jody could picture her wearing a mischief-inspired smile and shaking back her tousled mane of auburn hair, hazel eyes sparkling wickedly. She always had been the most forthright of the three friends who had attended the same schools and been brought up in the same market town. Like Jody, she had migrated to London and pursued a flourishing career in publishing. She had a reputation for being ruthless – Miriam Bowater, Killer Queen, using her brains more than her well-developed mammaries to clinch deals, but she headed for Heronswood whenever possible.

'You've not found a man yet, long term not one-nighters?' Jody asked, wondering how it was that she and Miriam, supposed to be the best looking of the trio, had failed in their quest, while Nicole, quiet and shy, was about to walk down the aisle.

'Sod that for a lark,' Miriam retorted. 'I'm still the only single woman at dinner-parties given by this couple or that, where I'm bored rigid listening to smug fat husbands and their smug pregnant wives droning on about the new house, the new car, the new job and how well they're doing. They manage to be so patronising.'

'I know. Been there. Done that. They probe, too, showing an unhealthy interest in one's love life.'

'The husbands do. Leery, and asking intimate, loaded questions. As if I'd tell them anyway, the dirty bastards.'

'What is it about young marrieds?' Jody mused. 'I guess I'll be on that treadmill again. As soon as word gets round that Alec and I are history, the invitations will start pouring in, with them very kindly and quite unnecessarily trying to fix me up with a date.'

'The thought makes me shudder,' Miriam agreed. 'They don't seem to realise that we might be glad to be free spirits, doing it from choice.'

'Independent and OK,' Jody replied. 'Who needs a man, anyway?'

'Who are you kidding? I do.'

'You can't be desperate. I thought you had loads of men queuing up to get into your knickers.'

'Don't exaggerate, darling,' Miriam drawled. 'I'll admit there's been a fair few, but no one new and interesting and challenging. I've been so bored I recently I put an advert in the Woman-seeking-Man column of a freebie holistic magazine that concentrates on Getting More Out Of life. All Health Revolution, and how to improve your body, mind and spirit. Full of self-help info, you know the kind of thing.'

'Miriam, you didn't?' Jody said, laughing. Trust her to come up with some crazy idea, but the Lonely Hearts column of an alternative publication was a new one.

'I did so, just for the crack. I wrote, "Who wants to come on a quest after truth with me? Mother's boys, alcoholics, sleaze-bags, clueless idiots and other no-hopers need not reply."'

'I'll bet you didn't have any answers.'

'Wrong. I had half a dozen, rang up three, dated one and ignored the rest. It was a waste of time. I drove to Kendal as arranged over the phone, and met him in a bar. Would you believe, far from being poetic and dishy, like he said, he looked like my father and dressed like him, too. Lying toe-rag.'

'It seems to get harder as one gets into one's late twenties. But then, I've got out of the way of it, being with Alec for so long. Having said that, I could have got laid in New York – several times by different blokes.'

'What, all at once? I've always fantasised about a gang-bang.'

'Don't be daft. It didn't happen,' Jody assured her, visualising the smooth, clean-cut boyish faces of some of the men to whom she had been introduced, her American agent detailed to fulfil her every whim.

There had been older ones who had chanced their arm. Husbands of clients, or clients themselves intrigued by having a talented, artistic English woman in their midst. None of them had appealed, or maybe she was still too raw about Alec. She had opted for the non-adventurous route and had gone to bed with her vibrator.

'Well, I suggest that you take a break and meet up with Nicole and me. She wants us to be bridesmaids.'

'Oh, no,' Jody groaned. 'You mean in daffodil-yellow taffeta with sweetheart necklines and puff sleeves?'

'Not quite. I think we'll be given choices, but her grandmother is adamant about it being traditional.'

'Not *her* mother?'

'You know Deirdre. Wouldn't say boo to a goose. Her husband's a control freak and so is his mother, the manipulative Maggie. What they say goes with regard to anything that happens in and around the family.'

'And they approve of Greg?'

'One hundred and twenty per cent. Maggie's a snob who would adore to have her granddaughter a politician's wife. She's getting more unbearable daily. Your mother can't stand her, always sticking up for Deirdre, but no one takes any notice, Maggie sweeping all before her like a juggernaut.'

The more Jody listened, the more she felt drawn towards Heronswood and its inhabitants. Once, she couldn't get away from there fast enough, so strong was the lure of London. Now, she found that she needed the quiet backwater of the country town. She drew strength from it to fire her imagination. A stroll among the ancient standing stones on the remote, windy plain was enough to inspire her. She reproduced the feeling of majesty and mystery in her own work – those solid concrete pyramids and ziggurats that she fashioned, inlaid with pieces of glass, or tiles, or pebbles, anything that reflected colour and gave a sense of natural grandeur to her creations.

'I've some designs to complete for Aaron Abbotson.'

'*The* Aaron Abbotson, the film director?'

'That's right. I did one for his Manhattan home and he wants another for his mansion in Los Angeles.'

'My, my, aren't we the namedropper? I suppose he made a pass at you?'

'He did, as a matter of fact,' Jody replied, aware that she had momentarily forgotten her woman-of-independence stance. She had honestly been flattered to have captured the attention of such a man, famous for his modern interpretation of classic tales such as *Romeo and Juliet*, and *La Bohème*. 'But I kept it together and turned him down.'

'What's got into you? Taken vows of chastity or something?'

'He's very much older and very much married, and I don't do married men. Too much respect for wives.'

'Me too. Anyhow, you can work in Heronswood, can't you?'

'With Mum wittering on?'

'Stay with me. I've moved into that cottage in Baker's Spinney.'

'Rented?'

'Buying.'

'Nice one. A love nest?'

'I should be so lucky.'

So it was arranged. After hanging up, Jody showered and dressed, but before doing so, she wandered into her studio, a wooden structure that had once been a summerhouse till she extended it. There she ran her hands over half-completed works, the stone smooth under her fingers, warming at her touch. She apologised to them as if they were children she had neglected. She had a couple of orders to complete for a high-flying footballer and his glamour model wife, who had chosen her over a TV garden designer who was all the rage. She had till the autumn to deliver. Home called her strongly. Or rather Heronswood. She needed to recharge her batteries.

'Tell her to get stuffed,' advised Nanette Hamilton, serving Deirdre with a cup of coffee. She then parked herself on a rush-seated stool, jodhpurs stretched round her backside, the heels of her riding boots hitched on the strut.

'I can't do that,' Deirdre answered from the other side of the kitchen table, appalled at the thought.

'Why not?' Nanette knew perfectly well why, but still hoped to inject a modicum of fighting spirit into her people-pleasing friend. 'Nicole's your daughter, isn't she? And you are the mother of the bride, not Maggie.'

Deirdre fluttered her hands helplessly, saying, 'You don't understand.'

'I do. Too bloody much, if you ask me. I know an interfering old harridan when I see one.'

'It's all right for you,' Deirdre said with a sigh, shoulders drooping, and Nanette fought the urge to shake her. 'Ronald does whatever she says.'

'Ronald is a wimp. I'm sorry, Deirdre. I know he's your husband and all, but he bullies you and everyone he contacts, be it in business or to do with the council, but he's under his mother's thumb. I wouldn't have it. Why d'you think I split up with Allan? It wasn't his adultery so much, or him thinking he had the God-given right to walk all over me. It was his way of comparing me to his mother and finding me wanting. No woman should be forced to stand that.'

She was surprised at how heated she became when Allan's name cropped up. They had been divorced for years and, fortunately, the Manor House belonged to her, inherited from her father, so he had had difficulty in laying any legal claim to it. He'd tried, of course. Didn't they always, despite their protestations to do the opposite? But when push came to shove and money was involved, all this went out of the window.

'I'm lucky to be comfortably off,' she said, thinking aloud. 'I haven't had to depend on him for a penny. The kids have been educated, flown the nest and done well for themselves, with no thanks to that dick-head. Jody's due back, by the way. See if you can grab her and talk over the vexed question of the bridesmaids' dresses without your mother-in-law being there.'

She refilled their cups and studied her friend across the table. Deirdre was one of those genteel women who had been taught that it wasn't the done thing to answer back or stand up for herself or enjoy sex. The feminist movement had passed her by and left her standing. Now she was fidgeting nervously, almost wringing her hands that were as slender as the rest of her. Long coltish legs were hidden by drab beige trousers, and her short nondescript-coloured hair with a natural wave, pale-blue eyes and a flawless complexion made Nanette think of her as a typical English rose – but one that couldn't weather a storm. She was a pretty woman, but she hadn't a clue.

When Nanette recalled the female members of the Heronswood Operatic Society, to which she belonged, she wanted to spit. The wives of doctors, lawyers, farmers and schoolteachers, they jumped at the chance of showing off, talented or not. Some were sincere, supporting the twice-yearly productions (a Gilbert and Sullivan comic opera and the traditional pantomime), but the rest were scheming and manipulative, using it as a cover for intrigue and social climbing.

Not that Nanette was innocent. She admitted to being as white as the driven slush, but then she was free to do as she liked. Running a riding school gave her ample opportunity to sample young male talent, like her latest groom, Kevin Moore. And there was her faithful standby, the more mature handyman, Shaun Sullivan. He serviced her as well as her swimming pool. All in all, she didn't go without, tossed her head at snide remarks and went her merry way. She was promiscuous, but it did not mean she had to be a bitch.

'Ronald has invited your ex to the wedding,' Deirdre murmured apologetically.

'I don't doubt he has. Birds of a feather and all that,' Nanette rejoined acerbically. 'And I guess he'll bring *her*, too.'

'You mean his wife, Patricia?'

'I do. Jesus, but they're well suited. Haven't two brain-cells between them. Only a kind of low cunning.'

She spoke ironically, but Allan's recent venture into matrimony had annoyed her, and this was unreasonable. After all, she never hesitated to screw any man who roused her own interest. But it was the idea of Patricia becoming stepmother to Jody, Adam and Sinclair that riled her. Not that either of them thought much of her, going to their father's wedding under protest, but Nanette was happier if there was no contact between them. Nothing had changed. Allan was still the same creep that she had divorced, except that there were now two of them.

'Is Jody staying here?' Deirdre asked, casting an eye round the rangy old-fashioned kitchen where Nanette had kept most of the original features, though updating it with the latest technology.

'I don't think so. Miriam's been in touch, and wants her to visit her holiday cottage in Baker's Spinney. Jody's very busy, of course, but is putting everything on hold.'

'I'll try to see her alone,' Deirdre promised, standing up and carrying her mug to the sink.

'Don't worry about that. Just bung it in the dishwasher,' Nanette said, almost impatiently. Deirdre seemed to be perpetually apologising for existing and trying to justify that existence by becoming everyone's personal slave. 'Look. You should get out more,' Nanette suddenly blurted out. 'Do something for yourself. Why don't you join the HOS?'

'I can't sing or act,' Deirdre exclaimed, horrified.

'No matter. We need people backstage.'

'I suppose I could make tea for the cast during rehearsals,' Deirdre said timorously. 'And I do play the flute a little. Although I'm very rusty.'

'That's better than nothing. We practise at the village hall on Monday nights. It'll get you away from Ronald and his dragon mother.'

'I don't think he'll approve.'

'Stuff him!' Nanette advised.

It was 1.30 when Deirdre left and Nanette went upstairs and changed into a minuscule bikini. Riding kept her in trim, but she did not deceive herself. Her hips were too wide, her buttocks too fleshy for such a brief garment, her naked breasts were large and, like everything else when one reached middle age, tended to slide downwards. She couldn't really pin all the blame on gravity. She liked her food and refused to starve herself. She secured her mahogany-tinted hair on the top of her head, then wound an Indian cotton sarong round her, knotting it across her chest. She heard a van drive up, the tyres spewing gravel as the pool man braked round the back. She snatched up her towel and bottle of tanning lotion, a little tremor of lust in her lower belly.

Shaun was down there, fiddling with the filter system in the pump-house. He had left the radio on in the van. The theme tune from *The Archers* infiltrated the sunny scene. Two o'clock in the afternoon and all's well; so much more the National Anthem than *God Save the Queen*.

'Hi, Mrs Hamilton,' he said, in his beguiling Irish lilt. 'And it's a fine day.'

This was about the limit of their conversation: the weather and the annoyance of wasps that landed on the water's surface – he was constantly fishing them out with a net. It didn't matter. Nanette wasn't interested in the contents of his brain; only what lay in his trousers.

She angled the lounger so that it faced the sun, spread out her towel and removed her sarong.

Shaun materialised at her side, one large hand restraining her as she went to lie down. She read the signals, saw the sweat glistening on his craggy face and wetting his gypsy curls. With that raven-black hair, olive skin and peat-dark eyes, she liked to imagine he was descended from the Spaniards who had traded along the Galway coast for five hundred years.

He kissed her neck and it connected with her loins. He cupped her breasts in his calloused hands and the nipples rose, hard as cherry stones. She could feel the sun's rays burning and wanted to apply lotion; this was only the second time she had been out, distrusting this freakish heatwave. This flashed through her mind and she weighed up the advantages. To have him now and oil up afterwards, kind of get it over with and then concentrate on acquiring a decent tan, or to make him wait? His lips travelled from her ears to her breasts, his stubble accentuating the tingling sensation. His mouth softened when it closed over one nipple, sucking and nibbling, and she decided to go for it.

There was no one about, the pool and terrace concealed behind stone walls and burgeoning bushes, but, 'Into the pump-house,' he muttered, surfacing from her breasts.

Nanette was accustomed to giving orders and Shaun's brusqueness was just what she wanted. It made her feel giggly and girlish, no matter how absurd, and she broke from him and headed for the small structure close by. Screened by shrubs, it contained the electrical equipment needed to keep the water sparklingly clear. It was cool inside, bringing her out in goosebumps, and she rather wished she had stayed in the sunshine. Then Shaun followed her and closed the door, plunging them into dimness, with rays of light penetrating the gloom from small windows in the walls. The machinery hummed and water sloshed till he pressed a switch. Silence descended.

She reached for him in the same moment that he opened his arms. Her breasts chafed against his soiled white vest. She pushed it up from the waist and caressed the matt of black hair that circled the wine-red discs of his nipples and sprouted to his throat. His arms and back were equally hairy.

In fact, as she had said to Deirdre, shocking her by this disclosure of her intimacy with the handyman, 'It's like shagging the shag pile.'

He chuckled deep in his chest, and tugged at the thongs each side of her tiny black bikini bottom. She felt it fall to the stone floor, felt his bulge pressing into her from behind the worn buttonholed fastening of his jeans. She loved that feeling; the heat and tumescence before the actual disclosure of the cock, the anticipation of confronting that one-eyed serpent, the longing to see it, touch it, guide it into her depths, but only after she had been satisfied. And here lay the flaw, the fly in the ointment, Nature's greatest disappointment – the fact that the clitoris rarely made contact with the cock-root during penetration.

Once, she had thought it was something to do with her physical make-up. Then she had read more and more outpourings from enlightened females who wanted to reveal the clitoral truth. She had experimented, shown her lovers what to do, and achieved orgasm by herself or with them by rousing her sensitive little organ in the right way. The first time she had sex with Shaun she had been delighted to find that he was that rarity – a man who already had a certificate in clitology.

He practised it now, his fingers parting her labia and caressing the sliver of flesh between. As she rose towards pleasure's peak, she thought she almost loved him. She trusted him; knew that he wouldn't suddenly stop and try to fuck her without seeing to her pleasure first. He'd never leave her frustrated and angry. He wasn't one of those men who imagined that she would climax when he did, and that penetration led to completion for her. Shaun waited, very obviously enjoying rousing her.

'That's it, *acushla*,' he murmured, his voice thickening. 'Come for me. I want to feel you do it.'

This did it. She came off like a rocket, moaning her pleasure into his mouth. Without taking his lips from hers, he clasped her round the bottom and lifted her till her thighs were round his waist. He reached down and unbuttoned, his cock springing out like an animal from its cage, nudging against her bare, wet and open delta.

She flung her arms round his neck and leaned back so that the angle of her body encouraged his possession of her. He bent slightly at the knees and pushed. She groaned as she felt the bulbous head and the first few inches of cock sliding inside her, giving her muscles something to clench around.

Her spine was pressed against the cold metal of machinery. This gave him greater purchase. He lunged and she rode him, going faster. And he responded, chasing his climax, while her body shook with the force of his desire. He threw back his head and gasped, face contorted, eyes closed, mouth wide open. Then he came, and she relished the feel of hot pulsing cock spurting inside her. He paused and then lowered her slowly till her feet touched the concrete. She smoothed her hair and retrieved her bikini.

'Will you oil my back for me?' she asked, as they left the pump-house and strolled to the poolside.

Closing the door of her bedroom – with its Neo-Georgian features that followed the style of her father's Neo-Georgian, five-bedroomed, conservatory-boasting, double-garaged house on the outskirts of Heronswood – Nicole went to the computer desk and took out a leather-bound book. It unlocked with a small key. She studied her name on the cover: Nicole Carpenter – Her Journal.

Intrigued by diary keeping ever since she dipped into that kept by the seventeenth-century gossip, Samuel Pepys, she had made several forays into keeping a record herself, starting enthusiastically, then finding it gradually tailed off. This year, however, she had bought herself a journal that looked like one owned by a demure, Edwardian miss. Now, at last, she had something worth recording. Magic had entered her life in the breathtakingly handsome shape of Gregory Crawford.

I should be using a quill pen, she thought, then wrote, Monday 20 April. Here she paused and flipped back to the beginning of the year, re-reading what she had written.

'This has been the most wonderful Christmas of my whole life. And to start the New Year with Greg! I simply can't believe it. Why should such a gorgeous man want to marry me? I wish I'd been keeping this diary when I met him at a church fund raising garden party last August. I suppose I didn't want to tempt fate. Couldn't credit that someone like him would be remotely interested in me.'

She stopped reading and went to the cheval mirror that topped her reproduction Chippendale dressing table. Her father didn't go in for antiques. As he was fond of saying, 'I like furniture that looks old but is new, if you know what I mean.'

That's Dad all over, she thought, for she was savvy enough to tell the difference between genuine and reproduction. But I can forgive him this, for it is him who has encouraged Greg and let us become engaged and is spending a fortune on the wedding. I've never been so happy.

But as she critically studied her reflection, she was again puzzled as to why Greg had proposed. He was older than her, thirty-four, well educated, well spoken and worldly, whereas she was small and timid. He even referred to her as 'Mousekin'. Her hair was fair and had a natural wave, like her mother's, but whatever she tried to do, it always reverted to falling to her shoulders from a central parting. Her face was kitten-shaped, her eyes blue, reflecting whatever colour she wore – sometimes turquoise – or greyish, even green. It's as well I don't go for purple or black, she thought.

Never satisfied with her appearance, she took any form of criticism to heart. She could be told a hundred times that she was attractive, yet one word concerning her tendency to put on weight or a pimple or a bad hair day and she was plunged into the depths of misery.

'This is why I love Greg so much,' she confided to her diary. 'He praises me to the skies and never, ever puts me down. Even Gran doesn't dare say a thing about me while he's there. He charms her anyway, just as he does everyone he meets. I've never met anyone so popular. To hear him talk makes me feel so feeble. He's an orator, a caring, concerned person and will make a fine MP. That's what Dad says, too. But when we're alone and he kisses me, I get feelings I've never had before – well, only when looking at pictures of actors I fancy or playing with myself sometimes. I want to go to bed with him and find out what all the fuss is about. I wish I wasn't a virgin, for he'll probably find this boring. I expect he's had loads of beautiful women. OK, so I'm twenty-five and that oddity, a virgin. It's not for want of trying. I've had boyfriends and enjoyed going out with them and being part of a couple, but when they tried to stick their tongues in my mouth or touch my breasts or get a hand under my skirt, I've always sort of frozen. I had begun to wonder if I was a lesbian, but Greg has proved me otherwise. The frustrating thing is that he says we must wait till our wedding night. It's all very romantic and lovely of him, but I want to do it now!'

She threw down the book and sprawled among the frilled pillows that matched the floral cotton curtains that draped the tester bed. The sun slanted through the diamond-paned windows, flashing off mirrors and gilt and all the other objects that decorated this bedroom. She had always lived at home, apart from a stint at college. Her father, though conceding that a smattering of education was advantageous for girls, had chosen to invest money in his son. But the wedding was another matter entirely, and he was prepared to spend lavishly to 'see her launched', as he jovially put it, making her feel like a battleship having a bottle of champagne smashed against its hull.

Although the date was some months off, the whole house had become a power station centred around the wedding arrangements. There was so much to do – the guest list, the wedding present list, the caterers, the florists, the cars (she wanted a white stretch limo while Grandma Maggie preferred a carriage and pair), the photographer, the journalists (Greg was an up-and-coming politician), the bridal gown and going-away outfit, the bridesmaids. So far there were two, Miriam and Jody, but Greg had unearthed a couple of nieces and nephews ranging from three to thirteen, and they had to be included. This necessitated communicating with their parents, who then had to be included in the invites. A venue had already been booked for the reception and it was to be held at Leigh Grove, an exceedingly classy, extremely expensive hotel. It was so much in demand that they had been lucky to get in. Harmony singers who went under the name of Bella Vista had been hired to entertain and there was to be a firework display by Star Burst. Nicole, always used to having money, didn't give it a second thought. Daddy was footing the bill.

As she lay there thinking, she held out her left hand and admired the cluster on her ring finger. Diamonds and sapphires flashed, and in early September they would be joined by a gold wedding band. Nicole continued to watch the gems scintillating as she eased up her skirt and spread her bare legs, allowing her other hand to dip down. Greg hadn't even attempted to storm her defences. She did so now. With skill born of practice, she held her pantie leg aside, exposing the sparse fair bush that covered her triangle. Her nipples ached and she used her ring hand to push up her T-shirt, dive into her lacy white bra and pinch those pink teats. Nicole gasped. Such pleasure was almost unendurable, yet so sweet. She had to continue, bringing herself to orgasm as Greg declined to oblige.

She didn't hurry; she enjoyed pleasuring herself in a leisurely manner, though sometimes she couldn't wait, and rushed towards her climax. Now, eyes closed, she circled her clit, patted and teased it, feeling it harden. She deliberately focused on Greg, mentally seeing his features so like those of the latest in a long line of James Bonds. His voice thrilled her, too, sending tremors down her spine to her core, making her feel that he had penetrated her as surely as if he had actually put his penis inside her. She imagined him lying there, his hand, not hers, cupping her mound. His middle finger, not hers, spreading moisture up her cleft and teasing her.

She sighed and concentrated on that spot, her lips parted as if he was kissing her, his tongue exploring the moist cavity of her mouth, his thumb rolling over her nipple. That heavy, needful feeling in her groin was growing more persistent. She couldn't help increasing the swift, light passage of her fingertip over her clit. Now it was erect and, using her other hand, she stretched it away from the labia, leaving it vulnerable and showing no mercy. Wait? She simply couldn't. Had her father walked into the room she wouldn't have been able to stop. What a thought! And if Greg had seen her? The thoughts were so powerfully erotic that she panted and groaned, unable to control her orgasm that exploded like the firework display hired for her wedding.

Jody set off early, trying to avoid the rush hour. She headed west, following the signs and reaching the dual carriageway. She had left Katrina in charge and set her up with contact numbers. In a couple of hours, all being well, she would be in Heronswood.

She was glad to leave London, far too tempted to get in touch with Alec. She was missing him, lonely and restless. It wasn't amusing to go out alone. Having become accustomed to being a twosome, she missed all the little things she had taken for granted. Him driving, for example, ordering the drinks, finding a table in restaurants, booking tickets for shows. Shopping for one was depressing, although she had grumbled like mad when forced to stop work and cook. Time and again Alec had done it, and cleaned up and put away. She began to seriously wonder why on earth she had let him go. Apparently, he had been an ideal mate. Then why hadn't he fulfilled her?

It didn't take a shrink to decipher this. She needed a man who would challenge her. He might drive her mad in the process, but she would never be bored. How stupid, she thought, as the car ate up the miles and she crossed the border into Somerset. Why is it that some women are drawn towards the bad boys, the Alpha males who are calculated to cause angst? Jody loved the ones who did as they pleased. They may be infuriating, but were all the more attractive for it. And that's why, she concluded, that Alec could never be right for her. He was too contained.

She stopped off at a motorway service station, went to the Ladies, ordered a coffee, then sat there sipping it and eyeing the talent. Once it would have been a luxury to travel like this, taking her time, but now she had too much of it on her hands. There were no fanciable guys in the building. Good-looking men were thin on the ground in such places, it seemed. It was ninety per cent hubbies and daddies, the wives and children demanding chips and burgers and milkshakes. Get a grip, she lectured herself, suddenly flushed with arousal when a brash young biker came in, unfastened his leathers and took off his helmet. He grinned over at her, and she found herself smiling back. But then he was joined by a girl in a black mini-skirt and fringed jacket, all blonde and sparkly and glaring at Jody.

No chance of a quick one with him round the back, then, she thought wryly, and left soon afterwards. The best thing she could do was go home and get herself involved in this wedding and stop thinking about herself all the time.

2

The basement of Willards Club was cramped and sleazy, but immensely popular and hip amongst a certain section of society. Scarlett sashayed down the stone stairs and eased herself into the hot, smoky atmosphere, where music thumped from overhead speakers and an Italian bartender showed off, shaking cocktails.

She cast a predatory eye over the men and stared in a barbed, calculating way at the women. Ah, yes, there was Laura May, looking the worse for wear these days, though she could well afford the full works now – face lift, nose job, boob enlargement – even go for a designer vagina. She could probably do with it after the way she had used hers, Scarlett thought wickedly. The gutter press had paid her an absolute fortune for her 'kiss and tell' story concerning an elderly statesman who had been, to say the least, indiscreet when it came to getting his jollies.

Scarlett, equally well bred and educated, would have 'come out' at eighteen if the archaic debutante system had still been in operation. She shopped in Harvey Nicks and Harrods, was seen taking lunch at classy West End restaurants, appeared at film premieres on the arms of celebrities, and moved in circles inhabited by West London's rich. She had a flat overlooking the City Harbour, the outrageous rent paid by a married man of some standing who got off on being her submissive. Because he treated her with scrupulous fairness, she respected his need for privacy. However, she had never promised him fidelity and was searching for the crock of gold that would make her independent. She had learned her trade, that of dominatrix, from a professional madam. She operated regularly, running her business with an efficiency that would have not gone amiss on the stock market. Tonight her protector was at home with his wife in the family mansion in Surrey, and Scarlett was on the prowl at Willards, one of the biggest hotbeds of vice in Mayfair. Anything and anyone could be obtained at Willards for a price, if one went below. Above, it traded as a most respectable gentlemen's club.

Scarlett recognised most of the regulars and could see there was no one new about. She sat on a high barstool, posing and watching herself in the large mirror behind the rows of optics. She knew the cocktail expert, Giovanni, and he winked at her and said, *sotto voce*, 'See that man over there? He was here last time you were in and he has the hots for you. His name is Lord Sutherland, though he's known round here as Birdy – don't ask me why. He's stinking rich.'

Scarlett looked beyond her own reflection and met the hungry gaze of a portly gentleman seated at a round table close by. She couldn't see his hands, they were hidden by the cloth, but she guessed at least one was in his pants. She pretended to be unaware, combing her fingers through her long, dark hair, and running her tongue tip over her poppy-red lips. She narrowed her eyes and gave him a haughty look. He brightened, almost slobbering because, at last, she had noticed him. She crossed her legs with a provocative glimpse of stocking-tops and a flash of denuded, pink pussy – just a tantalising peep, like the scene in the cop-shop in *Basic Instinct*.

Drawn like steel to a magnet, he rose and came

towards her. He was short and rotund, with thinning hair and a flushed face that spoke of indulgence and expensive living, a likely candidate for a heart attack. He was wearing a pinstripe suit, and the trouser zip was undone round his corpulent belly. From beneath it, half hidden by his white shirt, was a thin scrubland of reddish hair and a semi-erect penis of insignificant proportions. She had been right in her estimation. He *had* been playing with himself, using her as fuel for his low-grade lust.

She straightened her shoulders and thrust out her breasts. She wore a flimsy, sequinned dress with a deep cleavage. Sleeveless and 'distressed', it had a ragged hem and a torn bodice. It had cost her several hundred pounds, but was the last word in street fashion.

She nodded towards his cock and said, scornfully, 'Put that thing away at once. D'you hear me? You horrible little man. How dare you sit there playing with it while you look at me?'

'I'm sorry. I really am,' he quavered. 'But you are so lovely, commanding and slim and tall. I think I'm in love with you.'

'So you should be. I'm a goddess and expect to be worshipped,' she retorted fiercely.

'I do worship you. I *do*! How can I prove it?' he stammered, oblivious to the other club members who stood around drinking, chatting up the women or talking about their mortgages and investments, and the sorry state of the exchange rates.

'Buy me a drink, get down on your knees and kiss my boots, in precisely that order,' Scarlett commanded.

'Yes, goddess, yes. Anything you say,' he spluttered, signalling to Giovanni. 'What would you like?'

'A Margarita,' she snapped. 'I want it in a wide glass

with lashings of crushed ice, and the rim spiced with lemon and salt. See to it, Giovanni.'

Scarlett adopted the mantle of severe mistress easily. Once she had conquered her sense of the absurd, she took on her chosen part with gusto. Hurt early in life, betrayed by the one she had loved and trusted, she had turned her back on romance, discovering that she had an aptitude for playing various roles – headmistress, hospital matron, child's nanny, warrior princess.

She paid attention to detail and was scrupulous when it came to dressing as each character. Her flat was fully equipped with the accoutrements of her profession. There were wigs and leather gear, outlandish costumes and a cupboard full of accessories to the service she provided. Her generous lover got a kick out of this, and was often subjected to one or other of her 'toys' – chains, perhaps, or rubber masks and gags or whips. Looking down at the peer grovelling at her feet, she cynically observed that he would adore it if she invited him home. She considered the proposition. He'd pay handsomely and through the nose for the privilege. No doubt he had a chauffeur-driven Jag parked round the back, and they'd arrive at her pad in style. Everything would be hunky-dory, except for the fact that he turned her stomach, but even this would be added to the bill along with the cost of her time and attention. There was no room for sentiment in Scarlett's book.

With the drink to her lips, the tequila hit masked by lime juice and Cointreau, she sat there regally, casting an eye around the crowd and ignoring Birdy Sutherland. He crouched in front of the stool, took one of her black-booted feet into his hands and commenced running his thick, fleshy tongue all over it, sole, heel, the lot. The boots were made of leather and reached halfway up her thighs, laced at the sides and close fitting. They culminated in stilettos, spiky and wicked looking. There were occasions when her slaves whimpered with pleasure as she kicked them. Birdy looked like a prime candidate for a thorough booting, with special attention being paid to his balls.

The pace of the club was leisurely. Many of the men, by day the heads of corporations or government departments, longed to shuck off responsibility. The females were happy to provide for this – at a price that was not obvious at first. They chatted and flirted and flattered, making themselves available but in a completely lady-like manner. Fluttering like gaily-hued butterflies, they performed in much the same way as Japanese geishas, though without the submissive fawning. Most, like Scarlett, were motivated by the cash, though there was a sprinkling that were genuinely fascinated by the aura of power and authority these men projected. It had little to do with either good looks or charm, for the majority were middle-aged and balding, but ruthless when it came to matters involving finance or politics or holding on to their inherited or self-made millions.

Most of them were putty in the hands of someone like Scarlett. She knew it. They knew it. So did the women who eyed her jealously and even rushed across to embrace her insincerely.

'Darling!' they exclaimed, speaking in clipped tones that matched those of the men. 'How are you? Long time no see.'

Birdy was in heaven, apparently, and she wondered if he got off on the taste of shoe polish. His erection had burgeoned, filling the area behind his flies, and she enjoyed the thought of his discomfort. No doubt he was longing to take it out and give it a good hard rub. Not yet, sweetie, she thought and, when he advanced a hand above her boot top and tried to touch her cleft, she slapped him away. He shrank back, sweating as he made obeisance, apologising for being alive.

Scarlett felt decidedly flat. Birdy was just too easy a conquest. Even another drink failed to relieve her of that crippling sense of ennui. A faint flicker of interest stirred the crowd as the red curtains at the rear parted on a stage where a girl hung upside down, clinging to a pole. She was athletic and perfectly proportioned, except for a pair of enormous breasts that shrieked silicone implants. She twisted her lithe body, clasped the pole between her thighs, cavorted on it as if she was masturbating, rubbing her crotch up and down its shiny surface, while the beat had changed to a rock 'n' roll rhythm. Her mass of teased, twisted and bleached hair hung about her, turning her into a pagan. Agile as a cat, she landed on her feet, prowling round on the highest of high heels, naked apart from a tiny jewelled cache-sex.

She danced and postured and posed, and the men leaned forward and eyed her organ-stop nipples and over-firm breasts and hungered for her to remove the last bastion that protected her from their lust. She approached one, kneeling down, thighs widespread, turning her arse towards him and sliding closer till his face was almost pressed between her bottom cheeks. He reached for her thong, trying to push it aside, but she wriggled away and, instead of fingering her, he thrust bank notes into the gem-studded pouch.

'She isn't half as nice as you,' Birdy muttered.

'I know,' Scarlett replied, aiming a kick at him to relieve her irritation and general feeling of malaise. Then she looked across to where a newcomer had just come down the stairs. At once, every nerve, sinew and hormone woke into life. 'Who is that?' she demanded of Birdy.

'Oh, new bloke on the scene,' he grumbled, annoyed that she had taken notice of him.

'Name?' she demanded.

'Don't know, mistress. Haven't seen him here before, only in and around the City.'

'Go and find out, and don't come back without him,' she said harshly, and Birdy staggered to his feet, still sporting a boner.

She was startled at the mayhem in her loins. The stranger was, possibly, the most handsome man she had ever seen. She liked height, and he was above average. She liked dark hair and swarthy skin, and he possessed both. She liked arrogance, and he stood observing the crowd with such hauteur that she wanted to come, there and then and immediately, creaming his face with her juice as she sat astride him.

'So where's your boyfriend?' Ben asked, and Nicole ignored his dour tone; this was his customary way of speaking.

'He's away on business,' she answered breathily, her pulse quickening at any mention of Greg.

Ben made no reply, but she was used to this. He was, on the whole, not much good at communicating, except when fired by talk of the farm and his plans for its expansion. She valued his company. They had been friends since they were toddlers, though it had never turned into a boy and girl romance. He was like a big brother, much more so than her ambitious and pushy sibling, Jeffrey, who had become even more objectionable since their father had been elected Heronswood's mayor.

Sitting on the dry-stone wall near the cowshed, she glanced sideways at Ben. He was large and rangy, a strong individual with mid-brown hair, and a healthy tan that remained through the winter, but then he *was* out in all winds and weathers. His blue jeans stretched over his thighs, and he was wearing a red tartan padded shirt and substantial working boots as big as boats, for he took size thirteens, about right for someone of his build – six foot five and weighing in at sixteen stone.

She had driven to Northgate Farm after having had words with her grandmother and needing to get away and gain strength from Ben's down-to-earth, blunt manner, trying to hang on to a modicum of sanity before tomorrow's ordeal. She was being taken to a wedding gown fitting, and would be accompanied by her mother (which could have been fun) and Grand-mother Maggie (that expert in the art of mortification who would treat it like a military exercise). Miriam and Jody were turning up to discuss the question of the bridesmaids' dresses. The very first meeting of its kind, and Nicole anticipated trouble.

'Naturally, dear, you want your friends to attend you on your big day,' Maggie had said in that stoical, patient, I'm-talking-to-a-remedial-child way that meant she wasn't prepared to budge an inch. 'But I do hope they are not going to insist on wearing something wild and quite unsuitable for this kind of wedding.'

'What kind of wedding?' Nicole had said, wearily. Really, it was all getting a bit too much.

'A *proper* wedding, when everything is just right,' Maggie had replied.

As usual, she had been unruffled and in control, spruce in a cream trouser suit, and fresh from UpperCut, a salon in the High Street, where the proprietor always made himself available for her. He had landed the big order to do the main protagonists' hair on the wedding morning. Nicole thought he was a creep.

The farm lay five miles from the select residential area where she lived. A full orange moon hung in the sky and the air was warm. The road had been deserted, the bushes rustling with night-hunters, and shadows lying like inky pools beneath the trees. She had crossed the stone humped-back bridge, the car tyres making a hollow sound. Water had rushed below her, darkly swirling, rippled by moonlight. She had passed fields where horses, spooked by her car, had turned skittish, kicking and neighing and galloping behind the fences.

On turning into the lane that led to Ben's home, she had seen lights ahead, and shapes had gained form and substance, and the long, low house had come into view, its beetling thatch like thick eyebrows above the dormer windows. She had driven round to the back and parked up. Attracted by the noise, cattle had drifted across from the nearest field. They lifted their white horns expectantly, their tails swishing. They were ponderous, short-legged creatures, a rare breed that Ben cultivated. Now their chestnut coats were turned to rusty black by the moonlight.

The yard was paved with cobblestones and smeared with dung. The barns surrounding it dated from the time the house was built – circa 1500. The Templetons had lived there from the beginning, and Ben was the last of the line. He had inherited everything when his father died. There was no widowed mother; she had met an untimely end when Ben was five, and no brothers or sisters. People said he had been lucky to be left such an historic place, to say nothing of acres of grassland and water meadows and a river, cattle and sheep and cornfields. Nicole knew how hard he worked and didn't envy him.

The last thing she had ever wanted was to be a farmer's wife. The country was fine to visit but she appreciated Heronswood, big enough to be an interesting, well-stocked town yet without the obstacles to be endured if living in a truly rural area – transport being one. The inhabitants of the scattering of cottages that were North Farm's neighbours, were treated to one bus a week on Friday that dropped passengers in the Market Place near Heronswood's town hall, gave them two hours' shopping, and then headed back.

'Jezebel's due to drop her calf any time,' Ben vouchsafed into the dimness. 'She's one of my best and has won rosettes at agricultural shows, a fine example of the Dorset Red.'

Nicole nodded. There seemed to be no answer to that. She stuck a length of straw between her teeth and sucked it, her mind dancing with visions of Greg, her untried body aching to feel his arms around her and his mouth on hers, such an exciting, full, almost petulant mouth. His bridgework was superb and his breath peppermint fresh. He wasn't a countryman, though professed to want a house there in due course but, at the moment, was settled in his apartment in Chelsea and his partnership with a firm of lawyers. Nicole was happy to follow him to the ends of the earth if need be.

He was arriving at the weekend and she couldn't wait to introduce him to Jody who she had not seen for months. She was to be envied, so talented and sought after. There had been an article in *Homes and Gardens* with photos of her and her unusual pieces of sculpture. Though ashamed of her paltriness of spirit, Nicole had always been secretly jealous of Jody's stunning looks, and Miriam's, too, but above all she yearned to have their confidence. They had done well for themselves, the garden designer and the publisher, and she had gone through college and come out with a degree that offered her nothing more glamorous than to be primary school teacher.

'That's a very important job,' Greg had said. 'What could be more vital to the future of this country than the education of its young?'

Whenever Nicole remembered this she glowed, and loved him all the more.

The deep lowing of the cattle was echoed from within the barn. Ben looked across, brows drawn into a worried frown. 'The poor old girl's been in labour for hours,' he said, and stood up, blotting out the skyline with the width of his shoulders. 'Better go and take a look. You coming?'

Never one to pass up a challenge, even though playing midwife to a cow went against the grain, Nicole followed him inside. The herdsman, Stan, was leaning with his forearms on the stall wherein stood the mother-to-be. Hat pushed to the back of his head, his face deadly serious, he said to Ben, 'She's getting tired.'

'Where's the bloody vet?' Ben asked, scowling.

'I dunno,' Stan replied. 'I've rung and they're looking for him, but he's not answering his phone. Off chasing some woman, I expect.'

'Or run off his feet with work. He's short staffed,' Ben returned, and fished out his mobile. There was still no answer. 'Well, Stan, looks like it's down to us.'

'What can I do to help?' Nicole asked, caught up in the drama. It was like appearing on an animal programme on TV. She half expected a camera crew and Rolf Harris to arrive.

'Go and make some tea,' Ben said without bothering to look up, intent on examining Jezebel.

'You know where the kitchen is. Oh, and bring the whiskey, too.'

'For the cow?'

'For Stan and me.'

'OK,' and she was off.

The kitchen was large and warm, with cats snoozing on a rug in front of the Aga. She knew Ben had a housekeeper, but she was absent. She plugged in the kettle and found mugs, milk and sugar while waiting for it to boil. She added a half bottle of Jack Daniels to the tray, along with a tin of biscuits, then hefted it back to the cowshed.

Stan and Ben had fixed up more lights. Attached to cables, they were slung on hooks from the beams. Stan's lined face broke into a grin as he said, 'You done well, miss. Still, if you're going to be a farmer's wife, you've got to get used to the birthing. No good you getting squeamish.'

But I've no intention of becoming a farmer's wife, she repeated to herself. Heaven forefend! As for squeamish – she was that all right, as she saw Ben's arm disappearing up the cow's passage as he tried to budge the calf. It was stuck fast. He had thrown off his shirt and fastened a plastic apron round his waist and, when he withdrew his bare arm, it was blood streaked.

'Try the vet again,' he ordered and she jumped. He'd never spoken to her like that before. She used his mobile and this time there was an answer. He snatched it from her, bellowing, 'Where the hell are you, Luke? Jezebel's calf won't come. It's a breech! You're what? Well, get your bloody pants on and get up here. I told you she had started. Trouble with you is you can't keep it in your trousers. Right. See you in ten.'

Gosh! He's so to the point and commanding, Nicole thought, impressed. Till that moment, Ben had always seemed easy-going, if morose. This was an entirely different side to him, one to be respected, even admired.

He acquired new status. He was sweating with the fruitless effort of trying to move the wedged calf. Great wet arcs made half moons at his armpits, soaking his T-shirt. She had never heard him swear so much, frustrated by the patient animal's suffering as she stood there, head lowered, mournful moos coming from her.

Fuck a duck, I'm never, ever going to have a baby! Nicole resolved, shuddering.

At long last Luke arrived, smallish, dapper and attractive in an early-forties way. His hair was receding, and Nicole wondered who he had just been bonking. He took in the situation at a glance, nodded to Nicole, stripped off his anorak, scrubbed his hands in a pail of disinfected water and donned rubber surgical gloves.

'I can't shift the little bugger,' Ben explained. 'One of its legs is stuck in the way.'

'Give me hand here, and we'll soon get it out,' Luke said with that confident aura of authority and know-how that was part and parcel of being in the medical profession, be the patient human or, as in this scenario, bovine. He took a swig of whiskey and commenced.

It was brutal and Nicole felt sick. With the aid of a rope, Luke's considerable expertise and Ben's strength, the calf appeared, wet and bedraggled looking. Stan lowered it tenderly to the straw. It didn't move. They waited. Nicole prayed inwardly, Oh, God, please don't let it be stillborn. She wasn't much of a believer, but still asked for divine intervention if she wanted something badly. Should this work and her prayer was answered, she would dutifully think about God for several days after, promising that she wouldn't forget Him when things were going well, but she always did.

There was a tense silence, and then the cow's big soft tongue caressed, fondled and licked her baby. It jerked its folded limbs and gave itself a shake. 'Thank God,' Ben said, with a sigh of relief.

Indeed, Nicole thought. I'll light a candle or something when next I go to church, and that will be soon, as the vicar wants to see Greg and me.

She walked out into the yard where the moon had moved over, lower now, but still washing everything in blue-white radiance. She stood there for a moment, listening to the vet, Stan and Ben talking, while she pondered the mystery of birth – and death. Then they came out and Luke drove off in his FWD, while Ben stripped to the waist and Stan worked the pump. The water cascaded over his muscular torso and darkened his chest hair.

'Hell! I should have waited till I got into the house,' he shouted, gasping at the icy shock, but he was jubilant, Nicole could tell. Between them – and she took pride in being a small part of it – they had saved both the mother and the calf.

He ran his hands through his dripping hair and shook droplets from his face, and she stood there motionless, unable to drag her eyes away, her breath lodged in her throat and an odd feeling in the pit of her stomach. He was so different tonight, masterful, not shy and awkward. And it was as if the clothes he normally wore were a disguise he was compelled to adopt in order to fit in with his everyday persona. Without them he seemed even larger and much more powerful. His wet hair glistened and there was a sheen on his bare chest, wide shoulders and mighty arms. His musculature was that of someone who pumped iron, but she knew he didn't. It was manual work not sessions at a sports centre that kept him in peak condition.

Of course, Ben lacked Greg's grace, suavity and style;

he was rather awkward of movement, especially in company, and his features were rugged. Now, however, she was seeing him with a fresh eye, phrases flashing through her mind – 'gentle giant' – 'a fine figure of a man' – even 'built like a brick shit-house'.

The pump squealed and he ducked his head under it. His broad back rippled with muscles, forming a V to his narrow waist. His wet jeans emphasised the leanness of his hips, the taut lines of his trim buttocks. When he turned towards her, she could not avoid the package at his crotch – his genitals promising to be in proportion with the rest of him. The thought made her blush for she had spent hours roaming the fields and woods with him during halcyon childhood days and as teenagers, and there had never been any question of her fancying him or vice versa. But now, in stunned fascination, she watched as Stan handed him a towel and he rubbed it briskly over his torso, taking his time, in no hurry it seemed, aware of her. She was relieved yet disappointed when he dragged his T-shirt over his head.

'So, tell all. I'm here, and here I'm staying for at least a week,' Jody said, flopping down in the centre of the chintz-covered settee in Miriam's living room.

It was low-ceilinged and black-beamed, with magnolia emulsion walls, a wide stone hearth with a wood-burning stove, sloping, black-varnished floorboards brightened with Persian rugs, and a quantity of pictures, ornaments and knick-knacks purchased from car boot sales and antique fairs.

Jody had only just arrived, her bag dumped by her feet; there was no hall, one simply walked straight in the front door to the parlour. From there she glimpsed another room, and beyond that the kitchen. It was small, compact and homely. She wanted a cottage just like it.

'There's not much to tell. You know about my ventures into love, or should I say, bed, with various fellas. I'll take you down to my local later and you can view the talent. Not that it's impressive,' Miriam remarked, casual in combats and a khaki sweater. 'But it's not a lot better in London at the moment. The men are shit-scared of commitment.'

'Everyone seems to be so selfish lately,' agreed Jody. 'I guess they're all frightened of failure. Everyone I know seems obsessed with making money while they can. Grab, grab, grab. I guess it's partly a reaction to all the gloom and world disasters. The new millennium's three years old now and things don't seem to be much better,' Jody said, shaking her head. 'It must be something to do with planetary alignment.'

'You know, maybe we've been given too much choice,' Miriam opined in a rare moment of serious analysis, lounging beside her, feet propped up on the coffee table. 'Especially women. We have so much freedom to make our own choices, it's great! But it can also be a bit of a burden, too.'

'Women had a raw deal in the past,' ventured Jody. Imagine if we'd have been born a hundred years ago. It would have been awful! We'd have had to have had children until we dropped – that's if two World Wars didn't get us first.'

'You should read *The Cosmic Wheel* by Shani Palmer,' said Miriam. 'Diamond Press are publishing it over here. The jacket is fabulous, and Shani is dynamic. I'll invite you to the launch.'

'I thought you were fed up with comparative religions and the sex-war?' Jody continued, dunking a Rich Tea biscuit in her coffee.

'The books sell. They're one of our most profitable lines.'

'Yeah, self-help,' said Jody. 'I've only been more aware of the battle between men and women since Alec and I split. I like settled relationships. It leaves you free to work and not be bothered with finding a boyfriend, someone reliable who you can go out with or stay in with, the sex side sorted. I'm missing that. I've been flung back into the singles pool and it doesn't suit me one bit.'

'You couldn't have been that happy or you wouldn't have asked him to go,' Miriam pointed out logically.

'I know,' Jody answered, disgruntled. 'I didn't realise how difficult it would be going it alone.'

'Oh, fuck right off,' Miriam said with a grin. 'Look at it as the next stage on life's rich journey. It isn't all bad. You can do what you like when you like, cook or not, satisfy yourself, watch what you want on telly, read in bed, have the freedom to fart. We'll go down and eat in the pub and trawl the available blokes, guess who has the biggest cock. I can guarantee it won't be the one with the biggest mouth who's always banging on about it.'

The bedrooms were reached via a door by the dining room fireplace that concealed a winding staircase. It was steep and there were niches in the thick walls. 'That's for bringing the coffins down,' Miriam explained. 'Otherwise, how would the undertakers have managed if someone died upstairs? And they mostly did in the old days.'

'Quaint,' Jody commented, not liking to think about it.

'There's an en suite shower and loo attached to my room. You can use it if you want,' Miriam went on, lifting a latch. 'And the bathroom proper is downstairs, off the kitchen, a later addition. Did you call in on your mother?'

'I did,' Jody replied, admiring the charming guest-room with its flower printed window drapes and a patchwork throw on the double bed and a pine dressing table. 'She was just coming in from sunbathing by the pool, and the handyman, Shaun, was hanging around with a hard-on. Honestly, my mother and her men. I'm sure she's gone a bit batty of late. She's incorrigible.'

'Good on her. I wish mine was like that, but she seems happy enough with Dad, though he's busy as anything with his business and she is deeply embroiled with the WI. The most daring thing she's done in ages is to be photographed in a wet T-shirt for the calendar they brought out to raise funds for charity.'

'I saw it. Mother sent me one in the New Year. I thought it was hilarious, and attractive, too, unlike the one the men did just to show that they, too, could be sexy. Uuk! What a collection of wrinklies.'

'Few wear well,' Miriam agreed, and sprung a built-in wardrobe door under the eaves. 'I've made space for you. Stay as long as you like. I've got to go back at the end of next week. Sales conference. But this will give us time to meet Greg and Piers. We're all invited to dinner at Chez Carpenter on Saturday, where we'll have our pants bored off with listening to Maggie rhapsodising about the wedding. Anyone would think it was her getting spliced. Tell you what, it's going to be fun when it happens, if her ex turns up, that's Nicole's grand-father who managed to escape the Witch Woman's clutches years ago, and your Dad and his new wife. With any luck, sparks will fly.'

'I can't wait,' Jody answered, starting to unpack her bag. Now that she had paid her duty call on her mother, she could begin to unwind. She didn't want to think of the trench warfare that was almost certain to explode with these combustible mixes in the same area, let alone the church.

The public bar of the Yew Tree was bustling. Jody had visited it in the past and it hadn't changed. This was heart-warming, something permanent in a world where the goal posts were constantly shifting.

'It's a perfect hostelry,' she said as they found a table flanked by high-backed oak benches. 'The kind of place that fulfils the American dream of how England should be, picturesque, breathing out the ambience of Shakespeare, the Globe Theatre and Good Queen Bess. Their thoughts turn to dashing highwaymen and buxom wenches, Dickensian Christmases with stage coaches and merry travellers and forelock-tugging peasants.'

'The Americans are great for the tourist industry,' Miriam returned, then plonked her enormous leather bag on the settle, took out her purse and elbowed her way to the bar. Jody, following her instructions, clocked the men without appearing to do so.

She had adopted the style so prevalent at the moment – low-slung hipster pants and camouflage colours, browns and dull greens. When in town, she dressed up to the nines if going to a club, or out on the town. It took her a while to lower her guard when she was in Heronswood, and know that no one would be judging her on what she was wearing.

'Look who I've found,' Miriam carolled, returning with not only drinks but Nicole and Ben in tow.

'Nicole!' Jody got up and hugged her, registering that she had hardly changed at all, engaged or not.

She glanced at Ben, his tallness striking her afresh. He was certainly impressive and she wondered why he hadn't been snatched up as an extra by film companies making historical epics. Then she remembered his dedication to his farm. It had probably never occurred to him to try any other form of occupation.

'Hello, Jody,' he grunted, and she thought: He's still the same.

She shifted along the settle, making room for Nicole and Miriam. Ben took up most of the space on the bench opposite. 'We've just been delivering a calf,' Nicole announced proudly.

'You what?' Miriam questioned, winged eyebrows raised in horror.

'A calf. You know – a baby cow.'

'Bull,' Ben corrected her.

'Bull, heifer, what does it matter? The thing is, I was there,' and Nicole started to go into the gory details.

'Please! That's enough,' Miriam begged. 'You've put me right off my plonk. Will Greg be impressed?'

'I suppose so. I don't know.'

Jody noticed that some of the sparkle had left Nicole's face and little worry lines appeared instead. She had the sudden absurd notion that it was a pity Ben wasn't to be the bridegroom. The way he was glancing at Nicole spoke volumes, and his looks had improved tenfold since she had last seen him. He was quite a hunk. I might try there myself, she thought, tingling at the notion of his big, broad hands cupping her breasts, and that full mouth nuzzling at her clit. He'd probably be inexperienced and have to be taught.

The minute Ben went to the bar, Jody exclaimed, 'Fawh!'

'Did you say something?' It was Miriam eyeing her.

'No. Just thinking aloud.'

Indeed, thinking dirty thoughts. Jesus, she sighed inwardly. I imagined I was doing rather well, cutting men out of my life and bed, concentrating on my friend's wedding and being serenely self-contained, aided by my vibrator. Then I see this personable man, kindly, concerned, able to aid a labouring cow, and I'm creaming my knickers and having fantasies about fucking in front of a roaring log fire, and snowy mornings tucked up in his extra long and wide bed. I've known him for ages, God dammit! He's in love with Nicole anyway and I don't want him – not really. Nevertheless – Fawh!

'We thought we'd come down for a drink before I drive home,' Nicole explained. 'Luke Prosser came – the vet. Remember? But it was Ben...'

'And Stan. That's him leaning on the bar,' Ben cut in, as he returned to the table.

'And me. Well, I didn't do much. Only made tea and stood around.'

'You were OK,' Ben growled. Nicole blushed and looked down at her fingers.

'Hi, gorgeous!' shouted the man who now weaved through the drinkers towards their table.

'Piers. I thought you weren't due till the weekend,' Miriam returned, and there was a general shuffling around as he brought over a chair and joined them.

'Full of surprises, me,' he said, smiling in a self-satisfied manner that put Jody's hackles up and she hadn't even been introduced. 'No, darling, I was this way and Ronald has very kindly told me to drop by any time, so here I am.'

'Large as life and twice as ugly,' Miriam purred acidly.

'Aren't you going to introduce me to your sexy friend?' he asked, ignoring her snub.

'This is Jody Hamilton. She's to be a bridesmaid,' Nicole said, remembering her manners. 'Jody, meet Piers Latimer, Greg's best man.'

He was bold and brash, spoke with an Oxford accent, talked a lot about rugby, with which he was obsessed, and imagined that he was the answer to every maiden's prayer, besides those who had long passed their sell-by date. Jody understood why Miriam disliked him, and marvelled at her ability to hide this and flirt with him.

'Isn't Greg with you?' she asked, drawing her leg away when Piers tried to insinuate a hand on her knee. Khaki covered or not, she cringed at the idea.

'He's not here till Saturday,' Nicole sighed, and Jody did not fail to see the hurt in Ben's eyes.

Oh, dear, she mused. As the Bard wrote, 'Love makes fools of us all'.

3

It had the rapt and rarefied air of a sacred temple dedicated to Hymen, god of the marriage bed. Would its owner and her assistants resemble high priestess and acolytes, though hardly vestal virgins? Miriam wondered.

The shop was situated in an alley off the mall. Like a dowager duchess, it was old but well preserved. The buildings had bow-fronted windows of dimpled glass and glossy green-painted doors flanked by tubs of spring flowers. There was an art gallery, a whimsical babywear establishment, a bijou café, a shoe shop with nothing on display except a patent leather boot placed in the centre of a gilded chair, a supplier of animal paraphernalia, coyly called Purrfect Pets, and the boutique, Wedding Belles.

How twee, Miriam ruminated, stepping inside the door. Chimes announced her presence. God save me from ever going down this road. I'd have to be really desperate or drunk or have lost it completely.

Jody was behind her and Miriam deduced that she was feeling every bit as sceptical. They were given no time to compare notes, an assistant popping up on cue from behind a relic of days gone by – the highly polished counter.

'Can I help you, madam?' she enquired condescendingly, a stick insect with toffee-coloured hair twisted into a coil on the top of her head and artfully arranged ringlets bobbing about her ears like corks on an Australian bush-hat.

'We've an appointment with your boss, and with Mrs Maggie Carpenter, Mrs Deirdre Carpenter, and last but not least, Nicole, who happens to be the bride,' Miriam rejoined in her most crushing tone. Snobs like this made her gorge rise. What was she anyway? Nothing but a jumped-up shop girl playing at being manageress.

'I'll tell her,' the woman answered, climbing down but only marginally. She spoke into the intercom, and within minutes the proprietress swept through the hangings that divided the reception area from the workroom behind. Sewing machines could be heard whirring like agitated hornets.

'Hello. I'm Leila Penn,' she carolled, a flinty-eyed woman in a close-fitting two-piece, lavishly trimmed with bands of cerise-dyed rabbit skin.

Animal rights be blowed – fur is definitely 'in' this season, Miriam thought, and extended her hand. 'Hi. Nice to meet you,' she lied.

'You must be the bridesmaids. Come through,' Leila said, tossing back her mane of hennaed hair that was mostly extensions, streaked round the brow with shocking pink. The hand Miriam touched briefly had square-shaped nails lacquered sparkly purple, with chalk-white bands at the tips.

Miriam followed her across the fitted carpet, past a mannequin in full bridal regalia and a bank of shelves displaying hats, head-dresses, feathers, garters, underwear, gloves, and fringed and furry bags, either in pastel shades or making bold colour statements. Customers were supposed to relax when they set foot there, the white walls, willowy furniture and dreamy though sexy posters conjuring up an impression of feminine mystique.

Miriam's first love was clothes, but there was nothing in Leila's collection to remotely tempt her.

Weddings, she decided, were just not for her. If she ever did it, and God forbid, she'd settle for a beach in Jamaica, paddling in the shallows with her chosen one, the smell of ganja spicing the air and friends partying all around them.

And there was Maggie, front-seat-early-doors, in the centre of the holy of holies, posing with all the grace of a prima ballerina. There was a feeling of expectancy as they awaited the emergence of the bride from a changing room, the fortunate or unfortunate Nicole, whichever way one cared to look at it.

'Ah, there you are, dears,' said Deirdre, expressing relief that she wasn't to hold the fort alone. She was looking decidedly harassed, dowdily dressed in something mud-coloured – trousers and a blouse that did absolutely nothing for her.

Jeez! Miriam cogitated, is this what all middle-aged mothers become? Mine is bad enough, but because she is my Mum, I don't think about it much. I suppose it would rock my world if she did a seismic shift and appeared in dreadlocks and a red leather catsuit.

Miriam wasn't easily shocked, but the thought of seeing her mother in a wet T-shirt, charity calendar or no, hadn't seemed right, any more than when she heard about Nanette's antics with her toy-boys.

Deirdre was comfortable and comforting, baking fairy cakes in little paper cases, preparing tea and toast and hot chocolate, acting like a mother should. Now she stood there meekly, letting Maggie take command.

'Right,' Miriam said, getting the ball rolling. 'What have you in mind for us?'

Maggie condescended to look at her, flawlessly groomed, and dressed in a floaty chiffon frock and matching turban, flower-strewn against a navy background. 'Several designs will be suitable. We're spoilt for choice,' she replied blandly and gestured to Leila who lifted down examples and removed their plastic dust covers.

Miriam stared at them with a sick feeling in her stomach. Dear God, she and Jody were mid-twenties, not teenagers, and these samples of Leila's wares weren't right – either in colour or style. As she had feared, though joking about it with Jody, unable to believe that these still existed, both dresses were like something worn by Snow White on an off day – one was baby pink, the other pale blue. Both had huge skirts over crinoline cages, demure necklines with a coy little dip in the middle, and sleeves puffed up like meringues, the whole trimmed with hideous nylon lace. Just the kind of outfits to stir the loins of elderly, inebriated male guests using the occasion as an excuse to be avuncular.

'You don't expect me to appear in public in *that*?' she squealed. 'Or in private. I'd rather walk behind Nicole bollock naked.'

'No doubt you would, dear,' Maggie returned pithily, exchanging a glance with Leila that hinted they were privy to information about Miriam's love-life. 'But we can't have that, can we? What do you think, Jody?'

Miriam knew that Jody wouldn't let her down. They had both talked this over before coming to Wedding Belles, already put off by the name. Deidre had loaned Miriam a copy of *Beautiful Brides*, a glossy, up-market magazine crammed full of hints and tips, photos and florid journalistic flim-flam. Obviously no conscientious bride-to-be or her mother or (what a pity she doesn't drop dead) grandmother, should be without one. Mariam and Jody had flipped through it over a bottle of Chardonnay, getting ever more raucous. They had found gowns that they liked. Aubergine silk, strapless and banded with beadwork; they had been produced by a firm called Brides Are Us. That would do them nicely, and they had agreed not to budge.

They had leched over outfits for the groom and best man, modelled by gorgeous blokes who scrubbed up splendidly, attired in black or wine-red jackets and trousers with dandyish brocade waistcoats and loosely knotted cravats.

'I'm hell-bent on hard dicks at the wedding, and shall work on those stuffy ushers and whatnots,' Miriam had declared solemnly, swaying a little as she tried to stand. 'I'm going to lurk in the gent's toilets and give 'em a blow job.'

'What? All of them?' Jody had asked, owl-eyed and disbelieving.

'You bet your ass,' Miriam had boasted. 'You think I couldn't do it? I'll make you watch. It wouldn't be the first time I've sucked off more than one bloke in a session.'

Now she remembered both the conversation and the times she had milked men of their spunk, torrid scenes flashing across her mind while she was debating dresses with Nicole's grandmother.

Nicole interrupted them, stepping out shyly from the cubicle. She looked beautiful, all the fairy-tale princesses rolled into one, every little girl's vision of a bride come true. Miriam's heart did a flip in her chest. Old ambitions, daydreams, flights of fancy associated with childhood flooded back. And this was silly, because she was a hard-boiled cynic, not someone who came over all starry-eyed when she heard Mendelssohn's *Wedding March*. But Nicole was something else. Her face shone. She was Cinderella after Prince Charming had slipped the glass slipper on to her foot. She was the soul of ballet, where handsome men lifted lovely girls in white.

Miriam was impatient to meet the author of this transformation again. Gregory Crawford. Seemed like he walked on water.

'Darling!' Maggie gushed, leaping up. 'You look utterly radiant. Doesn't she, Deirdre?' and to Miriam and Jody, 'What do you think, girls? You can see why I am going to be ever so pernickety about her attendants, can't you? Nothing must mar this. Think of the photographs. The press, local radio and TV have approached us. Gregory is standing for Parliament next year. He's a very important young man.'

'You look perfect, Nicole,' Miriam assured her, for some of the sunshine had gone out of her smile and she was glancing apprehensively at Maggie.

'You like the dress?' Nicole asked nervously. 'I've tried so many before we – that's Mum and Gran and me – finally decided.'

'On the design, of course,' Maggie cut in. 'Made to measure, naturally. Nothing off the peg, as it were. It's slipper satin with that long, long train, and the boned bodice has a romantic laced back. Turn round, child, and let Miriam see. There now, note the details of beading and embroidery? And the tiara was designed especially for us, with a matching necklace, and the veil. Shoes, too, a pair of ivory silk mules.'

Let's make it as costly as we can, Miriam wanted to say. Ronald is footing the bill, so who cares? Just as long as Maggie's happy. Money being no object, I think Jody and me will stick to our guns and get what we want.

Leila, spurred by professional pride, was adjusting and tweaking, patting and smoothing the gown. 'There now,' she said on a satisfied hiss, stepping back. 'I've made those teeny adjustments at the waist and it is a perfect fit. I don't imagine you'll be putting that inch or so back before the Great Day.'

'She won't, I promise you,' Maggie vowed. 'She's coming to Pilates classes with me, aren't you, darling? And you, too, Deirdre. You're looking out of condition.'

Miriam had heard enough. 'So you'll see about those gowns, Leila? Order them or whatever?' she demanded, flourishing the magazine under her nose, opened at the relevant page.

'I can. Wedding Belles is the stockist for many famous makes, besides our own,' the designer answered in a tone that could have frozen steel, obviously put out because her creations had not found favour.

'I'm not at all sure,' Maggie butted in. 'That colour. It's too dark, more suitable for a funeral than a wedding. What about the four junior flower-girls and the two little boys?'

'Lavender or strong pink will go well with it, and the pages are wearing miniature tuxedos anyway,' Nicole piped up from the back, all eyes switching to her. It was as if a tailor's dummy had spoken.

'We'll talk about it and let you know,' Maggie started to say but Nicole broke in.

'What is there to talk about? I like the dresses. I want Miriam and Jody to decide. What does it matter anyway? By next day it will all be forgotten,' Nicole shouted, showing a rare flash of stubborn temper.

'All right, dear. Don't get upset,' Maggie replied, hauling on the reins of her faithful steeds, Common Sense and Respectability. 'You are not to worry. I expect you're tired and suffering from bridal nerves. It's a tremendous strain on all of us.'

'Then why do it?' Miriam burst out, unable to hold her tongue any longer. 'Like Christmas, weddings have become a commercial nightmare, losing their true meaning. Where are the solemn vows, the commitment, and the 'till death us do part?' It's turned into a fucking circus. *What's it all about, Alfie?'*

'Miriam! Your language! Really. You always were hotheaded and self-willed. I'm not sure it's a good idea for you to be a bridesmaid.'

'I want her,' Nicole muttered mulishly. Leila hovered, wanting to snatch the dress off her lest she cry over it. Emotional scenes were not the best environments for costly merchandise.

'Dear, please listen to what Maggie is saying,' interposed Deirdre, but so feebly that Miriam wanted to slap her. 'She knows best.'

'It's my bloody wedding!' Nicole fired back, cheeks red and tears in her eyes.

'This is all your fault,' hissed Maggie, glaring at Miriam and Jody. 'It was going like clockwork until you came.'

'And you imagined that you could decide what we were going to wear, something we'd look rubbish in? I don't think so,' Miriam retorted, standing her ground.

'No way,' added Jody, staunchly. 'Much as we love you, Nicole, it's a matter of principle.'

'And not wanting to look like clowns. You're so weird about this shit,' expounded Miriam, flashing her eyes at Maggie. 'Times have changed or haven't you noticed?'

Maggie remained icily calm. Miriam knew that she had marked her card, however, and she would have to pay for her defiance in the not too distant future. Probably during the wedding festivities. She almost decided to jack it in, tell them to go find some other stooge. But the appeal in Nicole's eyes could not be denied. A compromise had to be found. How, she didn't know, for neither she nor the Witch Woman were prepared to back down. It seemed she was the prime target, though Jody was her staunch supporter. Whereas Miriam throve on a fight, Jody was more easy-going, but she suddenly came up with a suggestion, plucking it out of the blue.

'Why don't you chew it over with the bridegroom?'

There was a second's stunned silence, then, 'It isn't lucky for him to have anything to do with the ladies' outfits,' said Leila, scandalised.

'I thought that was simply the bride's gown,' Jody answered, sweetly reasonable, levelling a 'shut-up' glance at Miriam.

'Well, yes, you may be right, but generally the groom concentrates on booking limousines and selecting sidemen and buying gifts for the bridesmaids,' Leila conceded doubtfully, thrown by this uproar.

'What do you think, Nicole? Shall we show him this magazine? Ask him to decide?' Jody said.

'Why not?' Nicole agreed, flushed with defiance as she faced her grandmother.

'It's most irregular,' Maggie grumbled, temporarily out-voted. 'But if it's what you want, then we'll see. But I insist on being there.'

Saturday night, and Jody had been invited to dinner at the Carpenter abode, whimsically called The Hollies. This was on account of a small bush of this species struggling to exist in the garden that had been ruthlessly attacked by a gang of overpaid professionals who had laid it down to blue decking and water features.

She and Miriam had spent a hilarious time deciding what to wear. It was obvious that Maggie would be present. 'Where does that woman get her va-va-voom? I don't know what she's on, but I want some of it. And if Greg's there, then his sidekick will come, too – Piers,' Miriam stated, standing in her bedroom, wearing a pair of briefs and no bra. 'There will be Deirdre and Ronald, Nicole, you and me and I don't know who else. Let's hope a few stallions turn up. I could do with getting some fun out of all of this.'

'So could I,' Jody sighed, wondering for the umpteenth time why she had let herself in for this charade. She should be looking up old boyfriends and maybe renewing their acquaintance. Soon, there might be a new significant other in her life, but it was unlikely to happen at a country wedding.

'I thought you weren't interested and had decided on celibacy?' Miriam rejoined, dragging a see-through top over her head and adjusting it round her breasts. 'I can't really wear a bra with this, can I? It's designed to show tit.'

Jody shrugged, envying her friend's insouciance. She had such a perfect figure that she looked amazing in anything. These latest fashions for showing as much of the female form as possible without being arrested suited her down to the ground. A few spangles discreetly position formed a screen between her pointed nipples and the onlooker. She added a fiercely expensive designer skirt made of tatty pieces of denim that had once been jeans, fly buttons, torn down pockets, a flashy belt slung round her hips and, miraculously, it didn't look scruffy. Her shoes were Milan made, spindle heeled with pointed toes. Her legs were bare, chunky jewellery draped her neck, wrists and hung from her ears. She should have looked like a brazen, scummy little tart. She didn't. She looked a million dollars. It just wasn't fair.

'Why so glum, chum?' she asked settling beside Jody on the bed, smelling very high of Givenchy's *L'Heure Bleue*.

Jody wanted to touch her smooth brown knees displayed as the skirt rode up. It wasn't yet summer, but Miriam's skin was naturally olive and never looked pasty white, whereas Jody had to struggle to get brown. Even so, 'Have you been under the sun-lamp?' she accused suspiciously.

'Thought you'd never ask,' Miriam chuckled. 'I had a session with the Mist-on Tan system. You simply go into a special shower-style cubicle and are sprayed for a minute by a tanning moisteriser. The colour comes on after a few hours and lasts several days. I'm well chuffed.'

'I want it.'

'When we get back. It's difficult to find outside of London.'

Jody had already slipped into a little black number, infinitely suitable for most occasions but with a modern slant, off one shoulder, spangled with diamanté glitter. In it she felt as sleek as a seal and topped it up with black seamed stockings, court shoes, and dangling chain earrings.

'You're looking fit,' Miriam commented. 'Why don't we do a lesbian scene some time?'

This threw Jody completely. 'I dunno – I never – have you?'

'Yes,' Miriam answered levelly, leaning towards the cheval mirror on its swinging stand and touching a trace more mascara to her already loaded lashes.

'I didn't know. Was it good?' Jody felt hot inside, picturing that lovely full red mouth eating pussy.

'The best,' Miriam said, arching her brows and squinting at her profile. 'Oh, boy, yes! Women know what women want. I have never been treated so well, before or since.'

'But you haven't gone over?'

'To the other side? Not entirely, but it doesn't mean

that I won't do it again given the chance. Why shouldn't we enjoy the best of both worlds?'

'I don't know,' Jody said dubiously. 'It must seem very odd – no cock, I mean.'

'Who said? Haven't you heard of a strap-on? Anyway, who really needs penetration when there are tongues and fingers to bring you off? Have you ever come with a man inside you? No? Well, neither have I. It's all down to the clit.'

Jody's own little organ began to tingle. She had never had this sort of conversation with Miriam before; they had been intimate, but not quite like this. Was it something to do with the wedding fever invading Heronswood via The Hollies? A kind of build up of pheromones, like in some great hive, where each individual was being taken over by primordial lust. What Jody had just said was true. Women refused to admit it, driven by some misguided desire to protect men and their delicate egos, but it was still common for women to fake orgasm. Yet not, apparently, if one was a daughter of Lesbos.

She felt decidedly horny. It was too long since she had had sex with someone else. She wanted to be held in warm arms, caressed as if she was a delicate blossom, giving and receiving affection and pleasure. And that time afterwards when, provided her partner didn't roll over and start snoring, they lay together in companionable peace, chatting of inconsequential matters, sharing a glass of wine or one of them getting up and making a cup of tea. Prosaic, but necessary to the human psyche.

She mentioned this to Miriam, who replied, 'Really?'

'Yes, and what's "really?" got to do with it?'

'You've just chucked Alec, haven't you? And presumably you had plenty of opportunity to cosy up to him.'

There was no answer to this, only what she had gone over before with her too-perceptive friend. Miriam gave herself a final check, hair, make-up and nails, then picked up her bag.

'Right. Hats and coats,' Miriam said, in the bossy tones of a games mistress. 'Have you got a pack of three?'

'No,' Jody answered crossly. She draped her pashmina round her shoulders. 'I'm not going to need them.'

'Chuh! A girl should be prepared,' Miriam advised, adding a short suede jacket cut Levi-style that part-covered her draughty top.

'Are you?' Jody was tired of this conversation.

'Me? I'm a love pariah at present. Nobody wants to bang me – except Piers, and I'm playing that fish real cool.'

'I think you scare them off,' Jody suggested, and they left the cottage.

'Enough, already,' Miriam snapped. 'Let's go.'

'There was a row at Wedding Belles. I sometimes wish Greg and I could elope to Gretna Green or somewhere, maybe Iceland, away from relatives and all the crap,' Nicole confided in her journal. 'When he asked me to marry him, I didn't realise the shit that went with it. Of course, it's heaven to wear a white dress, though I'm not sure about taking centre stage. I'll leave that to Maggie. Jody and Miriam are knockouts. Whatever they put on looks wicked. I wish it was over, yet don't, in a way. Greg arrived this morning. It's wonderful to see him. He drove me to the Dove Inn for lunch and we stopped on the way back. It was a quiet lane with no one about. He kissed me ... a proper French kiss, all tongues, and pushed up my jumper and I wished I had on a more glamorous bra, but the white cotton one from Marks and Sparks seemed to delight him. He sort of rolled his thumb over my nipples and it made me ache inside. I was in the passenger seat beside him, and he took my hand and put it on his crotch. I could feel his erection. It was so big and hot and solid, even through his jeans.'

She paused, reliving the moment, experiencing the ache again. It was as if there was a coiled spring deep in her womb, just waiting to be released. She wanted to go on writing, but used her left hand to repeat his actions, lightly cruising over her panties, feeling the springy bush that covered her mound, finding the divide, entering it, though it was still covered by her knickers. This is what Greg had done, at first.

She started recounting it, her right hand skimming over the page while her left continued that delicious frottage. She was ashamed of this tendency to play with herself, but had discovered it probably later than others, finding relief from the frustration of boyfriends, of which there had been few. They had been well meaning but clumsy, and had not lasted long. She had gained the reputation of being frigid. Watching late night TV, she had been fascinated by programmes about the clitoris and female orgasm. Secretly, using the Internet, she had ordered the accompanying books. These she had hidden and devoured. They had been a revelation and she had practised, viewing her genitals in a hand-mirror, using the prescribed techniques to bring herself off – not once at a sitting, but several times.

In the car that afternoon, Greg had been as skilled as any banner waving, Clit-for-President, fervent author-ess, working a finger into the side of her knickers, combing through her pubes and finding the seat of sensation. Nicole scribbled, getting faster and faster as her middle finger edged inside her gusset, excitement tingling from her heated, swollen bud to her finger and back again.

'He did it,' she wrote. 'He rubbed me there, and I didn't know whether to be embarrassed or come or what. I squirmed and he held me steady, saying, 'Relax, pet. Enjoy it. Do it for me. You're so smooth and wet down there. Do it, do it ... let me feel you come.' And I did. I couldn't stop myself.'

It was too much. She let the book drop on the bed, the biro, too, her whole being concentrating on her clit. It demanded to be rubbed harder, steadier, with no let up. 'Oh – oh – yes! Yes!' she whispered and great waves of orgasm got her and held her and tossed her on high, while she moaned and gasped and wanted nothing in the world but this – nothing else mattered. It lasted for a fraction of time, then she slumped back, replete, keeping her finger there while the spasms receded.

She dozed, her hand still inside her pants. After a while she woke, smelling her fragrance on her fingers as she put the diary away, reluctant to shower and lose the sweet odour of sex. She wondered how she would be able to sit next to Greg at the dining table without blushing, remembering the climax in the car and the more recent self-induced one. As for facing her grandmother? Dear God! It would be as if she had I've-Just-Masturbated tattooed on her forehead.

Chandeliers with crystal drops hung over the dining room. Electric candles flickered, throwing light on the Wedgwood blue ceiling, picked out with plasterwork in gold or icing sugar white. The walls were white, too, as were the damask curtains at the big sash windows, their heavy tie-backs consisting of gold cords with fringes twenty inches long. Jody, stepping through the pedimented cedarwood door, admired its flash, but was sensitive to its phoney nature.

Lovely to have so much money that you were in the position to purchase this replica of opulent eighteenth-century living, with all mod cons, of course. Who wanted to endure the sanitation of that era? No one, in their right mind. The estate was exclusive. No two houses were alike and the large gardens offered seclusion, garaging and the best security money could buy. Jody thought worriedly about her own system in London, keeping her fingers crossed that Katrina was not so obsessed with shagging Bobby that she forgot to switch it on.

Deirdre, wearing beige, had welcomed her and Miriam, leading them through the impressive hall to the drawing room. Sherry was served, and they mingled with the other guests.

'This is Chief Inspector Harrison and his wife Joan,' Deirdre said, introducing them to a quiet, intense-looking man in a dark suit. He was well over forty, with short greying hair and shrewd eyes, and a plump woman in green hung on his arm, looking up at him as if still bedazzled at having netted a policeman.

'And here is the vet, Luke Prosser. You remember him, I expect,' Deidre went on, while Jody nodded and smiled and wondered when she'd get to meet the blushing bridegroom.

'Nice to see you again. It's been a long time,' he said. He was small and thinning on top, but had that kind of nebulous glamour associated with medics, be they attending humans or animals. 'And Nicole behaved like a pro,' he continued, drawing her into the conversation and shouting to her father. 'Your daughter's a natural, Ron. If she gives up teaching, I'll take her on as my assistant.'

'We couldn't have that, could we, darling?' drawled a deep male voice from the door. 'You'll be far too busy being Mrs Crawford. No mucky cowsheds for you.'

'Greg!' Nicole exclaimed and rushed towards him.

'So, that's the ideal husband – superman hero and stud,' Jody murmured to Miriam.

'Yep. Can't you see his halo and wings? And here comes Piers. He never gives up trying to rob me of my virtue.'

'What virtue?'

'Eff off.'

Jody moved to one side a little to get a better view of Greg. He was handsome all right. Jody liked her men tall, with broad shoulders tapering to a lean waist. Greg possessed these qualities and an ease of manner that could have charmed the birds right down out of the trees. Oh, yes, a very desirable groom. Then why did she have this gut reaction? Not passion, or lust, but a presentiment as clear and dire as if Frankenstein's creature had suddenly manifested, dulling the lights, tainting the people and destroying the convivial atmosphere.

Nicole was dragging him over, Piers in tow, and she was smiling and lovely. Jody had never seen her more radiant, wearing a filmy cotton dress, predominantly white, with frills and flounces like an updated version of the Laura Ashley look.

'Jody, this is Greg,' she cried, her fingers locked in his.

'Hello,' he said, concentrating on her till it seemed that Jody was the only person present. 'You must be the garden designer. Nicole has shown me photos of your work. Very commendable, though not quite within my ken. I'm rather traditional, you see.'

'But you promised I could have one of Jody's pieces in the garden when we buy our home in the country.

Please, Greg, please,' Nicole pleaded, acting all feminine and Victorian damsel. It turned Jody's stomach.

'We'll see, Mousekin,' he said, an arm resting lightly across her shoulders, and he gave Jody a steady look from eyes that were blue and beguiling, set in a film-star face with high cheekbones and a strong jaw. His dark hair brushed his collar at the nape, and swept back from his forehead in carefully styled disarray.

He was a matinée idol type and no mistake, and he knew it and used it and made the most of it, she concluded. In other circumstances, he could even have been a gigolo. Perhaps he had. Into politics? Cultivating Ronald Carpenter because he was the mayor, and his business was that of making and ordering regalia for the Masons? He wants watching. Nicole, the poor inno-cent, will be no match for him and his machinations.

Giving no indication that she had his measure, she played the game. And so did Miriam. She was at her coolest, the sophisticated media person who knew what was what, who was in on the popularity stakes and who was out. Who was sleeping with who and how often, and who was fiddling the Booker Prize. They got round to Jody's sculpture.

'If you call it that,' he commented, and his fingers brushed hers as he handed her another glass of sherry.

He wore an agate set in a wide gold band on his index finger. For some unaccountable reason, she imag-ined him being pierced through the foreskin, a ring glistening there, wet with pre-come. She didn't want to think of this, but there was that about him which encouraged such ideas. She'd bet fifty pounds that he was the proud owner of a Prince Albert. I'll get Miriam on to it. There's only one way to find out.

'Piers will know,' Miriam said, when she told her about it in the cloakroom. 'They were at public school together, in the same rugby team. Rugger or bugger or something. Even if it was done later, they've hung around, bosom buddies, lots of male bonding, whatever that means, and Greg is bound to have shown his cock off to his old mate. Don't they just love flashing it? What do you think of him anyway? Apart from your fantasy about his piercing.'

'He's striking.'

'And to die for?'

'No. I wouldn't say that. There's a dark quality about him. He's got lots of secrets.'

'Not the man for our Nicole?'

'Ben would be better.'

'Ah, but there's one little problem.'

'Such as?'

'She doesn't love Ben.'

'You're right. Shit. We've got to get a suss on him.'

'He's been staring at you ever since you met. Not me. He knows Piers is there with his tongue hanging out. But you? I'll bet he sees you as a challenge, and is determined to add your name to his bed-post.'

'Bastard,' Jody replied, washing her hands at the basin, then holding them under the drier. 'He's engaged to Nicole.'

'Ha! Do you think that will stop him? They are locked in the cave man ethos. See a girl with strong hips and legs and they have her marked out as a breeder, a vessel for their sacred seed and the continuation of the race. That's why they don't usually go for older women. Without realising it, the out-dated breeding reason is behind it.'

'That's bleak,' Jody reflected, controlling one of her locks with a flashing sequinned comb. The unkempt look achieved by Miriam was much easier to keep, untidy and acceptable, an all right state of hair.

'Life is,' Miriam said, admiring herself. 'Décolletage is very much the thing at the moment. I'm glad my boobs are real and not implants.'

'So, I'd imagine, is Peirs,' Jody replied acerbically.

At table she found herself between Greg and Luke. Nicole was on Greg's other side and Miriam sat beside her, flanked by Piers. Ronald took the head and Deirdre sat at the far end. His mother Maggie was on his right, with the Chief Inspector and Joan, and another couple, Ken and Cathy Sugden who worked for The Compass, Ronald's business at the back of North Row. They were also members of the HOS. Nanette came late, full of apologies, smiling and effusive and, for Jody, excruciatingly embarrassing. After a couple of glasses of wine she insisted on singing snatches from the latest production. She'd never be cast as the heroine (soprano), but got the meatier roles (contralto).

Caterers had been called in to supply the dinner. 'We're having them do the reception, too,' Deirdre piped up. 'It's to be at Leigh Grove Hotel.'

'Five star,' cut in Maggie. 'Such a fine place and, if this food is anything to go by, we'll have nothing to complain about. After all, we are paying thirty pounds a head, aren't we, Ronald?'

How rude, Jody fulminated, wanting to say something. How pig ignorant to mention money in front of people who have undoubtedly been invited. Worse was to come.

'Remind me to give you the names of stores where wedding gifts can be bought. We have left lists with them to show to our friends who will then make a purchase without fear of duplication. No more risk of half a dozen toast-racks,' Maggie quipped, twinkling at the Chief Inspector, whose wife pretended to ignore her.

She has no manners, no finesse, no sensitivity, Jody

raged inwardly, and the food, fine though it was, stuck in her craw. She had an ally in her mother.

'My dear, how pushy,' commented Nanette, dressed to kill in a silk sari that fastened just above her breasts. 'It didn't happen when we were young. We were glad of toasters and toast racks, thinking the givers terribly kind. Even a hideous vase presented by my ex's great aunt was put on display. Granted, we gradually got rid of the superfluous, but as for this ridiculous nonsense of including washing machines, dish-washers, flowers delivered weekly for a year and all this other crap – it's flaky.' And she leaned across and added to Greg and Nicole, 'I shall search for something that isn't on the list, and you won't have it till the wedding day. We need to reinstate some of the old-fashioned values.'

'Your mother is quite something, isn't she?' Greg murmured in Jody's ear, his remark covered by the general laughter and controversy as Maggie struggled to turn it into a joke.

'She has her own strong views,' Jody answered, aware that he was pressing his knee against hers under table. Her instinct was to move away, but the demon of curiosity that had always been her bane urged her to keep it there, though not to return the pressure. He tried a little harder.

Scumbag, she thought. He's cheesy, shows lack of moral fibre and probably carries a lot of baggage. MP for the district? PER-LEASE! Would you buy a second-hand car from this man? Definitely not. But I'll go with the flow, though not too far, just enough to trap the two-timing bastard.

'Rather like yourself. Witness your garden orna-ments,' he went on, giving her a quirky smile that almost, but not quite, toppled her resolution to view him as potential trouble. His description of her statues annoyed her, making them sound like plaster gnomes, and she suspected this was done on purpose. He was challenging her.

'You don't want to go there,' she answered grittily.

'You're wrong. I'd love to,' he murmured, and squeezed Nicole's hand on his other side and added, 'I'm just saying to Jody, darling, how much I want to see her work.'

His expensive aftershave had been created to titillate the senses. Jody, while fully aware of the deliberate use of this to step up his sexual attraction, could not help responding. She was shocked. Nicole was one of her oldest and dearest friends, and yet she was letting her nostrils try him out, her sense of smell decoding what was artificial and what real – a concoction of perfume, shower gel and the personal scent of his hair and body.

I'm not interested, she told herself sternly. Not the real me, the spiritual me – maybe the rutting tart who is looking for cock. But I shan't do anything about it, just play him along a little and find out how far he is prepared to go to betray Nicole with one of her bridesmaids.

4

Dinner over, Miriam avoided Piers's amorous advances and got down to business. 'OK. We want your opinion, Greg.' She had brought along *Beautiful Brides*, with little yellow stickers marking the right pages.

'I'm at your command. What can I do for you, girls?' he replied, with a certain mocking condescension that roused her ire.

'Oh, Greg, it's about the bridesmaids' dresses,' Nicole burst in, bright-eyed and bushy-tailed, sure that he would wave a magic wand and conjure Disneyland.

'But isn't that your department, princess?' he said coolly, but his expression flickered and changed when he glanced at Jody, though he still smiled, as if finding the whole thing faintly amusing.

'Usually it is,' chimed in Maggie, her hawk-eyes on them as they prepared to leave the dining room. 'But there is such a wide variety to choose from and we can't make up our minds. Jody suggested that, as we couldn't agree, you should be asked to decide – rather irregular, I know.'

'Can we see you trying them on?' asked Piers, with a sideways leer. 'Shall I find some music? What do you usually strip to?'

'Give us a break, Piers,' Greg said, in a level tone with a warning undertow.

'Will you do it?' urged Maggie. 'We could use the conservatory. Not to strip, of course. Piers, you are so naughty – but to look at the designs. Come along, Deirdre.'

'Can't I take a look?' shouted Ronald, silver-haired and personable, one of the town's leading lights and chairman of the businessmen's breakfast club. Now he played mine host, radiating bonhomie.

'No, dear. It's out of bounds,' his mother replied. 'I don't really approve of Greg there. You'll have quite enough to do being the bride's father and giving her away.'

He shrugged and laughed and drank brandy with the Chief Inspector and Ken Sugden, his second-in-command at The Compass. The talk turned inevitably to work and, particularly, the ancient, threadbare banner that the skilled seamstresses were repairing. Ronald had his designer submitting sketches and swatches of material, proposing that this particular Lodge had a new one made. The debate was ongoing.

Miriam strolled into the conservatory. Such features were a must these days, along with trickle fountains and decking. It was reached via the drawing room; indeed, as Maggie exclaimed joyously, 'It's an extension to indoor living. So much light and glass and wrought iron and plants. One could imagine one was in the garden.'

'Or the jungle,' Miriam observed, glancing round at the tropical plants.

They jostled for supremacy – orchids, cacti, bougain-villaea, and a stunning, over-the-top lily, with almost obscene waxen petals and an orange stamen the size of an average penis. Its smell was overpowering, redolent of fecundity, luring bedazzled insects to enter its sexual orifice, drink of its honey-dew and fly away with spores clinging to their hairy little legs to be spread abroad and reproduce with others of its kind. Fat chance in England, Miriam mused, unless there's a rash of such blossoms breaking out all over, following this passion for glasshouses.

Does that mean we must keep our kit on and not throw stones? she questioned herself, though sure that she'd got the metaphor wrong.

'It's the last word in fashion,' Maggie continued, undeterred. 'I find it simply adorable, and have ordered one to be added to my own house.'

'Are you there enough to warrant it?' Miriam asked pointedly, finding a woven basket-chair with a deep, cretonne cushion, and getting out her cigarettes. She noticed an absence of ashtrays on the round wicker table.

Maggie narrowed her eyes, but said imperturbably, 'I spend a great deal of time at home, when I'm not travelling abroad. Though I'll admit to being always on hand should Ronald need me, as with the wedding arrangements, for example.'

'I could manage, you know,' Deirdre murmured, bringing in a tray with a jug of Sangria and several glasses. Anyone less thick-skinned than her mother-in-law would have backed off.

'Nonsense, my dear,' she said, sweeping this aside. 'It's a huge undertaking.'

'Can we get on?' Greg asked edgily, resting his shoulders against a green pillar that resembled a palm tree, arms folded over his chest, feet crossed at the ankles.

Miriam opened the magazine and handed it over. 'That's what Jody and I will be wearing.'

'Nothing is decided,' Maggie jumped in.

'Oh, yes, it is,' Miriam and Jody chorused. This stale-mate could not be allowed to continue. Both were returning to London within a day or two and they wanted to know the dresses were on order.

Greg gave the photographs barely a glance, then passed them to Piers who was over-enthusiastic. 'I say, that's nice. I like the low necks.'

All he thinks about is tit, Miriam decided crossly. Yet he had a certain something, terribly well bred with an accent only acquired through being born and brought up with money and titles and the right education. He was a loose-limbed man, who was already putting on weight. His face was that of an overgrown schoolboy, round and dimpled and rubicund. His hair was sandy and floppy, worn rather long, clipping the back of his collar. His eyes were pale blue and his ears stuck out. But, all in all, he had a great deal to offer. He, too, saw himself in the political arena, and Miriam had always fancied chancing her arm in this field.

'So, we are agreed, then?' Nicole piped up, blushing and fidgeting. Any mention of the wedding put her in a spin.

'Whatever you want, darling,' Greg said, hiding a yawn. Then he looked at Jody and added, 'That colour will suit you. I like it.'

Oh, God, Miriam moaned to herself. I hope she doesn't fall for his crap chat-up lines. She's far too sensible. Isn't she?

Maggie conceded defeat, quite graciously, as it turned out, and Miriam had to thank Greg for that. Nicole's pushy grandmother was a little in awe of him. Didn't he rub shoulders with the political bigwigs and wasn't Ronald prepared to back him all the way? She probably visualised herself canvassing for him in the not too distant future, Miriam decided. What party would he stand for? An Independent or a true-blue Conservative? Probably the latter, if Ronald had anything to do with it.

'Time we made tracks,' she said, victory assured. 'Are you ready, Jody?'

'Must you go?' Piers said, moving closer to her. 'I thought maybe you'd stay for another drink.'

'Sorry. I've had enough. Driving.' She fielded that one neatly.

'Then tomorrow. What about lunch?'

'Ring me. You have my number.'

Miriam wasn't entirely sure about going home alone, apart from Jody. She was curious about Piers. He knew how to kiss; their tongues had already shared a dance of desire, but the way he had groped her breasts had been amateurish. How would it be when they actually got down to basics? Would he be a fumbler? She wasn't in the mood for training newbies.

'Tell you what,' she said. 'Why don't we meet at the entrance to Sun Valley? They have a massive car boot sale there every Sunday. I might even find a wedding present. You wouldn't mind that, would you, Nicole? I've a suss on kitsch.'

'Looking at other people's cast-offs sounds like nothing to do. What time?' Piers grumbled, as Miriam swung away towards the patio doors.

She answered over her shoulder, without bothering to turn, 'Eleven. Don't keep me waiting. If you're late I'll walk.'

'"When Fredrick was a little lad he proved so brave and daring, His father thought he'd 'prentice him to some career seafaring."'

Damn, thought Nanette, struggling to remember the next line of the song. Why did I let myself in for this? She nodded to the bespectacled man seated at the upright piano side stage. 'OK, Bernie, let's carry on. I went a bit blank there, that's all.'

What she didn't add was that her lack of concentration had something to do with a new member of the HOS, also present at the rehearsal. His name was Stewart Ramsden and he had recently arrived in Heronswood. Gossip flew. Apparently he had gone into partnership with Lees, Marten and Crowther. They were dental surgeons who had been left one short when the senior member, Hector Lees, heedless of the drink/drive laws, had smashed into a lamp-post and killed himself.

Stewart was a welcome addition, and not only to the practice. He caused pulses to race among the female population whose teeth suddenly needed urgent attention. A bear of a man, but gentle with it, he was somewhere in his late forties. He did not have a wife or children, not visible anyway, living alone in bachelor freedom in a town house not far from the surgery. Nanette had met him when she went to have a filling. Even Novocaine, followed by the drill, had not detracted from Stewart's obvious assets. She had returned for a check-up.

'And are you getting used to our little community?' she had asked to a background of muzak drifting through the speakers.

'It's a very pleasant town,' he had replied, bending over her as she lay in the dentist's chair, so close that she could clearly see his craggy features and long-lashed dark eyes, and smell the clean, wholesome odour of him, slightly overlaid by disinfectant. 'Though I've not yet scratched the surface. It's a far cry from Taunton, where I had my last practice.'

'Do you like music?' she had asked, when he had finished prodding about among her lower molars. Her lips were numb but she managed to form the words.

'Oh, yes, but not that. I can't stand compilations,' he had replied, raising a strongly marked brow at the corner speaker and grimacing. 'But music is my passion.' He had turned away from her; his wide shoulders and broad back outrageously sexy under the crisp white overall.

'Well, then, perhaps you'd be interested in joining the Heronswood Operatic Society,' she had said, jumping in where angels fear to tread. 'Do you sing?'

The sour-faced dental nurse had rattled the tray of implements and treated Nanette to a gimlet stare, obviously staking a claim. Stewart, unperturbed, had answered with a smile, 'As a matter of fact, I do. I'm a baritone.'

'Splendid,' Nanette had mumbled. 'We're always on the lookout for men, and Aubrey, that's our producer, is still auditioning for the next production. Gilbert and Sullivan, you know. *The Pirates of Penzance.*'

'My favourite. I may give it a go, Mrs Hamilton.'

'Next Monday evening, at the church hall,' she had informed him, and that was that. As easy as taking candy from a baby.

Aubrey Blakeworthy had been impressed when Stewart sang for him, confiding to Nanette that he was up to professional standards and had been having lessons for years and, what's more, had acted in similar amateur efforts. The other men had accepted him, voting him one of the chaps and taking him to the pub. The ladies of the chorus were thrilled to have him join them, but Nanette had the edge, having introduced him. Nothing had happened between them – yet – but she was prepared to wait, setting her hopes on the adrenaline high of the actual performances, and the Last Night Party when most everyone let their hair down.

Now she was running through the beginning of Act One, where, as an ageing nursemaid named Ruth, she was explaining to the pirates how Frederick, due to be out of his indentures, had come to be apprenticed to piracy because of a mistake on her part.

Bernie Trent played enthusiastically, a church organist who revelled in Sullivan's tuneful music and Gilbert's witty words. He blossomed in the company of the lady members who, somehow, shucked off the burden of being wives and mothers and adopted new personas as soon as they set foot in the rehearsal room. There's an actress in us all, Nanette thought. A pole dancing, brazen strumpet. We become freer, less inhibited, and I don't know quite why, unless it is because we can pretend to be someone else. Ages ago concerned parents spotted this, warning their wilful daughters, 'You'll end up on the stage!'

'Nanette, dear, you're not paying attention,' complained Aubrey. He was a bank manager by day, but camped it up when donning the mantle of producer. 'You should know the words by now. Next week we're doing it without books.' His tone was faintly disappointed, as he went on, 'I hope you're not going to let me down.'

Though paunchy and with sparse ginger hair carefully combed over his bald patch, he fancied himself as a lady-killer, and was wearing corduroy trousers and a diamond patterned canary yellow jumper, courtesy of the Scottish Wool Shop that sported a branch in Heronswood. Sand-coloured desert boots completed this ensemble, and he placed an arm about her waist, gazing at her through pebble-glasses that made him look even more like a goldfish. But he knew his onions. G and S were his speciality, both their works and their lives, and he had grumbled throughout the film *Topsy Turvy* when the society rented it from Blockbusters and viewed it on his DVD.

Nanette was no slouch when it came to it, and learning her lines did not present a problem, unless Aubrey chose to make it one. 'Don't worry. I shall be all right. Can we get on now?' And she launched into the scene with Frederick and the Pirate King, played with swashbuckling gusto by Stewart.

'I say, it's going well,' he commented as they gathered in the brightly-lit kitchen at the far end, sipping tea and eating chocolate digestive biscuits. 'You're fine as Ruth.'

'Thank you, kind sir,' she said, dipping a mock curtsey. 'And you're not so bad yourself. Have you seen the film version where Kevin Kline plays the Pirate King?'

'Can't say I have,' he said, big and solid and having to stand close to her in the crush of tea and coffee drinkers. Her breasts brushed against his chest and, squinting downwards, she tried to make out the size of the package nestling at the fork of his trousers. If build was anything to go by, then he should be hung like a donkey.

Never one to let an opportunity slip, she leapt in. 'I've got the movie. Why don't you pop round and see some of it after the rehearsal? You could come, too, if you want, Danny,' she added, hoping the young man playing Frederick would refuse.

'Thanks, but I'm going to the pub with Aubrey and some of the cast,' he said.

Goodie, she thought. Then it's up to the Pirate King and me. She could feel that anticipatory sparkle that always danced along her nerves at the prospect of trying out a new man. She was nothing like as horny as she had once been. Getting older did make a difference – that and experience and developing a thick skin. But even so, there were times, like tonight, when she felt romantic and inspired and brimming over with desire.

Being my age is OK, she thought when, later, she poured two glasses of wine and sat beside Stewart on the wide Chesterfield in the living room after slipping in the tape and pressing PLAY. She loved sharing her favourites, the musical treat increased tenfold. But it wasn't easy to concentrate with his muscular body alongside hers, his trousers stretched over those substantial thighs (had he played football?), and her mind lighting up and responding to the intelligence of him. Like her, he knew the operetta from start to finish, and they sang along and commented and chuckled at the satirical lyrics. It was more than simply pleasant.

She leaned into him as they sat together, shoulder to shoulder and thigh to thigh, and she lit up a cigarette and he enjoyed a cheroot and it was as if they had always known one another, but with the added bonus of newness and novelty and uncertainty. She grew hungry for him, longing to feel that mobile mouth on hers and slightly troubled because he made no attempt to kiss her.

Was he gay? It was difficult to tell. Or was it that he didn't fancy her? She could hardly believe it. She was having one of those good days when she looked ten years younger, flushed with galloping across the plain earlier, putting a spirited horse through its paces. And the excitement of rehearsing, with all its petty squabbles, arguments and back-biting, never failed to stimulate her. All that she wanted to round it off was Stewart in her bed.

The video finished, and it was midnight. 'Coffee?' she asked, despising herself for trying to hang on to him just that bit longer. He lifted his arm from where it had been resting behind her, along the sofa back.

'No, thanks. Heavy day tomorrow,' he answered, and soon he was standing with her in the hall, glancing round appreciatively. 'Fine old house you've got here.'

'It's been in my family for generations. It was left to me when Daddy died, and thank goodness, for by that time Allan had left.'

'Your husband?'

She nodded. 'My ex-husband. It was a secure place to bring up the kids.'

'Are they still here?'

'No. Adam and Sinclair are long gone. One's an investment banker and the other's a property developer. My daughter, Jody, is around at present, but off to London again shortly. I shall see more of her over the weeks, as she is one of Nicole Carpenter's bridesmaids.' She wondered if this was the time to ask him along as her escort, then decided it would be premature, so, 'Do you have children?' she enquired, having heard that he hadn't, but wanting to have him say it.

'No. I'm divorced, too, and my wife was a barrister and into her career and didn't want to stop and have babies.'

Aw! She wanted to say. Such a shame that his magnificent physique should not be genetically reproduced by strapping sons. I'd have done it for him, she thought, and visualised having him mount her like a rutting beast, and becoming pregnant by him, later proudly showing him their new-born infant and seeing his rugged face wreathed in smiles.

You're daft, you, she scolded herself. There must have been a very solid reason why his wife didn't want to tie herself to him like that. Maybe he is a skinflint, or enormously insensitive, or useless in the sack. Even she was getting irritated because he was just standing there with the front door open, hovering on the threshold, but not attempting to make a move.

He stayed chatting of inconsequential matters, not even suggesting that they meet again, only at the next rehearsal. Nanette saw him out and turned back into the empty house. It was at moments like this she missed a companion – not necessarily a husband, for she liked living on her own, but someone with whom to share comments, opinions, and a bed.

You're getting maudlin, she lectured herself, carrying the glasses into the kitchen. Time to try Kevin Moore again. I'll go down to the stable early. He's learning fast, that boy. One day he'll thank me for it. There's nothing like sharing one's expertise with the uninitiated. The best thing about young men is their stamina. They can bang and bang away, whereas older lovers need a rest in between. Not that I'm giving up on Stewart, and I can't wait to see him in his pirate costume. Pillage and rape or what? Once aboard the lugger and the girl is mine!

Jody walked up the narrow, herringbone-patterned path bordered with rope-edged tiles, stepped into the porch and opened the stained glass panelled front door. 'Come on in, Miriam,' she said.

Tuesday afternoon, and they had driven back to London in convoy. Duty done in the country for the time being, work could no longer be avoided. Miriam had a studio flat in Knightsbridge and a busy schedule ahead. The launch of Shani Palmer's book, *The Cosmic Wheel*, was taking precedence over everything.

'She's on chat shows and morning TV and I don't know what all,' Miriam said, unfastening her fleece and getting out mugs in the kitchen. She always made herself at home. 'But, you know what?'

'What?' Jody obliged, opening a new box of tea bags.

'I need a man.'

'You do?'

'Yep!'

'And what are you doing about it?'

'I'm going to put a phone call through to Janine right now. She's a mate of mine. I discovered her when I started going to the gym. She runs a beauty parlour that's a little bit special. That's where I was sprayed with tanning lotion. You can get all sorts done, including massage and pampering and special attention from her male assistants, if that's what you want.'

'How come you haven't told me about this before?' Jody poured boiling water over the bags in the mugs.

'Honey, you were always so busy with Alec.'

'So what is this? A women's brothel?'

Miriam shrugged. 'That's a tad crude, but maybe.'

Jody found something repellent about the idea. She visualised men lining up to be chosen, rather like the whores she had seen in a TV documentary about The Bunny Ranch in America's West. How would they pose? In various get-ups, or nude? Would they be judged by their physique and the size of their cocks, or would something more be required? Surely not their intellect?

'It doesn't interest me,' she said. 'And anyway, I've a commission to complete pronto.'

What she did not add was that she was intrigued by Greg and wanted to be alone to think it through. There had been too much chatter and too much going on while she had been in Heronswood. Peace and reflection was required.

'Look. It'll give you a boost,' Miriam continued. 'No ties. No strings. Just business, but the boys know their job. There's nothing cheapskate about it. You can even use it as an escort agency, if you prefer, getting your hunk-of-choice to visit you at home, take you out to dinner or the theatre and wind up between your sheets. It's perfectly safe, though costs a bomb if you go for the whole works. They are vetted for honesty, cleanliness and all that jazz.'

'I take it you've indulged?' Jody could well believe it. Her friend never ceased to amaze her.

'On several occasions, when I got tired of my vibrator and wanted a solid piece of real live meat. It saved me from compromising myself with some man or other simply because I was mixing love with lust. Once I got the lust sorted, then I could see that love had nothing to do with what I was feeling.'

'It all seems so clinical. Where's the emotion?' Jody argued, still not convinced. There was enough of the romantic left in her to imagine that Mr Right would come along one day, sweep her off her feet and live with her happily ever after – sex and love combined.

'Who needs it? This is about lust, honey! Shall I ring Janine for an appointment? All you need do is enjoy a massage, if that's all you want.'

'I'll think about it,' Jody said, wondering how it was Miriam always managed to talk her into things.

She was already on the mobile phone, presumably chatting to her pick of masseuses. 'Oh, Janine? Yes, it's me, Miriam. What have you got on offer? You have? Sounds yummy. How old? Twenty-one? Great. Is Rickie still there? I need a full massage and extras, and I'm hoping to bring a friend along. OK. 6.30 it is. 'Bye,' and she beamed at Jody, slipping her mobile in to her pocket. 'It's all arranged. I'll pick you up at six.'

'Maybe. I'm still mulling it over. I'll call you.'

'Mind that you do. No chickening out,' Miriam scolded, and let herself out.

Jody was itching to get to her babies, neglected in the studio. She had several ideas she wanted to try out, the creative process churning away in her brain, despite the flurry of the last few days. Weddings be buggered, she thought irritably. What a farce. As for Greg? He did nothing but proposition me, right under Nicole's nose. Nothing said or done that anyone could put a finger on. He was all jocularity with her bridesmaids, but I knew and he knew what was really going on. It was deep-rooted in the groin. My cunt and his cock had the same idea. But I mustn't. I don't want to. He's a devious sod. Miriam's right. I probably need a good shag from some-one – and preferably not my friend's fiancé!

She wandered to the back of the house and quietly opened the studio door. The silence was absolute. Then she heard a sigh and a rustling sound. Jesus God! she thought, panicking. I've had a break-in. She froze, visions of TV newscasters describing how she had been found, battered to death by an unknown intruder.

She peered into the dazzle of afternoon sun pouring through the skylight. It was difficult to make out any-thing clearly. A solid slab of concrete blocked her view, one of several she was about to turn into decorative objects. Then her eyes encountered what her slow wits at first refused to register. Katrina and Bobby were there, and he was leaning against the wall, his bunched knuckles on his hips, watching Katrina who was on her knees in front of him. Bobby's shirt was unbuttoned all the way and his flies were open.

'Suck me, suck me,' he urged huskily, while Katrina flicked the exposed cock that pointed to the ceiling. 'I said suck it,' Bobby repeated. 'Not too fast. I want it to last.'

Katrina leaned forward and the large appendage disappeared inside her mouth. Jody saw how her cheeks caved in with the force of her cock-sucking. Her heart was pounding so much that she was afraid they might hear it. She was having trouble with her breathing. She moved forward a little, a dark skein of excitement unwinding inside her. Bobby used Katrina's hair as a bridle, holding her firmly and moving her head up and down. Katrina gripped him round the waist to steady herself. Jody could not resist slipping her hand down the front of her combats, entering her knickers and rubbing herself. She was wet and slippery, on the perilous brink of orgasm.

'I don't want to come in your mouth. I want to do it all over your face,' Bobby muttered.

'Not yet. Let's get undressed,' Katrina mumbled, then disentangled herself and pulled her vest over her head.

The sun glinted on rings piercing her nipples. A thin chain linked them. She unbuckled her belt and slipped her jeans down over her hips, kicked off her trainers and freed herself. She wasn't wearing panties. Bobby stripped, too, and then they caressed. Jody watched them, entranced, seeing them worshipping one another, while she adored *them*. Their faces expressed love, their hands encountered skin, and Bobby's cock was near to bursting, hard as iron, upright as a spear, springing from a forest of fair hair.

Envy pierced Jody, sharp as a butcher's knife. It was love she yearned for, the sort of love they were expressing. She needed to be sheltered, warmed by another's devotion, not leading a solitary existence and indulging in solitary sexual relief. Affection. Shared jokes and laughter. So what went wrong after a while? Why hadn't she become engaged to Alec? She might have been planning her own wedding.

The words of an old song echoed in her head: 'Why am I always the bridesmaid, never the blushing bride? Ding-dong, wedding bells always ring for other girls. But one fine day, oh, let it be soon, I shall wake up in the morning on my own honeymoon.'

Tosh, bosh and bollocks! She tried to get a grip on reality, slowed down the pressure on her clit, subjecting it to slow strokes from above, but could not have stopped being a Peeping Tom even if her life depended on it. Voyeurism had its own fascination, and she was indulging herself.

The lovers moved over to the couch. It was deep and wide and Jody had often fallen asleep there when working far into the night. Katrina lay on her back and Bobby lowered himself on top of her. He rotated his hips slowly, rubbing his stiff cock all over her body. They looked into each other's eyes and kissed, long and deep, while loneliness was like a raw wound in Jody's soul.

Bobby sat up, his penis straining back against his belly, the tip touching his navel. He was certainly well blessed, and Jody bewailed the fact that he was spoken for and all she could do was indulge in a little self-pleasure, but keep climax at bay. Then Bobby rolled Katrina over on to her stomach and she arched his hips and raised her bottom towards him, waggling it invitingly. Bobby knelt astride her and used his large hands to give her a back rub, and Jody stiffened, seeing him spit on his fingers as he reached the amber crease of Katrina's arse, dipping between the cheeks and inserting one into her anus.

Jody drew in a sharp breath, seeing Katrina hugging the cushion beneath her and hearing her moans, her hip movements becoming frantic. A hard slap reverberated though the studio and she yelled while Bobby ordered, 'Be quiet, you. Unless you want another one.'

'You are so cruel to me,' Katrina whimpered, but in a way that suggested enjoyment.

'And you love it, don't you, you slut,' Bobby answered grufffly, and brought his hand down on her rump again.

He spanked her several times and Jody saw the

suntanned skin turn fiery red. She wondered at this dichotomy between pain and pleasure, for there was no doubt that Katrina was revelling in it.

'Fuck me, fuck me,' she begged.

'Are you my slave-slut?' Bobby snapped, flexing his muscles and tightening his hold on her.

'Forever. Always yours,' she vowed, and Bobby reached under her and seized her clit. He rubbed it vigorously. She moaned and jerked and came.

Bobby smeared her wetness around her arsehole, then slid a condom over his dick and lubricated it from the same source. He took up position on his knees and guided himself into her, slowly and carefully, increasing the pressure until the whole length and girth of him had disappeared and his balls tapped against her. He pumped faster and faster, and Katrina clung to the couch, bracing herself for this assault. They made no attempt to mask the noise, locked in an embrace, and Bobby dug his nails into her back, leaving bloody scratches, and both of them were panting hard, as if running a marathon.

It looks so brutal, Jody thought. I didn't know Katrina was into anal, and her finger moved in time to Bobby's strokes, her excitement mounting with his. He rode Katrina, in and out, and Jody's finger kept up a light, swift flight. Then Bobby's breathing stopped for a second. He threw back his leonine head and let out a long series of grunts, juddering all over.

Jody was coming, too, a surge of release sweeping through her and carrying her to planes just visited by Katrina and Bobby. The same journey but reached by a different route. The couple lay on the couch, fingers entwined. She could hear their contented murmuring and crept from the studio before they became aware of her.

In the kitchen, she reached for her mobile and paged Miriam. She had made up her mind to visit the beauty parlour. What she had just witnessed had fired her longing to experience intercourse again, not with a rubber dildo but with real-live flesh attached to a walking, talking, living, breathing and, best of all, *fucking* man.

Jody stepped through the swing doors into reception. It was reached from the pavement, part of an elegant street in the heart of London. A posh address in a prestigious area. The rates must be sky-high, she thought.

Miriam gave her a broad wink and went to the desk, manned by a slender oriental in a white *gi*. This was sufficient to bring to mind martial arts movies, extraordinary agility and speed, tigers crouching and dragons flying. His hair was long and raven black and fell straight to his muscular shoulders.

He looked at them with slanting brown eyes and said, 'My name is Konane. May I help you, ladies?'

Indeed he might, Jody thought, intrigued by this exotic person. Though usually preferring Europeans, she found him very attractive. His masculine yet sensual looks instilled in her a feeling of security on the one hand and awoke her sexual passion on the other. Did he fancy the women who came there? Was it part of his job to service them? No clues could be glimpsed on his expressionless face.

'Hello, Konane. How are you? Are you a Second Dan yet?'

'I am. And there'll be further *Shotokan Karate* trials very soon.'

'Maybe I'll come along and watch,' Miriam murmured, reaching over the desk and stroking his silky hair. 'Meanwhile, we are expected and have appointments. Are you free this evening?'

'On duty here, madam,' he replied, and just at that moment a tall woman came in, walked up to Miriam and kissed her warmly on both cheeks.

Jody was introduced to her. So this was the enterprising Janine who had raised the male escort business to a fine art. There was nothing crude about her house; it could have belonged to an aristocrat and been handed down over the years. It was beautifully decorated and furnished. Being a procuress must be a profitable business, Jody concluded. Unless Janine was sponsored by someone rich.

The preliminaries over, Jody was taken along a corridor punctuated by closed doors, and then taken through one of them. The room was light and airy and contained a massage couch, mirrors and glass shelves holding bottles and jars of different shapes and sizes which probably contained oils and creams to soothe the skin and arouse the senses.

'I've brought along our portfolio,' Janine said, indicating that Jody should sit beside her on a chaise-longue. 'You may find someone here that you fancy. Take your pick and I'll tell you if he's free.'

It was confusing and embarrassing. Never before had Jody taken part in a commercial sex transaction. In the past she had got to know a man first, dating him several times before they went to bed. She was fussy and a little old-fashioned, maybe. Not a swinger like Miriam. She felt uncomfortable as she leafed through the file. There were at least a dozen shots of good-looking men, some dressed, some half-dressed and others naked, though there were no full frontals. Had the boot been on the other foot, she was certain that male clients would have demanded open-crotch poses.

'Is there anyone you'd like to meet?' Janine purred in her ear, a large-busted blonde woman who exuded a motherly air. She was as unaffected as if she was offering Jody a selection of fine wines.

'I'd just like a massage – to start with,' Jody said, nervously.

Janine smiled a wide crimson smile and patted her on the knee. 'OK. You call the shots. You can always change your mind. Just tell Kit what you want. He's your masseur for tonight.'

Oh, God, what have I done? Jody thought, as she undressed and entered the shower-stall when Janine had departed in a cloud of pungent perfume. She was nervous and jumpy, regretting coming, but the jets washed over her and the gel provided was top quality and smelled divine. After a while. her curiosity began to get the upper hand. Who was Kit? And what would he do?

She killed the spray and wrapped herself in a fluffy white towel bearing the salon's logo. She tiptoed back to the massage room, overawed and wishing she was at home in her studio, alone though, not watching Katrina and Bobby. Help! I wish I hadn't come. Bugger! Why doesn't this Kit dude arrive?

5

A tap on the door. 'Come in,' Jody called.

'Good evening, miss. I'm Kit,' he said, stepping inside. He smiled widely; his teeth were even and gleaming.

He fulfilled the image of the archetypal masseur; his T-shirt clinging to his muscular body, and white linen trousers, like an anaesthetist's scrub-ups, outlining his thighs. The material was thin. He wore nothing beneath, and the dark shape of genitalia was mesmerising.

'Hello,' she managed to say. 'What do I do next?'

'Leave it to me,' he murmured, his accent obscure, a hint of Geordie, perhaps.

He assisted her, his hands warm and firm. Then he took the towel away and replaced it with a smaller one that covered her hips and another to hide her breasts. So far, so good. Nothing to cause alarm. Kit took a couple of pots from the shelf. 'I think bergamot,' he mused. 'And a touch of ylang-ylang. Roll over, miss.'

She obeyed, face-down, aware that the rounded cheeks of her bottom were on display, and the dark crease between, and that deeper one that barely hid her furrow. She waited with baited breath, wondering where he would touch her first. She had had body massages before, but always carried out by a female. There had been a visit to an aromatherapist after she had strained a tendon, and Indian head massage to cure migraine and reflexology carried out by Katrina who was much into alternative medicine. But this one was entirely different, aimed at not only easing tension but satisfying physical cravings, too. Katrina would undoubtedly approve.

Kit ran a hand lightly over her, from base of the neck, down the spine to the tail-bone. She came out in goose bumps. Her nipples rose against the couch sheet, and her clitoris buzzed. She could feel wetness between her thighs, and it was nothing to do with the recent shower. He got down to work, and she lay with her head on one side, eyes closed, arms out. It was blissful. Kit had oiled his hands and his touch was magical. He knew every tiny sinew, each nerve and cartilage, which joined to which and where. His knowledge of anatomy was profound. He was a lithe, medium-sized man, dark haired and swarthy, stronger than he appeared. Jody was on fire, her naked pubis rocking gently against the firm surface beneath her.

'If I was a cat, I'd purr,' she remarked, and was gratified to hear him chuckle.

'I'm glad you're enjoying it. We haven't really started yet.'

The oil was fragrant, a combination of herbs mixed to suit her particular case. The smell was relaxing yet arousing. Jody wanted Kit to massage some of it into her cleft, making her slippery and sending ripples through her sex. He used the edge of his hands to hammer lightly up and down her spine, then kneaded and rolled her like a slab of dough. Nothing was missed, neither shoulders or waist, buttocks or legs, ankles or feet. It was a superb sensation and she slackened her thighs, the moisture pooling at her vulva trickling between her lower lips and staining the sheet beneath her. All thoughts of Alec or Greg were left behind. Nothing was significant except that this pleasure continue.

Kit leaned across and whispered, 'Roll over.'

She couldn't wait, though she was so rag-doll limp that it wasn't easy to move. Come on, brain. Where're your messages? Come on, bones. Get this body motivated.

She succeeded in turning with a modicum of grace, giving Kit a flash of her sex. Her nakedness thrilled her. It was as if she had never exposed herself to a man before. What absolute codswallop, she lectured herself.

As Kit came closer to the couch, the solid bar of his cock, though shielded by his draw-string pants, was eye level. She very nearly reached over and took it out, longing for him to show her, maybe even rest it on her bare belly. Would he be cut or uncut? That was the question. She never had been able to make up her mind which she preferred. I want to know. I *must* know, she repeated inside. But was his exposure part of the massage treatment? That's all she had requested. I was a fool, she thought. Can I change my mind at this late stage? Money talks. It always does. I'm sure Janine would be accommodating. Maybe it could be a private agreement between Kit and me. I could slip him a few extra quid and he could slip me a length.

Buying a man! It was an unusual concept and one that took some getting to grips with. Yet, didn't she know couples where he was a toy-boy, living off his older, career-woman lover? At least this was an honest transaction. Every room was linked to monitors and observed by Janine and her team. No one should leave with an anywhere near broken heart. It was sex, that's all.

Kit poured drops of lavender oil into his palm and she splayed her legs and lifted her hips encouragingly. He smiled darkly, and moved his hands over her in smooth sweeps. He lowered his head and fastened his lips round one nipple while his thumb revolved on the other. He pressed against her below the waist, making her aware of his erection. He shifted his attention to her shoulders, arms, wrists and hands, freeing any tension, then returning to her eager nipples. He flicked them, grazed the tender buds with his teeth, nibbled at them. Much more of it and she felt sure she would have an orgasm, and this would be a first for her, though she had heard of women who did just that – coming through their nipples.

She didn't – almost there but not quite. She was on fire below, decorum and modesty gone out of the window. 'Kit,' she gasped, gravid with lust. 'Janine said to ask for what I wanted.'

'That's right,' he said. 'Anything at all. The world is your oyster. Tell me what you'd like me to do.'

'Show me your cock,' she demanded, hardly able to believe it was herself speaking.

One of his hands left her and moved towards his trousers. He pulled the front down below his navel, where the dark pubic hair thickened. His penis uncoiled from the dimness. It was huge, fully erect. She grabbed for it, but he smiled enigmatically and moved out of her reach. His hands slid to her mound and he pressed his thumbs between her delta, spreading her labia like flower petals. Her clitoris burgeoned and he worked his fingers each side of it, then finally concentrated on the pink flesh, as expert there as he was with the rest of her.

This was to be for herself, then? True to her word, Janine made certain that her assistants put the client's needs first. OK, so Kit had a hard-on, but he wouldn't do anything about it till she indicated that she was good and ready. And if she wasn't? Then so be it. She called the shots.

She relaxed and gave herself over to enjoyment. Kit played on her like a delicately tuned instrument. Her clit was pampered and petted and rubbed, subjected to long, slow strokes, or short fierce ones. Using all his expertise, he eventually brought her to the most satisfying of climaxes. She convulsed and cried out, and then he was standing at the foot of the couch, rolling a condom over his bulging cock. He grabbed her hips and pulled her towards him.

She cried out again as she felt him push into her wetness. 'Oh, Kit – yes, yes!'

It was magic, and she looked up into his eyes, seeing them slightly unfocused, as if he was staring through her. He lost some of his gentleness, hell-bent on chasing his own release and she welcomed him, her core clenching around the thick, invading weapon. It wasn't over-long but had a girth that stretched her. His balls rapped against her anus as he held her up towards him and scissored her legs round his neck, obsessed about getting closer, as if wanting to be swallowed into her depths. It was wild and passionate, violent and loving and flattering. This man really was hungry, needing to feed on all she had to offer.

'But isn't this your job?' she panted.

'Nice work if you can get it,' he growled. 'You're beautiful. Don't talk. Just fuck.'

No more time for talking or even thinking. He reared and plunged and took his pleasure, riding to the crest of the wave and then straining back. His face contorted as he gasped in ecstasy and Jody felt the heat of his spunk jetting into the rubber.

He withdrew almost at once, unrolled the condom and dropped it into the pedal-bin, wiped his cock on a handful of tissue, then covered her with a fresh towel. 'Would you like a sauna now?' he asked, solicitously.

'I'll take another shower,' she said, wrestling with the problem of did she tip him? If so, how much?

He wasn't hanging about in that expectant, fawning manner of waiters or porters. Maybe male prostitutes had other criteria. She must ask Janine. She shut her eyes and drifted. When she came to herself, she looked for him in vain. Kit had vanished like a dream-visiting incubus.

Miriam was waiting for Jody in the bar. They ordered cocktails and sat at a small round table in the elaborately decorated room. Its was exotic and oriental, walls painted in jade and coral, drapes consisting of varied, costly materials, but all carrying the same theme. There was a great deal of gold leaf, and tassels, statues of gods and paintings depicting episodes from their lives. Aromatic oil-burners enticed the senses, and blue smoke coiled from the snarling mouths of bronze serpents. It was totally seductive and decadent, and the music was definitely Bollywood.

'Well?' Miriam asked, eyeing Jody, and trying to decipher from her expression whether or not she had found the experience fulfilling.

'It was OK.'

'Just OK? Not stunning, or mind-blowing, or even mind-boggling?' Miriam was disappointed by such a tepid answer. Her own session with Rickie had proved to be all of those things. He really did know how to do it, but then, he was a professional and it showed, putting to shame the ordinary men she had slept with. His younger assistant had proved to be dynamite, too, and at one point she had taken them in her pussy and mouth simultaneously, an eye-watering experience.

I don't know why I bother with dating, she ruminated. I've got my career, my friends, my male floozies.

Do I really want to get married and have children; kiss goodbye to all this fun and freeedom? But the notion of winding up as a spinster wasn't an inspiring one.

Jody smiled across at her, and her eyes were shining. Yes, she looked like a girl who had just had a session of something invigorating. Miriam sat back and sipped her drink. 'I enjoyed it,' Jody confessed. 'This masseur called Kit. Have you had him?'

'Yes. He's cool. Just the fix for our stress-ridden lives. Shall you visit again?'

'I'm not sure.' Jody said softly. 'I didn't know what to do about leaving him a tip.'

'Did he fuck you?'

'Yes. And I feel good about it. It wasn't one of those "Oh, my God, I shouldn't have done that" sort of moments. Ought I have given him a tip, though, and how much?'

'Janine will add it to the bill.'

'But I would have liked him to know that I appreciated what he did.'

'Don't be a nerd.' Miriam could feel herself getting exasperated. 'He's a paid shag, that's all. A dick on legs. Would you feel the same about tipping a vibrator? No? Well, then.'

Jody laughed, and added, 'It was fine. I'll be here again when the spirit moves.'

'When you're on heat, you mean. When you're in mid-cycle and ovulating, all hyped up and ready to conceive. Whether you're aware of it or not, Nature is playing her survival tricks,' Miriam said, then stopped in full flow, her attention drawn to a woman who had just entered the bar.

She was long-legged and striking with a mane of black hair, wearing a crimson leather jacket tightly laced over her generous breasts. She sported figure-hugging jeans that showed off her neat buttocks to perfection, and the soft suede ankle boots she wore screamed designer expense. She had the mien of an empress as she stood there, letting the full impact of her presence sink in. She considered the receptionist, Konane, eyes narrowed under lashes spiky with mascara. She then flipped through the photo-file, pausing at this man or that, the tip of her tongue wetting her pouting, aubergine-hued lips.

'Look over there as if you're not looking,' Miriam hissed at Jody.

Jody did so, then said, 'Who is she?'

'That's Scarlett,' Miriam replied, mentally pricing up the cost of her outfit. 'She's a dominatrix. One of the best, so I'm told. Makes a fortune with her strict discipline. Has lovers galore. Her stamping grounds are Mayfair clubs like Willards, where the politicians and important dudes hang out.'

'Then why come to a place like this?' Jody asked.

'Who knows? Because she gets fed up playing Nanny Whip to a collection of old codgers? Money is the tops, but I guess she needs boys with skin like velvet, or a hulking, tattooed brute who will dominate her for a change. That's when she's not shagging women.'

'She's a lesbian?'

'She's bi. Like me. Isn't she a wicked piece of ass?'

'How come you know so much about her? Are you in the SM scene?' Jody asked, suspiciously, but Miriam detected more than a passing interest.

'I'm pretty much open to anything,' she answered. 'D'you want another drink? I'm on orange juice.'

'That's all right. I'd better be getting home,' Jody said.

'You sound just like a man after he's shot his load and, balls emptied, wants to get away.' A dozen little vignettes flashed across Miriam's memory. 'They usually add that classic get-out clause, "Catch you later."'

'Oh, dear, I don't know whether to be pleased or sorry,' Deirdre said at breakfast, closing the airmail letter and placing it on the table.

'What is it, Mum?' Nicole asked, buttering a second slice of toast then glancing at the kitchen clock. It was 8.30 and she had ten minutes in which to walk to the primary school.

Ronald was in Birmingham on a business trip, and Jeffrey in Canada visiting the overseas branch of the computer firm he part owned. He'd promised to be back in time for the wedding. Deirdre was relieved. She got in such a flap when people were ordering her about, suggesting alternatives, asking her to make up her mind. Not Jeffrey, of course, he was a considerate son, though a tad like his father and, she feared, would probably become even more so as time passed. Maggie was still at the helm and giving no quarter, and this morning's post had brought a reply to one of the many wedding invitations.

'It's from your Aunt Clarissa,' Deirdre said, already anticipating Nicole's response.

'Oh. Great. Is she coming to my wedding?' Nicole sat there wide-eyed.

'Yes, dear. As it happens she will be in England soon for a film production. One of Jane Austen's novels, I believe.'

'Lovely. Shall I be able to go along to the set and see her working and talk to some of the other actors? I'll tell the kids at school. They'll be thrilled. Maybe she'd come down and meet them. They've never met a movie star before, though I've told them she got an award for Best Supporting Actress a few years ago.'

'She's flying over soon, and wants to visit. She'll e-mail me with the exact date of arrival,' Deirdre said, and that old, familiar, sinking feeling took a hold on her stomach.

Her glamorous, successful younger sister would soon be filling The Hollies with her larger-than-life personality, her beauty and talent, confidence and charm. Ronald would admire her, forgetting to show the bad-tempered, critical face he usually reserved for his wife. Maggie would be nauseatingly sycophantic. Nicole would be starry-eyed and impressed, looking at Clarissa as if she was a goddess condescending to grace mere mortals with her presence.

When Nicole had gone, Deirdre stacked the plates in the dishwasher, switched it on and phoned Nanette. 'Guess who's coming over from the States?'

'It's got to be your sister – Clarissa Howell,' Nanette replied, sounding reassuringly pragmatic.

'That's right.'

'Well, alleluia. God is in His heaven and all's well with the world. What is it with you and her? Dysfunctional or what,' Nanette went on, and Deirdre could hear the smile in her voice. This afforded scant comfort.

'I've told you that she broke free many years ago,' Deirdre said, reliving it in her mind. 'She'd shown promise in school plays and eventually passed exams and earned a place at RADA. Our parents were over the moon. They'd always been theatre-goers.'

'But weren't you talented, too?' Nanette asked, and Deirdre visualised her settling down to listen, cigarette smouldering away in the ashtray.

'I played the flute,' she replied, and remembered how she had been obscured and burnt to a crisp by Clarissa's fiery trail as she flashed across the firmament like a radiant comet.

'I remember. I've told you to come and join in with my lot on Monday nights. We could do with you in the orchestra. I know she's been in the papers and all that, and good on her, but you sound terrified at the thought of meeting her.'

'She always gets away with it – things, I mean.' Deirdre was voicing a resentment years old. 'I should have been pilloried by my family if it had happened to me. A couple of stormy marriages followed by divorce, a series of affairs exaggerated by the press and a spell in rehab. But, of course, she did win an Oscar and has been in many successful Broadway and West End plays, and films made on both sides of the Atlantic. She's still beautiful and still blessed by the gods. Everything she touches turns to gold.'

'She does seem to come up smelling of roses, doesn't she?' Nanette commented, then added, 'But karma is bound to catch up with her sometime. If not in this life, then the next. Don't despair, comrade. I'll be there to support you. Just call in the cavalry when she gets too much.'

'It's not only her, it's the whole shebang,' Deirdre sighed, finding, to her dismay, that she wanted to break down and cry.

'God! Weddings are the pits, aren't they? I suppose I shall be hearing from Allan and that addle-headed Patricia before long, but I'll tell you this for free – they are not staying at the manor. They can bloody well put up in a hotel. I wouldn't give her a pot to piss in.'

'I wish I was strong like you,' Deirdre said, fuming as she dwelt on Clarissa. It wasn't that she didn't love her, but sibling rivalry had gone very deep. 'It's stupid to feel so bad about her. After all, I've something that she hasn't.'

'And what's that?'

'Children,' Deirdre said.

'Big deal.' Nanette's sarcasm coiled, snakelike, down the line.

'Oh, you know what I mean. You wouldn't be without yours, would you?'

'Sometimes. Kids can be a pain in the butt, and it doesn't get a whole lot better as they grow up. Jody's going around looking as if she's lost sixpence and found a penny. She finished with that nice Alec, you know. On the loose again, and I know she ain't happy. But then, who is? Can I come over for a coffee? I want to tell you about Stewart Ramsden.'

'The dentist?'

'The sex-pot, though I'm only guessing so far. Will you be a love and invite him to the wedding? It'll be one in the eye for Allan if I turn up on Stewart's arm.'

'What about Shaun?' Deirdre reminded, teasing her gently, never knowing quite what to make of the men that Nanette termed 'rough trade'. For her own part, she had never been tempted.

One thing in Ronald's favour was that he was the first and only man to bring her to orgasm. They hadn't had sex till their wedding night and she'd never before experienced a climax. He had masturbated her and it had been a revelation. He still did this and, grateful but unaware that he was using it to control her, she had never once contemplated leaving him. Yet deep in the back of her mind she knew it didn't compensate for the times he humiliated and belittled her.

'Shaun?' Nanette gave a throaty chuckle. 'I don't think so, dear. Everyone in their place, and his is tending my pool, tidying my garden, and seeing to my other needs. OK?'

'I'll send Mr Ramsden an invite,' Deirdre promised, but it didn't make her feel much better about Clarissa, who was bound to outshine, out-talk and out-glamour every other woman present.

Deirdre hoped she didn't decide to add a dentist to her pack. Nanette wouldn't like that. Perhaps there would be a catfight in the middle of the reception. She brightened at the notion. An unseemly riot in the midst of such a stuffy, snobbish occasion tickled her fancy. That would serve Maggie right, and Ronald, too. Deirdre discovered a spirit of vengeance within her that she didn't know existed, and it had been brought to life by her sister's letter.

She poured coffee and waited for Nanette, opening the airmail and re-reading it. 'I'm bringing my new friend, Ed Brewster, with me. You'll like him. He's Australian and a stuntman.'

'Whoopee shit!' Deirdre said aloud, surprising herself with her vehemence.

'Can you meet me in town? The Daisy Coffee Shop. Make it 3.30 after the brats have been picked up by their proud mamas. I can never fathom why they think it cool to use heavy-duty four-wheel drives for such a piddling exercise.'

'It's a fad,' Ben answered, thrown because she had rung him. Never one for words, he now found himself stammering like a lovesick boy, which, he supposed, was precisely what he was. 'That'll be f-fine, Nicole. What? No t-trouble at all, glad to be of help. Jezebel? She's well, and the calf. I called him Nelson.'

'Why?'

'Dunno. Seemed to suit him somehow. He looks like a Nelson.'

'I hope I'm not around when you name your own children,' she said, with a throaty giggle that caused mayhem in his trousers.

He wanted to say: 'Not around? If I've got anything to do with it, you'll be their mother.' But some things are better left unsaid, and there are some itches that it's best not to scratch.

She was engaged to Greg Crawford and Ben steeled himself to having to listen to her rabbiting on about him over tea. But even this refined form of torture was better than not seeing her at all. Or was it? There were times when he simply buried himself in farm work, the harder the better, and others, like today, when she caught him off guard and he couldn't resist her.

He replaced the phone on its cradle and stood leaning against the battered kitchen table. Its pine top was rendered almost white by generations of women wielding scrubbing brushes. Usually, he took comfort from the peace, familiarity and ageless security found in his home. Not today. Hearing Nicle's voice had rattled him.

It was lunchtime and he made himself a beef and pickle sandwich, hacking the crusty bread into doorsteps, spreading it thick with butter and champing on it. He shopped and cooked and Mrs MacDonald 'did' for him. She was slapdash in her housekeeping and Ben didn't give a hoot – just as long as the floors were shown the vacuum cleaner now and again and the dust moved from place to place, his jeans and sweat-shirts available for wear: ironed or not he didn't care. Oil-fired central heating had been added and double glazing, but Ben continued to chop wood and stoke up the fire with logs the size of a man's torso. The wide-open stone hearth and ceiling-high cowl dominated the sitting room. He didn't much care for change.

As far back as he could remember he had wanted Nicole. In his mind, it had been a foregone conclusion that one day she would be his. Painfully shy and awkward with women, he did not consider himself attractive and his only sexual experience had been with the angry wife of a farming associate.

Twice his age, she had sought revenge on her adulterous husband who had sired at least one child out of wedlock and was at that time shagging the landlady of the local pub. Ben had first screwed her leaning up against a radiator in the hall. He had come almost as soon as he entered her and she had complained that she hadn't. Having taken his virginity she had led him down the pathways of pleasure and initiated him into ways of satisfying women. He had thought when she finally left her husband that he was in with a chance, but she found herself a tough, long-distance lorry driver and Ben was told to disappear, in no uncertain terms.

So it had been back to jacking off and wet dreams. He had felt tremendously let down, needing more than just physical relief, though he missed it. The luscious models in top-shelf magazines became his fantasies, and his fist was his mistress once again. Sometimes Nicole featured large when he was bringing himself to the peak, but he was always ashamed afterwards, fearing that he had besmirched her in some way. The large, quiet, shy man of the soil was a romantic at heart.

Restless after hearing Nicole's voice down the phone, he went to his room, undressed, and showered in the connecting bathing area. The water cascaded over him from powerful jets. Though nostalgic about the old way of life, he appreciated the benefits of modernity when it came to sanitation, water supplies, refrigeration and vehicles. Under the pump in the yard had been all very well, and he had thrilled to have Nicole watching, so much so that he had become hard despite the icy water. Thinking about it now, as he washed his hair and soaped his body, he was aware of that tightening in the groin that heralded an erection. It was happening, his cock rising, stiffening even as he watched, curving upwards, begging to be touched. He was an unusually large man, big at birth, so he had been told, and he'd never looked back. His height had been an embarrassment when he was a schoolboy but later this, coupled with his strength, had proved to be a boon. His penis was in keeping with the rest of him, a formidable weapon, and he sighed as he stroked it. He needed a girlfriend who would attend to it.

No, he corrected himself, he needed Nicole.

The very thought of her made his cock jerk. He held it in one hand and cupped his balls in the other. He had turned down the spray to a warm trickle that played over his shoulders and ran down his back and chest. He stood in the shower tray, enjoying the feel of soapy water, and handling himself, running a hand up the solid shaft and dragging back the foreskin. He watched the pre-come that oozed from the slit, and used this as a lubricant, massaging his cock, up the length of the iron-hard stalk to the acorn-shaped helm and back again. The skin was dark, the shaft knotted with a tracery of veins, and the cap had turned a deep, angry-looking red.

Ben smoothed a hand over it and pleasure made him groan. He stood with his legs apart and watched himself in the mirror tiles, or rather he watched that symbol of his manhood as it reared up, demanding release. It was fascinating, and so was the sight of his balls, tightening in their hairy sac. His chest was thatched with brown hair, a shade fairer than that on his head. This spread downwards, thinning out and scrawling past his navel, a thin, wavering line that thickened into a bush again at his lower belly, his cock sprouting from it.

If only it was Nicole's little hand caressing him. The

longing for her was like a pain in the region of his heart. He hated Greg, and wanted to see him dead, but knew this would be useless for then he would be canonised with Nicole worshipping at the altar of his memory. As these thoughts barrelled though Ben's head, he did not stop rubbing himself. Then, when the surge of feeling threatened to take over and make him come prematurely, he slacked his hold, deliberately refusing to touch it, using iron discipline. He saw how his reflected cock swayed, as if protesting in its spear-straight position, pressed back against his belly, needing someone, anyone, himself or a complete stranger, to massage it to completion. The urge was uncontrollable.

Ben couldn't wait any longer. He grabbed his penis impatiently and moved the foreskin up and down. At once the serpent fire that had been glowing in the chakra at the base of his spine started to leap, rising, rising, up and up, to his cortex, to his brain, where it exploded like shooting stars. He moaned and jerked, eyes rolling up in his head as he gasped in ecstasy. A stream of semen shot from him with such force that it spattered the mirror.

The phone jangled imperiously.

'Hold on, for Christ's sake,' Jody grumbled, padding across the carpet, wet from the bath, a towel wound, turban-wise, round her head.

Why was it that the bloody phone always went when one was either bathing, having sex or on the loo? She had taken to carrying the cordless with her constantly, but had forgotten it that morning, leaving it lying on her bed. Now she snatched it up.

'Hello. Jody Hamilton here. Who is that?' she said.

Her irritation was tempered with surprise when an

unfamiliar voice answered, 'It's Greg – Greg Crawford. I'm in town. How about I pick you up and we could go out for a bite to eat?'

Her first reaction was: what's he playing at? It was so strong that she said it aloud.

'I'm not playing at anything,' he replied, all injured innocence.

'Then why are you ringing me? Where's Nicole? Is she with you?'

'She's not. It's a working day and she'll be coping with the little junior school darlings.'

'I can't break off. Working on an important project. Have to get it finished,' she prevaricated, though this was true enough.

'I'll call in, shall I? I'm in your area.' He was nothing if not persistent.

'How do you know where I live?' Damn him, she thought. She hated interruptions when her ideas were in full spate. Even Katrina knew not to disturb her.

'Nicole gave me the address. She's keen for me to see what you do. Fancies a piece for our future garden.'

It was quicker to agree than to waste more time arguing about when and where and she agreed for him to call in an hour. She climbed into her working gear; a pair of blue denim dungarees over a black sleeveless vest, toe-post sandals, her hair scrunched, and very little make-up.

Carrying a cup of instant, she walked into the studio. She never did this these days without recalling seeing Katrina and Bobby at it. It wasn't annoying. It simply made her smile. She had never mentioned the incident to them.

It was peaceful there, her favourite place, steeped in the atmosphere she had created, filled with the tools of her trade, and shelves heaped with books relating to her craft. There were enlarged photos of her prize pieces and sketches of embryonic designs. A stereo was a must to encourage inspiration, though only between takes, not when actively engaged in tapping the source of her Muse. Miriam ribbed her for being a culture vulture, but Jody liked a variety of music, though, she had to admit, it was mainly classical, apart from Latin American and flamenco.

She put on a disc of Argentinean tango, the sexy rhythms speaking of the dance's origins in the bordellos of Buenos Aires. Humming the refrain, and doing a few steps, she took up her chisel and hacked at a corner of the monolith she was constructing out of cement and seashore pebbles.

She was lost in the world of imagination, happy as always when divorced from reality and residing in that headspace where anything was possible. Or perhaps it was more spirit-space, where her guardian angel waited to assist her when called by name. She had christened it (angels being reported as sexless) Juliano.

'Darling, you're so full of crap,' Nanette had commented when she had confided in her. 'Anyhow, I'm sure Juliano is a man's name. Sounds quite Italian and sexy and delicious. He can materialise at my bedside any time.'

'They are "it", mother. Androgynous. Neither male or female but combining both,' Jody had said, smiling ruefully, wishing her mother was not quite so liberal. She seemed to accept most of what Jody recounted, not in the least fazed by angel talk.

'Are you there, Juliano?' she whispered, preferring to think about this than dwell on Greg and the purpose of his visit.

There was no reply, not even the feathery rustle of enormous white wings, only an increase in peaceful vibes. She heard footsteps behind her and turned to see Greg.

'How did you get in?' she asked,

'Someone called Katrina answered my knock. One of your lesbian lovers?'

'My friend and lodger. I don't have any lovers.'

This is true, she thought. I can discount Kit. That was last week anyhow, and I've very nearly forgotten him. Well, not quite, perhaps, but haven't the urge to go back. Paying for sex still doesn't seem right.

Greg had his light-weight wool and cotton jacket slung over one shoulder, his cream shirt open at the neck and the sleeves rolled up to his elbows. His trousers matched the coat, and they were loose-fitting and belted. Jody didn't know much about men's fashion, but by the cut and verve she guessed it to be from the ateliers of a notable designer. He was looking so remarkably handsome that she regretted consenting to see him. Tempted? She might have been were he not engaged to her best friend. As it was, she kept seeing Nicole's face superimposed over his. It made her uncomfortable.

'You live here in solitary splendour?' he asked, hanging his coat on the back of a chair.

'Watch out for the dust,' she warned. 'You could hardly call it splendour, but I get by.'

'No man in your life?'

Oh, dear, not that hoary old question again. 'I was living with someone, but it wasn't working.' I don't know why I'm bothering to reply, she thought.

'His loss and my gain,' he said airily, then strolled round the studio and peered out of the opened French doors that connected with the garden.

'No one's gain, except my own,' she said grimly, riled by his assumption that he stood the remotest chance with her. 'You're out of the running anyway.'

He moved close by her, head to one side as he stared at the block on which she was working. 'It's pleasing,' he said condescendingly. 'I didn't expect to be impressed, but I am.' He stared down at her in a way calculated to melt the sternest resolve, a tactic that he must have found remarkably effective. 'As for my being engaged? That never stopped a good man, did it?'

One of his hands came to rest on her bare shoulder. The temperature was rising in the studio and she could feel wetness in her armpits, masked by deodorant. She disliked the odour of perspiration. Miriam rhapsodised about the smell of fresh sweat, but it wasn't for Jody. She liked men to use expensive body spray. Greg's skin breathed out a Calvin Klein fragrance. She took a step away from him.

'You're a rat-fink,' she said, putting down her chisel lest she be tempted to stab him. 'Nicole loves and trusts you. I wouldn't touch you with a barge pole, so quit coming on strong.'

He laughed, showing immaculate dentistry and bringing to mind her mother's new rave from the grave, Stewart. It was a fortunate remembrance, for Greg had pulled out all the stops and was at his most charming.

Jody almost wished that it could have been otherwise, with him an ordinary guy she had met somewhere else – nothing to do with Nicole. But even then, that radar system she had developed as a protection from falling for creeps would surely have worked. Greg was trouble with a capital T. He didn't know the meaning of the word fidelity. An opportunist, he would claw his way to the top of the political tree, stepping on anyone in order to attain his goal. Women would be preyed upon and then discarded. So why was he so damned attractive?

'Would you like a drink?' she said, pushing away the arm he was trying to insinuate round her waist.

'I've the BMW outside. Don't want to be breathalysed. Can't afford the inconvenience of being banned.'

'Coffee, then?'

'No, thanks. I didn't come here to pass the time of day.'

'Why did you come?' She didn't look at him. The way he pushed a floppy dark lock from his forehead was just too alluring, even though she recognised it as a crappy act.

His arm came round her again. He was like an octopus. She was drawn close to his chest, the heat of his body reaching out to enfold her. There was an almighty bulge behind his fly buttons. Jody was not going to dignify his grasp on her by struggling.

'I came because I want to take you to bed,' he murmured, his voice velvety brown and seductive. 'Come on, Jody. Admit that you want it, too.'

'You're wrong,' she said, any attraction she felt for him withering under his blatantly amoral attitude. 'I'm only involved because of Nicole. Her happiness is all that matters, and she should be warned about you.'

He smiled grimly, but tightened his grip. 'And who is going to tell her? You? She'd not believe you and I would say that you threw yourself at me, thinking that I was rich and determined to fuck your way into my wallet. You'd lose her, Jody.'

'You'd do that, wouldn't you?' She was perfectly still in his arms, refusing to afford him the satisfaction of a struggle. Though sorely tempted to use her nails and give him the fight he so richly deserved, she knew that if she marked him it would only serve to corroborate his story and gain Nicole's sympathy.

'In time, you'll learn that nothing stands in my way,'

he said, leaning closer so that his breath whispered past her ear and made her nerve endings tingle.

'Get out,' she snarled, enraged at his colossal impudence and her own unwilling but wanton response to him.

He raised a peaked eyebrow and stared down into her eyes. 'Is that what you really want?'

'Yes. It is. Shift your butt out of here and don't come back.'

'You'll give in,' he said confidently. 'If not before that wedding, then afterwards. Nicole and I will be seeing much of our friends, as young newly-weds do. You'll not be able to refuse our invitations to weekend parties.'

Before she could stop him, he captured her mouth with his, plundering her lips with his tongue. This was too much. He's like a bloody invader, she stormed inside, putting her two hands flat against his chest and pushing.

'Are you OK, Jody?' Katrina said, coming in from the garden, wearing a thong, nipple rings and sunglasses, a towel draped over one arm. She stopped, stock still, the blankness of her shades hiding eyes that didn't miss a trick.

'Yes. Greg was just leaving. I think you two have already met. He's Nicole's fiancé.'

'Oh, is he indeed,' Katrina said, sardonically.

'I'll see you soon.' Greg let Jody go, ignoring Katrina.

'Not if I see you first,' she snapped.

'You can't avoid me. You're one of the bridesmaids. Oh, and I shouldn't mention anything to Nicole, if I were you. I meant what I said. Good afternoon, Jody.'

'Goodbye, Greg.'

6

'What's wrong?' Ben asked, as he left the car park with Nicole.

He had picked her up at 3.15 outside the church school where she worked, and she had been a little late, keeping him waiting, a thing she never dared do to Greg. Ben seemed grumpy and she almost regretted phoning him and wasn't really sure why she had done so.

'Nothing's wrong,' she answered defensively. 'Did I say anything was wrong?'

'No,' he grunted and shrugged, and when she started out for the charity shop in the mall, he strode along beside her, though added, 'Do we have to?'

'I want to,' she said pettishly, and wondered why he put up with her.

She admitted that she sometimes acted like a spoilt brat. Teacher? Maybe, but to him, apparently, she was still the scrawny tomboy who had gone fishing and played around the farm before responsibility caught up with him and he put away childish things, forced to become a man.

The charity shop was neat, tidy, manned by blue-rinsed volunteers and over-priced. That was the trouble now; a plethora of daytime TV programmes about finding treasures in your attic, presented by smooth operators who gave the public too much information. Consequently, everyone was rummaging for that valuable painting or piece of china, and the charity shops had their own advisors on the bric-a-brac donated to them and charged accordingly.

'It's a con,' Ben grumbled and seemed bored, though he usually enjoyed bargain hunting, after anything old and interesting.

'Did you get out the wrong side of the bed?' she asked, waiting while the assistant took off the price tag, popped a one-eyed, one-armed, moth-eaten teddy bear into a carrier bag and handed it to her.

'Is this for your baby? How old is he or she? Or perhaps you're excepting?' Blue-Rinse asked, eyeing Jody's waistline, then twinkling roguishly behind her gold-rimmed spectacles at Ben.

'It's for me,' Nicole answered curtly, and took it tenderly, like a mother with her newborn.

'There's nothing wrong with me,' Ben grunted, glaring at her sideways. 'Did you really need another bear? You've already got a whole platoon, haven't you?

'One can never have too many bears,' she reproved, then laughed and grabbed his arm. 'I'm starving, and you can have the honour of buying me jam doughnuts, chocolate eclairs and toasted tea-cakes, in that order.'

She wished she felt as unselfconscious with Greg. Truth to tell, her fiancé scared her half to death. She denied it rigorously, pitched between heaven and hell, at one moment ecstatically happy, in the next cast down. I've led too retiring a life, she thought, as they strolled past the statue symbolising a wool pack, Heronswood having been a centre for the woollen industry, and came to the Daisy Coffee Shop. She had taken Greg there once and he had pronounced it quaint, which was worse than saying it was naff. Ben, however, accepted it as part and parcel of their heritage. His bad moods rarely had the impact or lasted as long as Greg's.

There were a few customers at the tables, drinking tea or coffee and smoking. This was one of the few places left that didn't make you feel like a pariah when you got out your pack and lighter. Not that Ben or Nicole indulged now.

'I sometimes feel like starting again. Don't you?' she said, when Ben had placed their order and returned to the table.

'Yes,' he said, staring at her. 'If I get uptight, like when Jezebel couldn't give birth to her calf. I nearly asked Stan for a roll-up.' His eyes sharpened and he added, 'Why did you want to see me?'

'I needed a chat with someone who isn't involved in the wedding,' she said. He had always been there for her, as far back as she could remember.

'Oh? Being a pain, are they? Your Mum and Gran?'

'Not Mum. She's the sweetest thing out, but there was a right royal rumpus about the bridesmaids' dresses the other day.'

'You still want to go ahead with it?'

Nicole couldn't answer for an astonished second, then, 'Of course I do! I love Greg and he loves me. That's all that matters.'

'You stick to your guns, in that case,' he answered, and she wondered why his eyes were so bleak. 'It's your life and you can tell 'em all to go to hell.'

'You're right. Thank you, Ben. You've always been my mate. I wish you could have been the best man, but Greg had already chosen Piers.'

'That wouldn't have been my thing, speeches and all,' he said, looking down at his hands. They were work-roughened and immensely strong, yet she recalled how gentle they had been with the calf.

She touched one on its lightly furred back, saying, 'But you will be there, won't you?'

He refused to meet her eyes, mumbling, 'Do I have to wear a monkey jacket?'

'Just come in something tidy, that's all.'

'The suit I had for Dad's funeral?'

She remembered that sad occasion, with herself standing by him in the crematorium. A rainy day. Many mourners, for Denis Templeton had been a popular man. The wake held in a pub. She wished Ben had another outfit. It seemed unlucky to wear his mourning suit on her special day that was supposed to be filled with joy and happiness.

He picked up on her thoughts, helping himself to a doughnut and then saying, 'If I come at all, and I'm not promising – shall be busy with the harvest – then I'll get myself new clobber. But you know that such bashes don't appeal – dancing and making small talk. It was never my style.'

'You don't have to stay to the disco in the evening. Greg and I will be gone by then anyway. On our honeymoon. A secret location. He won't tell me where it is, just hints that I should pack my bikini and sun-oil.'

'I don't like hot countries,' Ben rejoined, while she poured tea from a small china pot and handed him a cup. It seemed lost in his large fist. 'Spain and all that. It's never appealed.'

'You might be surprised,' she said, elbows on the table, holding her tea to her lips in both hands. 'Think of swimming in a warm sea, and sitting outside your villa on starlit evenings, watching distant fireworks. There's a fiesta every night during the season, honouring some saint or other.'

'Too hot. Too foreign,' he snapped. 'Give me soggy old England any time, 'cept I want it dry when we're getting the corn in.'

This riled her. He had always been such a stick-in-the-mud. 'How do you know if you've never tried?' she demanded, suddenly angry because he was throwing up these barriers between them. 'I'll bet I could make you change your mind.'

'Well, you can't, and anyway, you'll be there with your bridegroom. You wouldn't want strangers hanging around.'

He studied her mouth intently, then leaned forwards and wiped a trace of chocolate from her top lip, using his little finger. To her astonishment, he transferred it to his tongue, sucking it in. The gesture was curiously intimate and totally unexpected. It left her feeling hot and disturbed. It was as if a faithful dog had suddenly turned disobedient, showing a will of its own and trying to hump her leg.

At that moment, she noticed that three girls seated at a nearby table were looking at Ben admiringly, whispering and giggling. Nicole saw him in a new light. He was impressive, if one liked height and a big frame. She had taken this for granted, along with the fact that he was always there for her. Now he seemed embarrassed, as if regretting his impetuosity.

She placed her hand on his arm, trying to convey that she wasn't in the least offended, saying, 'I hope my being married won't make any difference to our friendship.'

Nicole had rarely known him angry, but now his brows drew together in the blackest scowl she had ever seen on a man's face. He dragged his arm away, snarling, 'It'll ruin everything. You'll be Mrs Crawford, canvassing for your husband, no doubt, and like Caesar's wife, you'll have to be above reproach. Do you really believe that he'll take kindly to you coming to the farm on your own?'

'He trusts me,' she said indignantly.

Ben laughed, and it was bitter. 'More fool him.'

'What are you suggesting? That I'm a slag?' Nicole could hardly believe her ears.

'No, not a slag. Just someone who deludes herself, lives in cloud-cuckoo-land and feels let down when things don't turn out as she wanted.'

This was profound, coming from him, but it hurt, too. She had always had and expected to continue to receive, his unquestioning support. 'You make me sound like a brainless idiot,' she muttered.

'That you're not,' he vouchsafed, the frown dissipating slightly. 'But you do get carried away, Nicole. Life isn't a fairy-tale, and we don't all live in toyland.'

'But it's seems like that, ever since Greg proposed to me,' she said earnestly, hands clasped in the lap of her cotton dirndl skirt, feeling the warmth of her thighs and that unsatisfied throb between them that appeared whenever she thought about Greg and visualised their wedding night. 'I've met my prince and shall soon be his wife. We'll live in London and buy a house down here, too. I love him, and we'll have children . . .'

'And live happily ever after,' he added, with a cynicism rare for him. She remembered reading somewhere that the greatest romantics become the greatest cynics. She had never thought Ben in the slightest way romantic, but maybe he had unplumbed depths.

'I hope so,' she said, in a small voice.

He stood up, his height impressing the interested girls even more. 'I've got to go,' he said abruptly, and picked up the bill, leaving a tip for the waitress. 'I'll drop you home, if you like.'

'I'll walk, thank you,' she answered stiffly. He had changed. Their relationship would never be the same again.

One day, he, too, would marry. A sensible girl, most suitable to be a farmer's wife. And I'll go to his wedding, she thought, just see if I don't, and I'll wish them well from the bottom of my heart. Yet her lips still tingled from the touch of his finger when he had wiped away the trace of chocolate and that irksome throb remained. When she moved to leave, she was aware that her panty-gusset was damp.

'She wouldn't let me shag her when I called in the other day,' Greg said, his eyes flashing angrily.

'Who are you talking about, old lad?' replied Piers, shifting his bulk on the lounger facing the sun on the balcony of Greg's riverside penthouse. He was shoeless and his trousers were rolled up, his shins already turning pink. He reached for his glass of ice-cold lager.

'Jody. Who else?' Greg muttered, lying back, stretching out his long legs and crossing them at the ankles. He had nothing on his feet and was wearing shorts and acquiring an even tan, easy for him to do with his swarthy skin.

'Ah, the reluctant bridesmaid,' Piers drawled, adjusting his shades. He imagined they made him look cool, even sinister, but this was impossible with his typically English, upper-class features.

'She's not reluctant. That's the problem. Got this bloody loyalty thing about Nicole.'

'Who you haven't poked.'

'I'm saving it for the honeymoon. Christ! She's so damn pure, I've got to get my prick up somehow. I think she wants me to fuck her, but I'm keeping her hanging on. Can't let this one slip the net. Her father's too influential for that. He's my sponsor for joining the Masons.'

'I wish my old man would do the same for me, but he's always putting it off.'

Greg shot him a blistering glare. 'It's because you're such a prat. If you'd only put your back into it, he'd make you a partner in his firm. But you won't, you lazy arse, and he knows it. Jesus, Piers, can't you play along with it? That's what I've done, and look where it's got me. Wine, women and politics. I'm almost there, matey. And dear little Nicole is helping me, though she doesn't know it. She's falling more and more in love with me. Do you know, for all her manners and graces, she comes like the clappers when I diddle her clit.'

'You're a bastard, aren't you?' Piers commented. 'But I like your style.'

'Years of practice,' Greg said, grinning across at his sidekick. He could be himself with Piers, talk dirty, talk politics (which was pretty much the same thing), and indulge his sexual predilections without fear or favour.

'I'm sorry for your bride-to-be,' Piers commented, taking off his shirt.

'You're putting on weight,' Greg remarked, running an eye over his friend's torso. 'Almost developing a beer gut. And you'd better protect that fair skin or you'll be red as a lobster and that's not going to give the girls the hots.'

'OK. I know. Have you any lotion? As for this,' and he patted his belly, 'I don't fancy dieting.'

'What about exercise?' Greg suggested, lifting his face to the glory of the sun, then admiring the River Thames glinting below.

What a view, he thought, giving himself a mental pat on the back. The apartment was most desirable with its high security, underground parking and fashionable address. He had bought it at the right time and it was now worth a cool million.

'Gyms are boring,' yawned Piers.

'Not fencing classes, they're great,' Greg observed. 'They give you stamina and poise and it impresses the birds. They associate it with swordsmen and types like Errol Flynn, who was reputed to have had an enormous dick!'

Greg was a fan of old films, and had a large collection of videos and DVDs. He modelled himself somewhat on the rugged heroes of the past – Robert Mitchum, Clark Gable, and Errol, of course. He found, too, that it stood him in good stead with older people and he was very much aware of wooing his constituency when the time came for him to stand for Parliament. He needed elderly as well as young voters. He knew which side his bread was buttered, proud of himself because he was so two-faced, using this ability and gaining through it.

'Why don't you give over?' Piers grumbled, beginning to sweat and obviously wanting to go inside. 'I do my best. Have a round of golf occasionally. We can't all be Adonis.'

Greg was amused by his friend's discomfort. 'It's for your own good,' he said calmly. 'You want to fuck, don't you? You want to be lean and keen, like me. You'll have to put some effort into it.'

'I don't have to bother. I can buy it. You do, despite your success with the totty.'

'Only when I want specialist treatment,' Greg answered, and his cock stirred in his pants, the material rubbing against his helm as he remembered the last time he'd indulged himself in that way. Maybe he'd do so again tonight. Why not? He had to perform his duty the coming weekend, visiting Heronswood again. Time for a treat first.

'You fancy a trip to the country?' he asked.

'Will Miriam be there?' Piers perked up.

'Give her a bell and find out. I shall be meeting Nicole's aunt, who happens to be Clarissa Howell.'

'The actress?'

'The very same. She's still beautiful, though must be forty. I might stand a chance there.'

'Aunt and niece?'

'Why not? I've had mother and daughter before now.'

Memories of mature women were making him randy. He'd always got on well with them. They were so grateful if a young man shafted them, and generous, too. Money, clothes, gold watches, cars – he had found nothing wrong in being a kept man, though this was years ago now.

Piers turned his face towards him, but it was impossible to read his eyes behind the shades as he asked, oddly eager, 'Have you ever done it the other way? You know, the Tradesmen's Entrance?'

'Arse-fucking? Oh, yes.'

'And you'll not tell Nicole about this, or your involvement with the pervy scene?'

'No. It has nothing to do with her. I might introduce her to anal, though, if the horseplay moves in that direction. God, can you imagine what a shocker that would be, her so prim and all.'

There were times when Greg found Piers simple beyond belief. He was certainly a shilling short of a ten bob note. He sat up and refreshed his drink, enjoying the sun, enjoying that hard, urgent feeling in his cock. He placed a hand over his bulge and gave it a tug. His mind streaked ahead to the evening's entertainment and his prick stood to attention.

'Another half hour here and then let's get cleaned up and take a trip to Willards,' he suggested.

'What about dinner?' Piers protested, and Greg smiled, knowing that food was almost as vital to him as sex.

'We can eat there, though I don't intend to make a pig of myself, or get bladdered. I've other, more stimulating things in mind.'

It's funny how it happens, Jody reflected. There you are, minding your own business, and suddenly, out of the blue, like it says in the song, you look across a crowded room and bingo! Lightning strikes, thunder rolls and you're saying as you are introduced to him, 'Hello. I'm one of the bridesmaids,' and blushing like a fool.

'Are you OK?' Miriam said, coming out to join her where she was sitting on the terrace wall.

Miriam always dressed for events, and her stylist had charged her eighty pounds for making her hair look as if she had just got out of bed after a frantic night with a sex-maniac. Her shift dress was short and figure hugging and showed her arms, her back and most of her bosom.

Jody had not attempted to compete, adding a sleeveless top with a flower motif and spaghetti straps to a calf-length skirt, cut on the cross and with a handkerchief-pointed hem. She had added pendant earrings and a coral necklace and, though not wanting to bother, was glad she had taken the trouble to doll herself up for this informal gathering at The Hollies. A barbecue was on the menu, with Ronald officiating and Deirdre running around, doing most of the work while he took the credit.

In answer to Miriam's question, she replied, 'I'm all right, though the day started with Katrina spewing up in the bathroom. She staggered out and no, it wasn't a hangover. It was morning sickness. She's up the duff, in the pudding club, with child. Bobby's the father, apparently, and he's as proud as a dog with two dicks, and she asked if they could stay till they find a place of their own.'

Having handled the initial shock, Jody had been pleased for them. She had stood there, offering her congratulations and thinking about how she had seen them at it in the studio. She could have sworn they'd been doing it anal. This must have happened some other time.

'How far gone are you?' she had asked.

'Eight weeks. We did a pregnancy test, didn't we, Bobby? And it was positive. Then I went to see the doc, and it's definite. A New Year baby. We'll start at antenatal classes soon.'

We? Jody had thought, bemused by the change in them. 'Are you attending, Bobby?'

'Sure,' he had answered from the depths of the couch placed at a precise angle to the TV. He was watching a football replay. He had managed to drag his eyes away long enough to look at her and smile. 'Got to get ready for the birth.'

'But it's Katrina having it, not you.'

'The modern father wants to be included every step of the way,' Katrina had replied smugly. 'We shall opt for natural childbirth, of course.'

'He may,' Jody had retorted acerbically. 'But it's not his body that will go through the mill. I should keep an open mind on this, if I were you. Wait till you get there and scream out for painkillers, if you need them.'

'I don't think so,' Bobby had said, putting an arm round Katrina as she took the seat beside him. 'You'll cope wonderfully, love. I'm sure.'

Now Miriam expressed surprise bordering on disbelief at the news. 'Here's a turn up for the books. I thought she was a go-ahead career girl.'

'She is. I think this was a blip. She intends to go on working and, after the sprog's born, Bobby will be a househusband.'

'Lucky old him. As long as you don't get roped into brat-sitting.'

All these options had jostled for place in Jody's mind, but she was willing to help them out while they were property hunting. 'They'll soon get somewhere. Both of them are in the money.'

'Bobby, too?'

'He's a model and does TV commercials. It's all OK, but I'm feeling wrung out after meeting Greg again. I was ready to vomit, seeing him being so charming to the Carpenters and the famous auntie. God, I believe he fancies his chances with her.'

'He's despicable. We should grass him up to Nicole,' Miriam said, perching beside her but with a, 'Fuck! This stone is cold! You must be freezing your butt off.'

'We can't tell her. She'd never believe us. We'll just have to catch him out some other way.'

'I'll give Piers a hand-job and get information out of him while I'm pumping him dry.'

'How noble of you. Such self-sacrifice,' Jody teased, but she was abstracted, thinking about the newcomer who had taken her fingers in a firm grip, looked into her eyes and made an instant connection. 'What did you think of him?' she added.

'Who?' Miriam was sitting on her hands to keep the chill from her bottom. 'Oh, you mean Clarissa Howell's friend, that Australian dweeb – what's his name?'

'Ed Brewster,' Jody supplied. It was carved in letters of fire across her brain.

'You fancy him, don't you?'

Jody's face was growing hot. She wished she could flirt and engage in complicated mating rituals as naturally as Miriam. I'm just too honest and wear my heart on my sleeve, she decided.

'I thought he was a bit of all right,' she answered, trying to brazen it out.

'Yep. I'd give him breakfast,' Miriam nodded. 'But Clarissa! What a snobby tart. And the others bowing and scraping. She looks good for her age, though. What is she? Forty odd? Has had face-work, by the look of it, and can't eat more than a crumb and has probably brought along her trainer. I wouldn't mind her life. I could cope with the red-carpet treatment.'

Jody shuddered. The press had descended on Heronswood at the first whisper of Clarissa's touchdown at her sister's house. She hadn't been ensconced many hours and already there had been a flash on the local TV and an earnest newscaster giving a run-through of her life and times and return home to the West Country.

'She's been in rehab at The Abbey,' she pointed out.

'Several times,' Miriam chorused gleefully. 'Lost weight, put it on, becomes bloated or anorexic, drinking like a fish or on the wagon. Popping pills or prescribed antidepressants. The woman's a mess. If you shook her, she'd rattle. Can't think how she can possibly be Deirdre's sister.'

'Genetics. A throwback along the line,' Jody offered. 'Anyhow, it's Ed I want to get to know, not Nicole's aunt.'

'You'll have to bottle her to get at him.'

'We'll see. You concentrate on Piers and I'll make sure Greg pays attention to Nicole. Clarissa is busy being a movie star and I shall talk to Ed, offer to show him round the place or something equally pathetic.'

'Careful, girl. You don't want anyone with a shit-load of emotional baggage,' Miriam warned.

Jody clung to this sensible advice as they went into the drawing room where they were jostled by the other guests and pigeonholed by Maggie. Their dresses had arrived from Brides To Be, and were even now awaiting them at Wedding Belles.

'You'll be here Monday?' Maggie challenged, brooking no refusal. 'We'll see them, and you can try them on. They should fit perfectly as your measurements were sent and they were made especially for you.' She gave a disapproving sniff, as much as to say, 'Had it been down to me, you'd have worn what you were offered.'

'We're staying for a long weekend anyway,' Miriam said bluntly, snatching a glass of wine from the tray of a passing waiter. The Carpenters are loaded, she concluded, and can well afford to pay, and they will. There's no way I'm going to fork out for a dress I'll never wear again. Aloud she said, 'There's Piers. Excuse me. I promised him the Last Waltz.'

Her irony was lost on Maggie who looked puzzled and said, 'Really, dear? But there's no band.'

Jody was coming back from the toilet when she rounded a corner and collided with Ed. 'Steady she goes,' he remarked, catching her under the elbows. 'Jody, isn't it?' His voice was low-pitched, his accent a cross between an American and a native of the antipodes.

'That's right. You've a good memory,' she answered, flustered.

'Only when I want,' he said cockily and she decided that she didn't like him. He was too full of himself.

'Have you been to England before?' She escaped into empty chitchat, a thing she despised, and here she was, in the trap and all because of an arrogant, swaggering male. It was galling.

'Was over here a couple of years back. I love your countryside, so green after brown old Oz. Lots of arid spaces in the bush there. That's why the imported camel took to it. They just about fit in, too, bad-tempered old buggers, stubborn as mules and ready to spit in your eye when you least expect it.'

What am I doing here, discussing the bad habits of camels? she asked herself, and disengaged from him, though her body wanted to stay.

'Excuse me,' she said, in her best private school accent.

'I don't think so,' he drawled, and pressed her back till her spine touched the wall, then boxed her in with his arms braced on either side of her chest. The corridor was deserted. If she screamed no one would hear, and her pride wouldn't let her do that.

'You're joking, of course,' she said coolly, though her blood was racing and she fought the desire to lift her ribcage and push her breasts against him.

He was tall, angular, and ruggedly handsome, in *Indiana Jones* mould. His nose had been broken, in a scrap, she assumed, and he had a little scar on his right cheekbone. His hair was straight and brown and untidy, brushing his nape and falling over his brow. The tropical sun that had given him an even, coppery complexion (all over? she speculated) had put blond streaks in the top layers. Long, strong tendons sculpted his throat, running down over his collarbones and meeting the neck of his blue denim shirt, open over a tawny chest with a coating of crisp hair. He was designer scruffy, his chin stubbled, and a pair of torn jeans were slung low on his hips, fastened by a wide leather belt with an eagle-ornamented buckle. It laid emphasis on the generous swelling behind the faded fly.

He was perfect, if you yearned for a rough and ready seeing-to. Jody couldn't imagine sophisticated foreplay, or any at all, for that matter. It was probably a case of 'Brace yerself, Sheila,' if you had the misfortune to be seduced by him.

'I never joke when I meet someone who I know is going to play a big part in my life,' he averred.

'What's with you? Psychic or something?' She used sarcasm as a form of defence.

'Maybe.' A smile hovered about his firm lips, and she hated him for making mock of her.

'You're with Clarissa, aren't you?' she asked, determined to take the wind out of his sails.

'Could be,' he replied laconically.

'You arrived with her.'

'So I did. We're working on a movie together.'

'You're an actor?'

'I'm a stunt man.'

What else? she thought, and said, 'How macho.'

'It pulls the sheilas.'

'Does it? Some girls have no taste.'

'Why are you so prickly?'

He hadn't let her go, still caging her with his arms and she was forced to look up at him. His bright blue eyes had tiny lines at the outer corners, as if he was constantly searching the ranges for enemies.

'Prickly? *Moi?*'

'Yep. Prickly as a damn old porcupine.'

'You'd know about that, I suppose, grubbing around in the outback? What do they call it? Going walk-about?'

'My, my. And whose rattled your cage, lady?' he asked, regarding her through a masked expression.

She wanted to scream, You – *you*, with your exciting newness and bravado and devil-may-care. And you're just the kind of man I loathe. You probably look down your damaged nose at women. I hope it was one who broke it for you. Did she hit you? To you we're sheilas, inferior creatures to be kept pregnant and bare-foot in the kitchen.

'You don't know anything about me. Strewth! You're assuming a lot. And why shouldn't I feel that way about you? You've not told me who you are or what you do, so I assume you're an empty-headed bimbo – a party girl – an easy lay.'

'And if I were to tell you that I'm an artist, producing garden sculpture, and respected in my field?'

'I'd say, good on you. Show me some.'

'Over my dead body. I don't want to see you ever again once this wedding is over. Go back to America or wherever with your mistress. Keep her sweet, so that she can get work for you.'

He lowered his arms, and eyed her steadily, a sardonic smile lifting his lips. 'I don't reckon you'll believe me when I say that I'm as well known as she is in the industry. There's no way I need her, except for . . .'

'Eddie! There you are! I've been looking all over for you,' cried Clarissa, in her rich, dramatic voice, as she materialised from the direction of the conservatory. She was slender and superbly turned out in a Lazaro cocktail dress, her honey-coloured hair carefully arranged to look shaggy and informal.

He was totally unfazed, turning and saying, 'I've been chewing the fat with Jody here. She's one of Nicole's bridesmaids, and a renowned sculptress.'

'How clever,' Clarissa replied with a blatant air of disinterest, and she linked her arm with his.

'Off you go, Fido,' Jody muttered. 'Do what Mummy says.'

'I'll see you later,' he growled. 'Don't think I've finished with you. No way.'

Nanette had declined the Saturday night invitation to
The Hollies. An extra rehearsal had been called and she
had headed off for the church hall.

A quick glance round showed her that Stewart was
already there, running through one of the Pirate King's
songs, but quietly, in the background with Bernie. The
rest of the cast were chattering and laughing till Aubrey
clambered on to the stage and banged on the rostrum.

'Calm down, ladies and gentlemen,' he began sternly.
'As you know, I've called this additional rehearsal as
time is running on and a number of you are still
clinging to your books. It's high time you knew it by
heart. It really won't do. G and S has to be played
deadpan and absolutely straight, or it simply doesn't
work. Familiarity with the words means that you are
free to concentrate on the dancing and movements,
under the guidance of our choreographer, Peggy Watts.'

Peggy, a devoted member of HOS, nodded and smiled
and backed him up. She was unmarried and ran ball-
room dancing classes at the fitness centre. It was
rumoured that she was carrying a torch for Aubrey, had
been for years.

Nanette had heard him scolding before. Every time
they did a production there were mutterings and dis-
content among the ranks, and Aubrey tearing out what
was left of his hair. It was traumatic and exhilarating
and was always 'all right on the night'.

Stewart had stopped singing to listen, and he stood
beside her and she responded by an almost impercepti-
ble movement of her hips. Her nipples thrust against
her black brassière, twin peaks aching to be caressed by
his agile, dental practitioner's fingers. So far nothing

had happened between them, though they had chatted a great deal, partaken of coffee together, shared the delight of watching videos in her cosy, old-world lounge.

They had progressed from G and S to the works of Verdi and Puccini. She had even put on the passionate dancing of Spain and quite explicit modern ballet, but so far hadn't been able to raise a bean in his trouser department. This was an intriguing novelty. Ever since she entered her teens, Nanette had found no difficulty in having any man she wanted. Stewart was proving a hard nut to crack, but I'll do it, she vowed, I'll crack his nuts for him!

Suitably chastened by Aubrey, the cast assembled and the men's chorus of pirates kicked off with the start of Act 1. Then Nanette made her appearance as Ruth and was on stage throughout with Stewart. Even Aubrey had admitted that he was up to professional standards, a perfect Pirate King.

Having finished her scene with Frederick – after he and she landed on the seashore and she had declared her love for him, only to be spurned as too old – she had a break while he cavorted with the Major General's daughters. Stewart was not due to appear again for a while, and she contrived to get him outside, on the pretext of cooling down.

'What a beautiful evening,' she declared, sitting on one of the solid green-painted park benches erected by public contributions in order that those who wished might rest in the churchyard and contemplate their mortality.

It wouldn't be the first time she had been bonked on a gravestone, but she glumly reflected that it was hardly likely to happen tonight, her companion being of a retiring nature, despite his occupation. She fished in her bag for her cigarettes, lit one and blew the smoke heavenwards. Stewart followed suit with a thin brown cheroot that made him look more like a bandit than a pirate.

'All you need is a sombrero,' she remarked, thinking how personable he was, on her wave-length. It was all very fine to have an uncultured lover, but as one became older, then other things mattered besides the length of his todger. I'd like the chance to measure Stewart's though, she thought.

'I could sing Ramerrez, the outlaw in *The Girl of the Golden West*,' he suggested.

'You could, but there's one problem.'

'And what is that?'

'Ramerrez is a tenor role, not a baritone.'

'Of course. Silly me,' he replied, and moved a tad closer to her on the bench. Bats skittered and swooped from the bell tower, and the twilight was hushed and mysterious. 'It's like a Hammer House of Horror set,' he added.

'I should be scared, if you weren't here,' she whispered, playing the frightened, helpless poppet that was so far removed from her earthy reality, hoping this might get him going.

'I can't imagine you frightened of anything,' he said jocularly. 'You always seem so self-sufficient and brave.'

Oh, damn, she thought, I've put him off by being Miss Super Efficient. What does he know of the lonely nights and the things that go bump therein when one cowers under the covers, too frightened to move? I'm like that sometimes, and always sleep with a cosh beside me.

'Most of living alone is good, but there's a part of it that isn't,' she said.

'You have many friends, surely, besides your family. I have heard . . .' Here he paused.

Nanette was on it like a ferret down a rabbit hole. 'What have you heard? Who has been dishing the dirt? Not that I care,' and she flung back her head and ruffled her hair.

'Well, someone said, I can't recall who, that you are having an affair with your pool man.' He brought this out hesitantly, adding quickly, 'Not that it's anyone's business but yours.'

'Too right it isn't,' she answered angrily, running through a list of possible suspects. 'If I deny it, you won't believe me.'

'Yes, I will,' he said staunchly. 'I know what it's like to be on the receiving end of gossip. That's why I'm cautious in what I do.'

'Like showing an interest in me,' she replied, grabbing the bull by the horns.

'That's right. I like you a lot and want to spend more time with you, but I'm new here and have my reputation to consider.'

'Oh, sod that,' she declared, flung her arms round his neck and kissed him, long and deep. To her delight, his lips parted under hers and she felt the urgent press of his tongue.

He lifted his head, and held her to him and his hands were trembling. 'Look here,' he whispered unsteadily. 'We'd better take this slowly.'

'Don't worry about a thing,' she assured him, running her hands over his chest and letting her fingers brush across his trouser closure. She was rewarded by a promising swelling that hadn't been there before. 'One of the few advantages of maturity is patience. We'll see what happens, shall we?'

The tempo of the music had changed and both recognised that they must be there on cue. 'You're a lovely woman, Nanette,' he said as they walked back to the hall, hand in hand.

'And you're not so bad yourself,' she said with a laugh. 'How about coming back to my place, just for coffee and videos, you know? I recorded a new production of *Madame Butterfly* from Covent Garden last Saturday night. It went out on BBC2.'

'I'd like that,' he replied, and did not release her fingers until they were inside.

7

'It was super to see Greg. I hate the times when he's away. He's been so loving tonight, but didn't take the hint when I offered to leave my bedroom door ajar. In a way this impresses me, but on the other hand I want him so badly. Clarissa arrived. What a star! I'm so lucky that she's coming to my wedding.'

Nicole put her pen down and stared into space, then she took it up again and continued writing, 'Ben's in a strange mood these days. I suppose he's up to his eyes in it, running the farm practically single-handed. Tomorrow, Daddy has suggested that some of us go riding, borrowing horses from Nanette's stable. I'm thankful that I've been around ponies since I was eight. Would hate to make a fool of myself in front of Greg. He says he's used to them, but Ed, that's Clarissa's boy friend who claims to be a stuntman, boasts that he was practically born in the saddle. She's taking a rain check, far too busy. They are staying at the hotel where we shall be having our reception eventually. It's very up-market. I wouldn't be surprised if she has bodyguards. There were a couple of tough-looking men hanging around, and staving off the press. She's only here for the weekend, then on location. I'm not sure about Piers riding, though he's been included. Miriam and he were thick as thieves this evening. A budding romance? Love seems to be in the air, and I can't settle down to anything sensible.'

* * *

'I thought you'd never ask,' Piers said as he followed Miriam into the guestroom placed at her disposal so that she could drink and not drive.

'Don't push your luck,' she retorted, not quite sure why she was doing this. It was partly boredom, a slice of lust, a hefty dollop of curiosity – oh, and her promise to find out all she could about Greg, via his buddy-boy.

Piers advanced towards her unsteadily, his breath laced with alcohol. She sidestepped neatly and he lumbered past, tripped over the dressing table stool and landed on the floor. He dragged himself to his knees, bleating, 'Sorry, sorry. Don't send me away.'

He was gazing at her in that besotted fashion she had seen on men's faces before. They recognised her inner strength, and the forceful aura that surrounded her. Some simply accepted her on equal terms. But there were others, and Piers was numbered among them, who had the urge to worship her, to become her submissive and obey her every command. She had not yet indulged in the dominatrix role, though she admired women like Scarlett, but now it seemed she had been given the opportunity to practise these skills.

She pointed towards the double bed and said, 'Get your kit off and lie there.'

As she watched him unlacing his shoes, peeling down his chinos and unbuttoning his shirt, she was puzzled by her mixed feelings. She recognised him as a toady, brown-nosing like mad when it came to Greg, but in many ways he was more likeable than that wily individual, probably trainable, too. And she wasn't above using her influential publishing connections to make or break a rising politician. Piers lacked the drive to become a party leader but, with a little help from a resourceful partner, he would make a satisfactory secretary, aide and general dogsbody.

And now he was hers. She decided to go for making, not breaking.

He had removed his socks and then his boxer shorts. Despite his bold assertions to the contrary, he seemed shy, covering his cock with one hand. That's all it took – one hand – she observed. The flash she had got of it showed it to be small, curling like a shy snail in the nest of scrubby pubes coating his lower belly.

She wanted to see if she could make it grow, and stood at the foot of the bed, doing a fair imitation of a strip-tease artiste. Piers remained still, mouth open, eyes bulging, while Miriam indulged in one of her favourite fantasies, that of removing her clothes, piece by piece, slowly, sensually, in front of a crowd of randy men. In her mind, she heard the bump and grind music and moved to its compulsive rhythm. She slid down one shoulder strap, letting it fall a tantalising inch from her nipple. Piers gave a strangled gasp. She ignored him, moving in a world of her own, lascivious, narcissistic, admiring her body, letting her fingertips trail over her puckered teat. Then she dropped the other strap and the bodice slithered to her waist. She arched her spine, cupped her breasts and played with them.

'God, Miriam!' Piers sighed, struggled to his knees and reached for her. His cock no longer flopped. It was hard and aimed towards his belly button.

'Get back!' she shouted, and whacked his cock. It jerked and oozed. 'Did I say you could touch me?'

'No,' he murmured, grabbing at his appendage and fondling it.

'Let's get this straight. You do so only when I give my permission. Is that understood?'

'Yes.'

Miriam was taking fire from his excitement, her own heat rising. The dress was sliding lower, exposing her flat stomach, the prominent hipbones, the dimpled navel and then the dark pubic floss that gave the lie to her russet hair. She was no natural redhead. Standing tall on her high heels, she tormented Piers further by diving her hand into her crotch, massaging her clit vigorously, head thrown back, eyes slitted. She stopped before she reached the point of no return. She intended that he should lick her to orgasm.

She smiled down at him alluringly, and ran her fingers under his nose. 'You like the smell of me?' she asked, her voice low and sultry.

Piers seized her hand and pressed it to his face. 'God, yes,' he panted, and sucked her fingers into his mouth. 'And I can taste it, too. All salty and spicy and gorgeous. I want some more. Let me nibble you.'

'Will you do anything for me, if I agree to have your big, fat tongue slurping at me?' she asked, smiling and closing her palm round the velvety skin of his shaft. He moved his hips, driving it in and out of her hand, as if he was inside her.

'Anything,' he vowed. 'Anything at all.'

'Firstly, does Greg have a Prince Albert – a cock-ring?'

'Why d'you want to know that?'

She slapped his dick again, shouting, 'I'm asking the questions.'

'Sorry,' he groaned, then gulped and added, 'No, he isn't pierced.'

'Really? I would have thought him up for it.' Then her tone changed and, 'Tell me where you get your kicks in London,' she said pleasantly, still manipulating his organ, but slowly now, tightening her grip on his root to prevent ejaculation.

'I go to several clubs. Willards mostly,' he grunted, while she slipped her fingers between his legs and lightly handled his balls. When she touched him in that sensitive place between his sac and his anus, she did so for a mini-second. It was too extreme a pleasure, and she didn't want him coming yet.

She freed her legs from the skirt, naked now except for her stilt-heeled gold sandals, her necklace and pendant earrings. She felt like a pagan goddess and it was empowering. Piers lay beneath her, and she clamped her thighs round his hips. He was straining upwards, trying to poke his one-eyed monster into that heavenly entrance he desired so much. Miriam settled herself down on him, her wet slit connecting with his belly but not yet permitting his cock to worm its way in. She enjoyed the pressure on her wide-open crack. It excited her clit. In control, she wriggled up and down.

'Let me, let me,' Piers begged and his hands reached for her breasts and cradled them tenderly, his thumbs rotating on the nipples.

'What is it you want to do?' she murmured, surprised at his performance. He had more finesse than she had imagined.

'I want to have you sit on my face. I want to lick you out, suck your clit and bring you to a screaming crisis,' he said, and his urgency was arousing.

'Not till you've told me more about Willards,' she said, stopping all movement, pushing his hands away.

'What d'you want to know?'

'Tell me what you do there.'

'One can eat and there's always a bar open,' he began.

She drove her nails into his forearms, grating, 'Just like any other club. What's so special about this one? Don't lie to me. I shall know, and be angry.'

Sweat beaded Piers's face. He looked distinctly uneasy. 'There's nothing much happens – not on the ground floor, anyway.'

'And below? There's more, isn't there?' Miriam was beginning to like the role of interrogator.

'There's a basement, sort of thing, and I meet women there – not prostitutes – girls from my own class. We have a few drinks, have a few laughs, and it sometimes ends up in sex. Two girls, three . . .'

'But you pay through the nose, or through the cock, for it. So they *are* whores, no matter that they act and talk like Sloanes. Do you do it with them there, or go back to their places?'

'Look here, Miriam, why are you wanting to know?' His attitude was so fraught with guilt that it convinced her there was more – much more.

'I'm the quiz master, not you,' she rapped out, bouncing on his belly.

The breath left him in a rush and he went red in the face. 'There's a bit of dungeon play, sometimes,' he blurted.

'S and M? Chains and gags and whips? Where? Below the respectable club?'

'Maybe,' he grunted, obviously sworn to secrecy by someone. Who?

'Do you go there alone?'

Now he dug in his heels, turning stubborn. 'Not always.'

'Who goes with you?'

'I'm not going to tell you. Damn it, Miriam, you can't expect me to snitch.'

'Is it Greg?' She was acting on a hunch.

'I'm not saying,' he replied mulishly.

Well, the little fucker's loyal, she concluded – or is he motivated by fear – or promise of gain?

'I think you're telling porkies,' she announced, pinching his nipples hard. 'And I don't like naughty boys who lie. You deserve to be punished.'

'Be fair, Miriam,' he begged. 'Finish me off, please. My cock's nearly bursting. Don't be so cruel. You know I'm mad about you.'

'Crap!' she exploded, and grabbed his wrist and stretched his arm above his head, tethering him to the bedhead with a scarf.

'Hey! What the hell are you doing?' he protested, but there was no droop to his cock. If anything, it had swelled more.

'Be quiet,' she ordered, slapping him across the face and sitting on him. 'Don't pretend this is anything new. I'll bet you enjoy bondage.'

She fixed a cord round his other arm and fastened it securely. 'Bitch,' he hissed, heaving and kicking, but Miriam was prepared, looping a thong round one ankle and then smacking him across the tops of his thighs and his fat, throbbing cock. The end was tied to the footboard.

She got up and searched through the tallboy, returning with a necktie and a leather belt. She used the tie to secure his free foot. Now he was spread-eagled, and she stood beside him, admiring her handiwork, then flicked the end of the belt over his belly, catching his penis that stood up like a flagpole. She took further aim, striking his balls and the underside of his erection.

'Are you going to talk?' she murmured, and the lash landed on his ribs and chest. He made no sound and she added, 'I get where you're coming from, Piers. You're enjoying this, aren't you?'

'It's because of you,' he whimpered. 'You're amazing. They'd love you at Willards. Why don't I take you along?'

'Maybe, but the other girls sound like crap. I couldn't stand their flakiness, lack of values and baggage. Welcome to their world? It's not pretty,' she answered grimly. She knew about these clubs, and had seen predators like Scarlett, fierce-eyed and greedy, patrolling their territory.

Piers's lack of co-operation was frustrating. So was her desire. She had made a start with him. Soon she would have him eating out of her hand, but now she needed an orgasm. She climbed aboard, sitting on his stomach, then slid higher, leaving a trail of juice that wetted his sparse brown chest hair. Now, poised over his face, she parted herself and exposed her large blush-pink clitoris.

'Good doggie,' she instructed, her voice unsteady. 'Give it a licking.'

Piers moaned and seized it eagerly between his lips and rotated the tip of his tongue. The feeling was exquisite. This isn't the first time you've done this, she thought, while it was possible to think at all. She arched her back, sighed and encouraged that tantalising tongue to play havoc with her ultra-sensitive clit. She was coming – coming – chasing her climax, the feelings rising and rising through her loins, up her spine, into her brain and then exploding into stars.

'Ah – ah –' she cried, her fingers circling her stone-hard nipples, prolonging the sensation that was filling her whole body with delight.

Piers turned his face aside and drew breath. She could smell her essence rising between them. Climax achieved, she was recovering fast, back to normal now for the time being at least. She withdrew from him entirely, stood up and retrieved her dress. Piers glared at her in disbelief and tugged at his bonds.

'You're not leaving?' he exclaimed.

'For a while,' she answered, as cool as the north wind blowing over the tundra.

'But what about me?'

'I shall be back shortly. Meanwhile, think over your stupidity. It's no earthly use lying to me. I shall find out.'

'You're mad!' he shouted. He was angry, and it suited him, hardening his features and making his eyes spark. She could feel her inner walls pulsing, needing his cock to stretch them.

'I shan't be gone long,' and, fully clad now, she leaned over and kissed the tip of his cock, then left the room, still tasting the sour-sweet flavour of his pre-come.

'It's a heavenly morning,' Maggie rhapsodised, repeating this mantra each time a guest arrived in the breakfast room.

Jody hadn't wanted to stay at The Hollies, but as Miriam had decided to sleep over, there was no way she could avoid it. Forewarned, they had packed suitable riding togs in their overnight bags. Not the whole kit; it wouldn't have been practical to keep jodhpurs and headgear as permanent fixtures in their wardrobes, just in case they decided to take up riding again. One day, perhaps, when they had retired from the town, returned to their birthplace, or somewhere similar, and settled down.

She was dressed in stretch jeans with straight legs, flat-heeled boots, a T-shirt and a fleece. Nanette had promised to provide hard hats. Miriam was wearing something similar, but Nicole had the whole outfit, a horsey girl from head to toe. Greg was in denims and trainers and had borrowed a hacking jacket, and Piers had managed to rustle up adequate clothing.

Jody had been given to understand that Clarissa had declined, but Ed had promised to be there. She had a cup of tea and a slice of buttered toast, listening to

Maggie going on about the weather. There was no sign of Deirdre; impossible to think she might be enjoying a lie-in. It was more likely she was overseeing the preparations for lunch with which to greet the brave heroes on their triumphant return. Ronald was conspicuous by his absence, too, reminding Jody that he was a jumped-up tradesman who had bought his way into Herons-wood society. Riding wouldn't be his bag. He was probably meeting cronies in the clubhouse before partaking of a few rounds of golf. Nouveau Riche – New Money against Old Money, she thought, astounding herself by this non-PC notion that had dropped into her mind.

'Has everyone had an elegant sufficiency?' Maggie quipped whimsically.

Oh, yes, everybody had. They rose and walked outside to the garage. Piers was following Miriam around like a lovesick puppy and Jody assumed that the deed had been done. 'Not quite at first, but eventually,' Miriam said mysteriously, in answer to Jody's aside. 'There's nothing I care to share, except that he's wicked at going down on a girl, and we got it wrong about the cock-ring.'

With that thought-provoking remark ringing in her ears, Jody climbed into the car. There was still no sign of Ed, but when they ground to a halt in Nanette's stable-yard, there he was, dressed up to the nines and looking like a member of the hunting, shooting and fishing brigade. Nanette had fetched him from the hotel in her Range Rover.

'Isn't he splendid?' she asked all and sundry, beaming at him proudly. 'He could be part of the aristocracy ...'

'Instead of descended from transported crims,' he

quipped, with a lop-sided grin that made Jody's heart somersault.

Horses were selected, great beasts with noble heads, rolling eyes and snapping jaws. They had slender legs and glossy coats and flowing manes and tails. Some were docile, others remembering that they were flight animals, easily alarmed, running with the herd, afraid of being alone and prey to carnivores hungry to rend and eat their flesh.

'Silly old darlings,' Nanette murmured fondly, stroking and patting, breathing down flaring nostrils and whispering sweet nothings. 'No one's going to hurt you, so just behave for the nice ladies and gentlemen. No bucking, no throwing, and no flying off the handle. I expect reports of impeccable manners.'

With her help, Jody selected a piebald mare named Flossie. 'When I bought her, she was called Maggie, but she has too sweet a nature to answer to that, nothing like Nicole's grandmother,' Nanette murmured, smiling as a personable young man introduced as Kevin helped with the harness.

Greg insisted on choosing the most high-strung and powerful animal, ebony black and with attitude. 'That one looks a right handful,' Jody remarked, her left foot in the stirrup, rising like a feather as Kevin gave her a leg up.

'Oh, he is, miss,' Kevin answered, looking at her with a disarming grin. 'We call him Old Scratch – that's a name for Satan round these parts. I hope the gentleman don't get thrown.'

'That would be the quickest way to make an angel out of an arsehole,' she returned sharply, and Nanette threw her an amused glance. It was as if she was colluding, unimpressed by Nicole's betrothed.

When everyone was upsaddled, the party clopped out of the yard and took a gravelled road leading towards the scrubland and moors beyond the Manor House. Maggie was right about one thing, Jody thought, it certainly is a glorious day. The few clouds dotting the blue sky were no more than picturesque additions, making one think of woolly sheep. She was aware of Miriam and Piers jogging along side by side, and Greg in the lead with Nicole keeping up with him easily, a fine horsewoman who had won many an equestrian event, silver cups, certificates and all the trimmings.

At least this gives her the chance to put one over on him, Jody mused. He obviously knew his way round a horse, but was probably rusty. Nicole would out-ride, out-race and leave him standing and Jody silently cheered.

They reached higher ground and sat their mounts who fidgeted beneath them, heads lowered to chomp on the fresh grass. Greg proposed finding a flat area and racing, laying bets on the outcome. He deferred to Nicole. 'What do you think, Mousekin?'

'That sounds fun,' Nicole agreed, flushed by the sun, but mostly from her own emotional turmoil.

'Not for me,' Jody said. 'I want to explore.'

She wheeled Flossie round in the opposite direction, nudged her heels into the mare's sides and set off at a gallop. She could see a copse with a meadow beyond, and headed towards it. She crouched low over Flossie's flying mane, the wind plastering escaping strands of her own hair over her mouth. She wanted to snatch off her hat, but prudence prevailed. The speed was thrilling, the power-packed flanks rose and fell under her. She relished this strength, and the smell of leather and the stench of the animal's foam-flecked haunches. It made her feel horny, deciding that – yes, horse riding was essentially sexy. Hadn't she always known it, right from days of innocence when she had wondered what was causing that hot feeling between her thighs as they were chafed by the saddle of her pot-bellied pony?

She was excited now, gripping with her denim-covered knees, wondering how it would be if she was naked and Flossie devoid of harness. Then the beast's hairy, knobbly spine would rub against her cleft with each stride, causing ripples in her bud. Sometimes it would be squashed by the rough hide, sometimes free as Jody jogged up and down, and the sensations would rise sharply. They were doing so as she thought about it, and she was fully clothed.

She slowed Flossie to a walk and entered a glade. It was brushed by sprouting undergrowth and she ducked under the lower branches of trees that were heavy with blossom. This secluded spot was filled with sunlight. It was like riding into a golden sphere. Maybe this is what happens to people who go through near-death experiences, she pondered. They describe the glory of the light, the happiness and universal love they experience. They don't want to return to the mundane ball of rock we call Earth.

She fought the urge to take off her clothes and free Flossie from her trappings. This was ridiculous. She had come out for a ride, nothing more, then admitted that her spirit had soared and her pussy throbbed when Ed hove into view. It was odd, for she didn't rate him. He was rude and arrogant and too cocksure. That was it. He was absolutely sure of his cock and it irritated. No one had the right to be like that. He must harbour a doubt or two about its prowess and size, mustn't he? Most guys did. She had had her fill of cocky men; Greg was a prime example.

She pulled on the bit and Flossie stopped, only too

happy to lower her head and graze. Jody looped the reins over a convenient branch and flung herself down on the short, springy turf. It was blissful, a regular sun-trap and, disliking strap-marks, she took off her shirt and bra, used them as a pillow and settled back to soak up the rays. It really was hot, and soon her boots and jeans were discarded, leaving nothing but a minute black thong that cupped her pubes and narrowed to a string passing between her bottom crack.

'Lovely, lovely scorch,' she crooned, stretching out and glorying in the heat. The English weather was so unpredictable that one literally had to 'make hay while the sun shines', or in Jody's case, get a base tan.

In the distance she could hear the others shouting and laughing and the drumming of hooves as they raced. She wasn't bothered if anyone found her nearly nude. She had covered her breasts with one hand and dipped the other down to cradle her pubis, not through modesty, but because she was contemplating playing with herself. Warm, peaceful, had she been a cat she would have purred. Reality was slipping away and she entered that hypnagogic state between sleeping and waking, too idle to stir a muscle.

Something impinged on her dreams. She struggled with its significance, then realised that a shape was standing between her and the sun. She opened her eyes, seeing the silhouette of a man throwing his shadow over her. Annoyed by this invasion of her privacy, she shouted, 'Move over. You're blocking the rays. I'm sunbathing and don't want to be disturbed, so please go away.'

It was Ed, and he dropped on his hunkers and said, 'Mind if I join you?'

'Yes, I do. I like to do it alone.'

'Does that apply to everything?' he asked with a smile.

She didn't flinch. 'Most things. Sex, too, if that's what you're getting at.'

'You're hard to please.' He was mocking her, she was sure, so tanned and handsome and very masculine. Even the bleached crest of hair didn't make him look effeminate, though it could have done so on others.

'Why aren't you racing and where's your hat?' She answered one question with another, then added: 'I'm easy to please if you press the right buttons.'

'My hat is with my horse, over there,' and he jerked a thumb towards a screen of bushes. 'I came to find you.'

'Oh? Am I supposed to be flattered?' She was throwing up defences against this infuriating man who was just too attractive.

He shrugged and sat on the grass beside her. 'Feel what you like. I can't stop you. All I'm saying is that I want you and what I want I usually get.'

'Ha! You may be in for a shock, laddie. What about Clarissa? I thought you were her latest mount,' she said nastily.

He didn't bat an eyelid and, if anything, his smile deepened, showing up the tiny scar and making the bump in his nose more prominent. 'Clarissa and me are not an item. We work together, play together and sometimes sleep together. That's all there is to it. If she fancies screwing around, that's fine by me, and vice versa.'

Jody pulled a dubious face. 'I'm not so sure. I think she's jealous of you. If looks could have killed, I'd have been dead at her feet the other night.'

'She won't mind. I promise you,' he insisted and leaned closer.

She wasn't convinced, but what did it matter? She wasn't intending to have sex with him anyway.

'Why don't you sling your hook and leave me in peace to enjoy the sun?' she suggested irritably.

'Because I'm not sure that's what you really want.' He rested back on one elbow, long legs stretched out.

This last remark fired her feminine freedom fighter instincts. 'And who the hell gave you the right to tell me what I want and don't want?' she stormed.

'Calm down, lady,' he replied. 'No one's going to make you do anything.'

She tried to recapture the enjoyment that had been hers, but the atmosphere was ruined. I might as well have stayed away, she complained, but silently. No one knew how much she had grieved when Alec and she split up. She was a very private being, an artist, sensitive and creative, and now this brash Aussie was treating her like a strong, vibrant person, not a victim or a prisoner of her own feelings.

She made to sit up, searching for her discarded clothes but Ed stopped her. She glared at him, shouting, 'Get out of my way.'

'Not yet,' he said, and touched the tip of her breast with one finger.

Jody was taken aback by the rush of heat that tingled through her nipple and down to her loins. She tried to wriggle away, but her heart wasn't in it. She wanted the caress to go on and on. Ed moved to the other nipple and repeated the pleasure. Jody glanced down to where he lay on the grass. His legs in the beige breeches were apart, one knee raised, the other slack. The close fit of the jodhpurs emphasised the firm bar of his promising-looking penis.

He placed a hand behind her head, and pulled her down to his mouth. She didn't struggle, falling into him as if it was pre-arranged, her lips parting, her tongue and his seeking each other out like two small animals in a cave.

Clarissa? Who was she? Jody's self-respect? What was that?

She was wet, she was eager, no matter how loud the warning bells clanged in her head. She reached down between their bodies and unzipped him. He made no attempt to stop her. Drawing back so that they no longer kissed, he took her hand and guided it to where his cock protruded through the gaping fly. She grasped it, working the foreskin up and over the shiny swollen helm, and was rewarded by the sticky feel of his arousal.

'Not too hard,' he warned, breathing unevenly. 'I want to hang on, not lose it in seconds.'

'We shouldn't be doing this.'

'Afraid of being caught at it in broad daylight?'

This was not the reason, but she was too overwhelmed to explain something that she didn't understand herself. It was an instinct, a gut feeling that she might fall too far, too fast and too hard. He was sweeping her along, rushing her towards a future that she wasn't sure she wanted. Different from any man she had yet met, full of outward confidence, yet no doubt flawed in ways of which she had no comprehension. But it's not a life-long commitment, she told herself, if it happens and I'm not yet sure, then it will only be a passing dalliance.

The sun burned with increased force for it was high noon, and she regretted not being left alone to soak up the rays. Why did he have to find her there, upsetting her routine and impinging on her life? It wasn't too late. She could still tell him to leave.

'Go away,' she said, and freed herself, drawing up her knees and hunching her shoulders.

'You mean it?' He seemed genuinely baffled.

'I do.' She refused to look at him, keeping her eyes lowered.

'Why?'

'I have reasons that you won't understand.'

'Try me.'

'No.'

He got to his feet and fastened his zipper. He looked more sorrowful than angry. 'Are you in love with someone else? I could understand that. I've been in love several times and it hurts like hell, doesn't it?'

'I'm not in love. I've been there, done that, got the T-shirt. I don't need it. I'm happier on my own,' she said, glancing up and finding herself speared by his amazing, all-seeing eyes. She dressed hurriedly, using her clothing like armour to protect her – not from him, but from herself.

Ed leaned against the bole of a tree, loose-limbed, rangy and relaxed. She envied him his cool, and wondered how sincere he had been. A girl in every port or on every movie set? Probably. You've had a lucky escape, she told herself, but was only half convinced.

'I shan't give up, you know,' he said, the cadences of his voice penetrating her core.

'That's down to you. I can't stop you,' she replied frostily.

When she was ready, she untethered Flossie and vaulted into the saddle. It was hotter than ever. She thought of Nanette's swimming pool with a longing that resembled ravaging lust. They cantered back to where the others were still charging up and down, trying to beat each other. Piers was red in the face and sweating profusely, and Miriam looked uncomfortable and cross.

'Do you think it would be OK, if we went back to Nanette's and used the pool?' Jody said.

The idea was voted for unanimously, and the tired riders retraced their steps to the Manor House.

Nanette was there, topless on her lounger by the water, a parasol adjusted to protect her face. Shaun was hanging around in the background, using a long-handled net to free the surface of suicidal wasps and flies. She took one look at the weary party and said crisply, 'Trunks and bikinis, towels and sun-lotion in the changing rooms over there.' Then she ordered Shaun to, 'Go inside. Find Doris and have cold drinks brought out.'

It must be satisfying to be in her position, Jody thought, as she wandered in the direction of the changing rooms. She's rich, she has a housekeeper who takes care of the chores and a poolman who takes care of her. Probably Kevin does it, too, when she feels like a different banquet.

'What about lunch?' Nicole piped up. 'I think Mum is expecting us.'

'I'll ring her,' Nanette offered. 'If it's a cold spread, and I expect it is, then it will keep till later. Maybe she'd like to come over for a swim, too.'

'I don't think so,' Nicole declared. 'She'll say she's too busy.'

'Leave it to me. Off you go and enjoy yourself,' and Nanette waved a kindly but dismissive hand and then picked up the cordless phone.

'Are you OK?' Miriam asked Jody, when they had changed from skimpy underwear to even scantier swimming gear.

'Yep,' Jody answered briskly, taking a colourful towel from the shelf.

'You don't sound it. Is it Greg? I've told you, I'm going

to have another go at Piers about this club he goes to. Willards. I'm sure he's not telling me everything. Maybe we should go along. It might be a giggle.'

'Putting ourselves about as high-class whores? I don't think so.'

'There must be worse ways of making a living,' Miriam said blandly. 'I think I shall take a look-see. Where did you go earlier? Ed was missing, too. Is it what I think it is?'

'No way,' Jody shot back, riddled with guilt and for no concrete reason.

'But you like him?'

'That isn't how I'd put it.'

'Have the hots for?' Miriam supplied an alternative, cramming her breasts into a bikini top two sizes too small for her. She took it off, adding, 'Dammit. Why am I bloody bothering? It's tits out time, isn't it? Why are you being so cranky?'

'I'm not.' Jody sometimes wished Miriam didn't have this sixth sense that always seemed to know when she was upset or lying or just plain bored.

'You need a new man,' she now pronounced, posing in front of the wall mirror, sucking in her stomach and lifting her ribs. 'I need a new man, though I've a feeling I've got one. Piers likes bondage. I left him tied to the bed for two hours last night. When I got back he was dying for a pee, and even then I made him wait to shag me. He did, finally, and he's not bad at it. I may keep him for a while. Come on. Let's have a dekko at them in bathing shorts. This should be good for a laugh.'

'Put the salad back in the fridge, Helga,' Deirdre said, after taking Nanette's call. 'Our guests won't be in for lunch. We'll serve it up later. I'm going out. Can you manage? Mr Carpenter is eating at the clubhouse. You can have the afternoon off.'

'Thank you, Mrs Carpenter,' said Helga, a foreign student employed by them during the college vacation. She was dumpy and efficient and Deirdre was glad that she was plain, never quite trusting Ronald when it came to pretty young women.

When she arrived at the Manor, she went round to the rear, attracted by the sound of laughter and splashing. She had her costume and towel in a beach-bag, and it wasn't her first visit to Nanette's pool. It had become something of a summer ritual, though she wasn't as obsessed with obtaining a seamless tan, and always felt twinges of guilt when she lay around doing nothing.

It was an idyllic scene. The water glittered, reflecting blue from the turquoise tiles, reflecting azure from the overhead sky. Its surface was broken here and there by swimmers, gambolling like children or unruly dogs. She recognised Nicole, with Greg's dark head bobbing beside her, and was relieved to see that she was wearing a bikini top. There was so much nudity around these days, and Deirdre didn't really approve. A glance at Jody and Miriam confirmed her worst fears. They sprawled on loungers, bare tits pointing to Jesus.

As her mother-in-law had once said to her, 'Bodies look so much better when they are covered up.'

She recognised Ed as she walked across the terrace towards Nanette who was also displaying herself with complete disregard for modesty. And where was Clarissa? Still at the hotel being busy with the media, she guessed.

'Hi, Deirdre,' Ed called across, muscular and extremely fit, hair streaming, his bronzed body covered in shining droplets, his very brief jockstrap leaving her in no doubt as to the shape and size of his equipment.

'No sign of my sister yet?' she answered conversationally, striving to sound unaffected.

'No, though I did see her before I left. She gave me an ear bashing for waking her up,' he said, grinning unrepentantly. 'She's coming to yours later.'

'Deirdre! Bully for you! You chucked away your distaff and came out to play,' Nanette shouted, and Deirdre reached the lounger and looked down at her friend who had all the magnificence of a mature tigress.

She envied her. Nothing seemed to upset her. She took everything in her stride, whereas Deirdre got flummoxed. She was experiencing pangs because the lunch plans had misfired, though in reality, she hated cooking, had been doing it for far too long and could see no end to it with Ronald in his exalted position as mayor and leading light in the Masons. People like him were expected to entertain and, as his lady wife, it was her supposed duty to organise such events.

Rebellion stirred and she practically ran off to the changing rooms, already hauling her costume from her bag. There was no one there and she stripped without her usual reserve. Her body was pale-skinned, her waist slim and her legs long, and her swimsuit was a flattering all-in-one, cut very high at the sides. It was black polyester, with large pink flowers here and there, and she was pleased with the mirror image flung back at her. She pinned up her hair, popped on her sun-glasses, picked up her towel and headed back to the poolside.

Nanette was no longer alone. A big man wearing faded shorts, terrain sandals and nothing else had joined her. He was fair and ruddy and Nanette introduced him as, 'Stewart Ramsden. I've told you about him. He's my dentist and Pirate King – a baritone, darling, and a very fine one. We're singing together in the forthcoming show.'

Stewart bowed with old-world gallantry and wheeled over another lounger so that all three of them lay in direct line of fire from the sun. He wore a panama hat and dark glasses and was entertaining company. Nanette wondered where Shaun and Kevin were. Really, Nanette was incorrigible. Now she was involved with this new man, a dentist, no less.

Deirdre applied screening lotion to her arms and legs and tried to get comfortable under the parasol. Her attention was drawn to the water play, where Greg and Ed were circling Jody like a pair of sharks and Nicole was circling them, looking anxiously at her fiancé. Miriam was lounging voluptuously beneath the small waterfall that cascaded into the shallow end, up to her knees in water. She glistened like a maiden from the Hawaiian Islands, brazenly flaunting her nakedness. Not only was she topless, but bottomless into the bargain.

Piers wallowed about below her, then took one of her feet in his hands and kissed each toe. He tongued the arch, her shin and up, up to the inside of her thighs, until he rested his face on her pubic mound, then buried it between her legs.

Deirdre felt bereft. No one had ever done that to her, not even when she was young. What must it feel like to be adored? It simply wasn't fair. She had equally fine qualities, but that's not what men were seeking, was it? They wanted youth and a gorgeous figure. She sank back and closed her eyes, tears burning behind her lids. No one would ever want her now. It was all too late. She might as well settle for what she had and support Ronald, much as she hated his pomposity and self-righteousness.

She regretted coming. It would have been far better to have pottered about in the garden at home, engaged in dead-heading the flowers. Why couldn't she slip gracefully into middle age like others around her seemed to do? With the exception of Nanette, with her stage performances and her poolman, her groom and her dentist. It simply wasn't fair.

Brooding on her life, she kept her eyes closed and endured the unremitting heat of the sun. She wanted to cool off in the pool, but wondered if she dared. It would be fine if they would all disappear and she could be there alone. Then she woke fully, hearing Nanette saying, 'Hello, Derek. So glad you could make it. Isn't it a glorious day? D'you want a drink? Stewart, be an absolute lamb and fetch some more ice, would you? Are you awake, Deirdre? Here's a face from the past. I think he knows you. Do you remember Derek Glover?'

Deirdre hurriedly covered herself with her towel. She looked up into a pair of amused grey eyes set in a weather-beaten face. He was wearing a straw hat, an open-necked shirt, slacks and sports sandals. When he smiled, he looked boyish, and very kind.

She was puzzled and only half awake. 'Derek?' she repeated. 'Do I know you?'

'We were at college together,' he said, and his voice was warm and pleasant. 'Lost touch, unfortunately. I married and so did you. Now I'm free again, widowed last year. What are you up to these days?'

He was easy to talk to, and this had been one of his qualities when they had both attended college. So long ago now, and yet, as she related the relevant facts concerning herself, it seemed that they were continuing a conversation started years before. How did I lose contact with him? she wondered, then remembered that she had met Ronald round about graduation time and he had taken her over, hook, line and sinker. There had been no room for anyone else.

Stewart returned with fresh orange juice and Derek explained how he had settled in Heronswood a while back and had joined the operatic society, playing oboe in the orchestra. 'You used to play an instrument, didn't you?' he asked, and Deirdre couldn't believe that he was interested in her.

'The flute,' she rejoined promptly.

'There you are,' Nanette butted in. 'Didn't I tell you to come along to rehearsals and help us out?'

'Do join in,' Derek insisted. 'That is, if your husband won't object.'

'I'm sure he won't,' Deirdre answered, surprising herself with her eagerness.

She could feel her shoulders burning and got out the sun-cream, pouring a puddle into her palm and applying it. Her arms were coated, and she turned away from Derek, embarrassed at doing this but knowing she would burn if not.

'May I help?' he offered. 'I always did this for my wife.'

He took the bottle from her, and she felt the lotion sliding effortlessly over her back and reaching into the awkward places. She let the towel drop, enjoying the feel of a man's firm hands massaging unguents into her skin – a nice man, a kind, understanding man.

'I'll come to the next rehearsal,' she promised, frightened by her boldness, yet unable to help herself. She had found a new friend – nothing more than that, she insisted. A friend from the past, who would share her interests and support her. There was no harm in that, was there?

8

'You know that we're destined to go to bed together, don't you?' Ed said, catching Jody under the elbows and drawing her into his warmth before she had time to avoid him. They were in the lee of the changing rooms, supposedly heading back to get into their clothes, the bathing episode over.

His skin was wet, his bulge solid behind that inadequate pouch. He had been showing off in the pool, diving from the side, doing dags under water, impressing her despite herself. Then there was Greg, so careless and inconsiderate, heedless of Nicole's feelings as he flirted outrageously. Nothing female was safe from him. He left Miriam cold, however, and he had picked up on her antipathy. But Piers was enslaved, and Jody knew Miriam was working on him to get the information they needed to bring about Greg's downfall.

All this was such a pity, for Nicole was desperately in love with him, and it was going to be hard to convince her that he was a scoundrel, a cheat and a liar.

Were all men thus? Ruled by their blind urge to put as many notches on the bedpost as possible?

'I'm going to get dry and changed,' she said, severely. 'Isn't it time you made a move? Clarissa is expecting you, isn't she?'

Ed frowned and pushed back his hair. 'OK. Sure, I know that. I'll be there for her, but this doesn't mean

I'm not wanting to get to know you better.' He threw her a look that was hard to resist, and curled his fingers in hers before she could stop him. 'Give me a break,' he insisted.

'We'll see,' she said, nothing like as resolved now. 'But I don't know how we can possibly meet, apart from in public. I'm a very busy person, and so are you, besides being committed to Clarissa.'

'I've told you already, we're not doing the commitment thing,' he said forcefully in his Aussie twang, and pulled her closer to him. He captured her mouth before she had time to stop him, using his lips to part hers, and delving into the warm cavity with his wet, agile tongue.

Someone was coming, and it wasn't her – or him. Deirdre rounded the corner and they broke apart, while she stopped and stared, too polite to say anything, but no doubt wondering why her sister's beau was embracing someone else.

Jody said the first thing that sprang to mind. 'I had a lash in my eye. Ed was trying to get it out.' She went even further in this crazy fabrication. 'He's done it, too. Thank you, Ed, that feels much better.'

'Any time,' he replied gallantly. 'There's nothing I like better than helping a damsel in distress,' and he winked and disappeared into the male changing room.

'Shall we get dressed, too?' Jody said, while Deirdre gave her a puzzled stare, then to Jody's enormous relief, Miriam joined them.

The incident passed without comment, but Jody had the uneasy feeling all evening that Deirdre was wondering about her and Ed though, strangely enough, she seemed abstracted, as if there was something else on her mind.

* * *

'Well, lover boy, and what have you been doing today?' Clarissa demanded when Ed got back to the hotel, and she ordered drinks to be sent to her room. His adjoined it.

The suite was lavish, the best in this upper income bracket establishment that had once been a coaching inn and retained something of the ambience. Because she was a star, the bedroom and reception area were swamped with bouquets from well-wishers. They spilled from Chinese vases and antique jardinières – carnations, roses and Star Gazer lilies ravishing the senses with rich aromas. Unlike Maggie and her plebeian son, the members of the chain who owned the Leigh Grove Hotel appreciated objets d'art and original décor, and everything was in perfect harmony and flawless taste.

Ed shrugged and took off his tweed jacket. 'Riding. Swimming. D'you like my rig?' And he paced about, posing in his breeches and sweatshirt.

He picked up his crop and made a few practice swipes through the air. Clarissa shivered and stared at him with wide, glittering, slightly out of focus eyes. She was on her third gin and tonic and he played up to her, well aware that she liked him to be dominating. He was sincere in his feelings about Jody, but cynical enough to forget her when he was with his beautiful, famous mistress, who had so much clout in the movie industry. Sexually frustrated, too, for consciously or unconsciously, Jody had been tormenting him all day.

Clarissa stretched seductively, and her lids drooped as she held out her arms to him. 'I've missed you,' she pouted and her lips glistened provocatively, reminding him of the many occasions when she had given him head.

'You could have come along,' he answered smoothly, going to her, running his hands around her bare shoulders and starting to unfasten the buttons at the front of her dress, quite slowly, one by one.

She was seated on the arm of a gilt-framed chair, and now parted her legs and gripped his thigh, her taut, finely tuned muscles closing strongly as she began to rub her crotch up and down it. She worked out daily and kept her trainer busy so, despite her binges, she was in good shape. Ed could feel her heat through her skirt and his jodhpurs, and smell the pungent odour of her arousal punctuating the costly French perfume with which she always drenched herself. She was horny as an alley cat.

Ed liked women, found them much more interesting than men, their complex minds as well as their bodies. He had made a study of sex, finding out exactly what turned them on, and the way in which their clits responded to the right treatment. He had become conversant with breasts, nipples, ear lobes, and all the other not so obvious erogenous zones so often shamefully neglected during lovemaking. But he always returned to the seat of sensation, that little pearl at the top of the female cleft, equivalent to the penis, but a hundred times more sensitive. It was small wonder that he never lacked girl friends.

Clarissa was fickle, changing her men as often as she changed her panties, but Ed appeared to be longer lasting. He didn't know whether to be pleased or sorry. Despite his assertions to Jody concerning their free relationship, Clarissa sometimes showed disturbing signs of possessiveness. Like now, for instance. She wanted him to service her, and service her he would, whether or not he felt like it. But Ed was willing to oblige, highly sexed himself. His cock was in an almost permanent state of tumescence. It could be quite an embarrassment at times.

'Oh, darling, you're marvellous,' Clarissa crooned as he sat her in the chair, legs apart. He hauled aside her knickers and knelt between her thighs, inhaling the strong scent of pussy, parting her pink, hair-fringed delta and fondling her clit with his tongue-tip.

She squirmed a little, wanting something else before she climaxed, and Ed guessed what it was: she was excited by his riding gear – the boots, the tight pants, the whip. He'd come across this with her before, when he had been doing the stunts for the actor who was her leading man. It had been a costume piece, and both he and her co-star had worn the same outfits – that of a Regency buck in his hunting gear. This roused her to screaming pitch, especially if he gave her a little taste of the crop.

He left her abruptly, scowling as he said, 'You're a dirty slut, Clarissa. What would your fans say if they could see you now? You need punishing.'

'Do I?' she breathed, flushing.

'You certainly do,' he answered, striking his right leg with the whip. It made a satisfying swish.

He went over to the outsized bed; a viceregal couch draped with purple and gold swags, the overhead tester fitted with mirrors. Seating himself, he unzipped and took out his erection, fondling it while she watched. He beckoned and she obeyed. He turned her away from him, ran a hand down her back, then bent her over, holding her firmly. She was weighty on his lap, his bare cock nudging her side, her breasts pressed to his knee, her long hair dangling towards the carpet.

Ed made her wait, deliberately winding her up, tickling round her ears and caressing that tender spot where her neck joined her shoulders. He raised her skirt and hooked a finger into the elastic at her waist and pulled her panties down and off. He heard her sigh, felt the frantic movements as she gyrated her mound against his thigh. She wanted it. Oh, yes. She wanted it very badly. Odd to think about it really – this woman, whom her admirers worshipped, was nothing but a bundle of hormones needing release, just like any other female.

Ed took fire from this thought, his cock swelling uncomfortably. Whatever else she might lack, Clarissa was a superb lover, giving as well as taking pleasure. He guessed she'd snorted at least one line of coke that day, probably more, and this made her even more rampant and able to go on longer.

He caressed the firm white globes of her buttocks, and dipped a finger between them, finding the moue of her anus and the deep fissure that gave access to her vagina. Clarissa moaned and wriggled, wanting him to go lower and bring her off. He changed to his left hand, keeping her hanging on, then raised his right. The crop landed on her skin with a whack. She jerked and gave an agonised yelp. He struck her again, and once more, seeing the scarlet welts springing into being.

'Oh, don't mark me, sweetie,' she pleaded, her voice thick with tears. 'My dresser will see and know I've been a very bad girl.'

He fondled the blazing stripes, then tempered his strokes till they were mere taps, falling on her bottom like summer rain. Slipping a hand under her, he found her swollen clit. It was like a slick wet gem, and he frigged it harder and harder. She started to wail and then he felt the convulsion that told him she had reached her zenith. She flopped across his lap, sighing and panting and groping for his penis.

He rolled her off and she fell to the floor. He stood above her and she dragged herself up, her hands on the smooth stretch fabric that went all the way to his crotch and beyond. His cock jutted out, and she rose high enough to lick it, her hands at his waist, pulling him closer.

Ed could feel the blissful ache in his balls, groin and penis. He was losing himself in that urge which knew no restraint. Give Clarissa her due: she had practised on hundreds of men during her climb to fame.

Now she held off and went to the drawer in the bedside table and produced a condom. She took it from the packet and, returning to her subservient position, formed her lips into an O and held the rolled up rubber there. Then, slowly, almost reverently, she took it to the tip of his penis and, again extremely carefully, worked it till the helm was covered completely. Her hand came up then, assisting her mouth and tongue till, gradually, Ed's shaft was fully protected.

She left him, running to the bed and sprawling there on her back, gripping the rails of the headboard. Ed followed, and fell with her into the depths. Her legs came up, fastening round his waist as he plunged his cock in and out of her velvety channel. It was perfect, tight, clasping him like a slick vice, and she tipped up her hips and lifted her legs higher, resting them on his shoulders. Ed was beyond reason now, following the instinct to rid himself of his spunk. She had been satisfied, so all he had to do was concentrate on his own completion.

He rammed at her, speeding up while she gave short, sharp cries. 'Yes,' he grunted, as the feeling overwhelmed him, spilling his seed into the condom.

'Yes, yes!' she echoed, her inner muscles clasping him at just the right moment.

He gave a final lunge, then slumped on her.

With athletic agility she untangled her legs from his neck, and rolled on her side, gazing at him fondly. Then she sat up and finished the half-full glass of gin. 'And now, pet, I shall shower and put on my glad rags and visit that terribly boring sister of mine. You, too, beloved. I simply couldn't endure it on my own. What d'you say to a toot before we go? That should brace us against the ennui of Deirdre, her old bag of a mother-in-law and those tedious friends.'

'I'm free – free!' Nicole exclaimed, bouncing into Jody's house and dropping her bags on the hall floor. 'No more teaching – ever. The summer vacation has started and that's my lot. Thank you for offering to let me stay. It means that I shall be able to visit Greg's flat, and it wouldn't have been the done thing for me to have slept there, not yet – not till we're married, and then it will be my home. I was hoping to meet Greg's father. He's a widower and lives in the Bahamas, but it seems he can't get over, though he's promised to be at the wedding.'

'You're welcome,' Jody said, and she meant it, though her work was pressing and she was due to fly to Los Angeles at the end of September, to deliver the sculpture to Aaron Abbotson. By that time, the nuptial furore would be over, and she wouldn't be sorry to see the end of it.

Miriam called in as Nicole was getting settled. Katrina and Bobby were there, too, and her bump was beginning to show. Nicole was enchanted. 'A baby. How lovely,' she said, looking at Katrina as if she was the Madonna. 'I'm so excited about having one myself, in the not too distant future.'

'Let's get you hitched first,' Miriam returned, and exchanged a glance with Jody.

So far the wedding plans were gathering momentum. Try as she might, Miriam had not been able to persuade Piers to divulge his and Greg's secrets, though she still suspected there were plenty. However, both she had Jody were rushed off their feet, Nicole's emergence into a bride only a part of the equation. They had their dresses, time off had been arranged, and it was all going full steam ahead. Jody wanted to whisk Nicole round London on a shopping spree. She and Miriam had organised a treat for her – the full treatment in Janine's salon, sans strapping lovers, of course. This would not have been appropriate for a virgin bride.

Nicole was like a kid in a candy store. They stayed up late, watching a video and, next morning, it was off to Harrods, then lunch with Greg. There followed a whistle-stop viewing of the flat with Nicole in awe of such a film-set venue that was to be her home and, in the afternoon when he went back to the office, Miriam met them at Janine's.

'What a place!' Nicole whispered on meeting Konane, and being welcomed by Janine.

'I'm leaving my friend here,' Miriam said. 'She's shortly to be married and this is a special treat for her. But straightforward beauty treatment, nothing special. A masseuse, I think, not a male.'

'I understand perfectly,' Janine answered, smiling at Nicole in that special way woman of all ages and professions reserve for a bride. It sprang from old traditions and origins, to do with fertility rites and the replenishment of the earth with virgin blood.

'Maiden, mother and hag,' Jody remarked to Miriam from the side of her mouth.

'I reject that. Who are you calling a hag? It must be me as I'm neither of the others,' Miriam retorted. 'And that means you as well.'

'Aren't you staying?' Nicole said nervously, overawed by the sophistication of the beauty parlour.

'We'll call back for you at the cocktail hour, and have a drinky-poo in the bar. Enjoy.' And with that Jody backed out, glad to leave the responsibility for Nicole's wellfare with someone else.

'Follow me, Miss Carpenter,' said a sleek, soft-footed Japanese girl in a brightly patterned kimono, and took her to the area given over to the gym, the Jacuzzi, the sauna, cold plunge baths, solariums and massage couches.

Why haven't I done this before? Nicole asked herself. I've reached my present age and, come to think of it, I haven't done anything much. Non-adventurous, that's me. I like a quiet life, not an interesting one. Isn't that what the gods give one as a punishment – an interesting life?

That's not true, though. Greg's a part of it and he's very, very interesting indeed. He's taking me out to dinner tonight and on to a show. Will we go back to the Chelsea apartment later, or will he still respect me? I hope not. It wouldn't matter if I got pregnant now. We shall be man and wife in a few weeks. Then suddenly she had a vision of herself and Ben on the farm together the night the cow was struggling to give birth. The thought of that raw masculinity sent a little shiver through her consciousness. She couldn't imagine Greg being so earthy. He'd be too worried of messing up his tailored jackets to get stuck in to anything. He was what they called a fop, and Nicole knew it. She suddenly felt sad.

'Please to undress, Miss Carpenter,' lisped the Japanese girl, when they entered a curtained cubicle. 'My name is Susuki, and Konane is my brother. We have worked for Miss Janine for a while. I shall help you to shower first, then we will progress to the massage, followed by the Jacuzzi, and finally facial cleansing and make-up and a manicure and pedicure, plus our stylist fixing your hair.'

Nicole would rather have showered alone but was too much in awe of this dainty creature to say so. The ordeal was not too bad. Susuki chatted amiably as she soaped Nicole's back and worked the foamy lather into her skin, then washed it off with the invigorating force of the power shower. She gave her an enveloping towel and then guided her to the massage table. She took off her kimono, wearing track suit bottoms and a string vest beneath, and then requested that Nicole lie down.

Nicole felt extremely vulnerable, handing her body over to someone else's ministrations. The up-side was, should Greg want to make love to her that night, her skin would be silky soft, her limbs relaxed, and her confidence boosted by knowing that she had been made to look as beautiful as possible.

Susuki worked on her spine and shoulders first, those small hands proving to be immensely strong as she probed, pounded and released muscular tension, freeing tendons and knots until Nicole felt utterly boneless. The woman's touch was entirely professional. There was no hint of sexuality, nothing but the sole purpose of releasing Nicole's tension, and this continued across her buttocks and down the length of her thighs to her knees, calves and feet.

At her bidding, Nicole turned over, keeping a small towel across her private parts. Susuki was equally businesslike, treating Nicole's breasts like any other part of her, kneading her waist but not venturing below the towel. Then her front thighs were pummelled, and finally her ankles.

Susuki straightened, wiping her hands, smiling widely and saying, 'All done, Miss Carpenter. Rest for a moment, and then I will conduct you to the Jacuzzi.'

'I don't feel as if I'll ever be able to stand again,' Nicole exclaimed. 'I could lie here for ever and never stir an inch.'

Susuki slipped her arms into a zipped, fleecy jacket and tidied the cubicle, putting away the tools of her trade, then, 'Ready?' she asked, and held out a dressing gown.

Nicole sat up and put it on, her own clothes in a grip bag that Susuki carried for her as they followed the sounds of water and women's upraised, laughing voices, coming to a room where marble gleamed and light fell from a stained glass cupola. There were several Jacuzzis positioned here and there, and all were occupied, the agitated water swirling round the naked bathers. Several young men were in attendance, each clad in shorts. Some squatted on their hunkers near the sides of the pools, chatting to the women. Others adjusted the mechanism that kept up the constant motion, while the rest simply leaned over and flirted, using their hands on breasts, nipples and even diving further to fondle their clients' deltas.

'Are you ready?' Susuki asked, hands on Nicole's shoulders to whisk off the robe as she stepped gingerly into the warm, whirling water.

She was far from ready, aware of eyes on her, male and female, wishing she wore a bathing costume, but it was too late now and she sank down quickly, up to her chest in concealing wavelets. That was better, and she started to enjoy the sensation, gradually adjusting to the sybaritic luxury of her surroundings.

There were three other women sharing the pool, each lying back with their heads resting on the rim and

Nicole lost her shyness, loving the feel of those impudent watery fingers playing with her body, dipping into her secret places and rippling over her skin. It was invigorating and totally enchanting.

'It's a buzz, isn't it?' the woman nearest to her remarked, lifting a hand from the water and adjusting the band that swept her dark hair away from her face and secured it on top of her shapely head. 'Your first time?'

'Yes,' Nicole breathed, impressed by this sleek beauty, with her sun-kissed skin and those perfect breasts glimpsed through the transparency of the blue-tinged water. 'I've never visited a beauty parlour before. My friends are treating me. I'm getting married soon, you see,' she rushed on, encouraged by the woman's apparent kindly interest. 'And tonight I'm going out with my boy friend. He lives in London . . .'

'And you don't?' the woman asked, straightening one of her legs and lifting it to the surface, turning it this way and that, examining it critically. The gold lacquer on her toes sparkled.

'Oh, no. I'm from the country – a place called Heronswood, but Greg, that's my fiancé, is a lawyer and wants to be a politician, too. He's frightfully clever. I'll move in with him when we've tied the knot.'

'And what do you do?' the woman asked, giving her a lazy glance.

'I'm a teacher – *was* a teacher, I should say. Greg doesn't want me to work once we're married.'

'You say his name is Greg?'

'That's right. Gregory Crawford. I can't wait to be Mrs Crawford.'

One of the splendid young attendants came across to kiss the woman's shoulder and murmur, 'Shall I see you later? In the bar, maybe, and we'll take it from there.'

She reached up and caressed his lean jaw, murmuring idly, 'Maybe, Dean. Depends on my mood. Now go away, darling, I'm talking to my friend.'

He cocked an eyebrow at Nicole, saying pointedly, 'Ah, I understand.'

The woman cupped a palm full of water and threw it at him. 'No, you don't. It's not what you think. She's new here and we're just chatting. Hop it, sweetie.' She turned to Nicole and said, 'Tell me more about your wedding. What's your name, by the way? Mine is Scarlett.'

'Do I have to go back to Jody's? Can't I stay here with you?' Nicole pleaded and Greg almost said yes.

Why was he holding back he wondered? The silly little thing was besotted with him. If he robbed her of her precious virginity tonight, what possible difference would it make to the wedding? The event was rolling inexorably nearer by the hour. He took her jacket and wondered what excuse he could make. The truth was that he didn't fancy her all that much. She was his pathway to success, and that was about it.

'Mousekin, you know I've promised your father and mother that I'd look after you,' he began.

She was on to this like a shot. 'They needn't know.'

He adopted a sorrowful face. 'But I should, and feel that I'd let them down. Please, poppet, don't make it any harder for me than it already is. I'm a full-blooded male, after all, and you're looking particularly pretty tonight.'

This is true, anyway, he thought, while she wound her arms round his neck and kind of hung there, mouth parted for his kisses, her eyes hooded. And she'd only had a couple of glasses of wine, too! he thought. Cheap to run, unlike some he could name, girls who had taken to behaving as badly as lads, getting drunk and carousing around town centres being loud and picking up blokes. He didn't know which was worse, their brash behaviour or Nicole's naivety.

'I spent the afternoon at a beauty parlour, having myself made lovely for you,' she cooed. She flung back her head and stared into his face, adding, 'Do you think I'm sexy, Greg?'

Oh, Lord, he groaned inwardly, glancing at the antique malachite clock set slap-bang in the centre of the modern marble fireplace. He was hoping to be able to bundle her into a cab and then link up with Piers at their customary watering hole and fun-house.

'I shouldn't be marrying you if I didn't,' he answered glibly.

'Why are you marrying me?' she persisted, and he was supporting her almost fully now, for her knees were buckling.

'I love you.' The answer came out pat and he felt not the smallest twinge. Most women had always been satisfied when he said that, melting like chocolate mousse.

Yes, it was working again. 'Oh, Greg,' Nicole sighed. 'I'm so lucky to have you. Let me sleep in your bed.'

Tricky, he thought. The easiest course would be to fuck her, but he had decided to play this one very cool. There was too much at stake to blow it. He sat on the white leather couch and drew her down on his lap, cradling her like a child.

'That's so tempting,' he murmured into her hair, and indeed the sweet smell of her and her utter devotion to him was making him think twice.

Soon to be his wife; not such a big deal these days for women were so goddamn independent and feisty, yet this one was from the old-fashioned mould. He knew himself well enough to realise that he'd soon find this a drag. He needed sterner stuff in a woman. Without doubt, he'd end up being unkind to Nicole and making her life a misery. As for her offering her virginity, pre-ceremony – well, he'd had a few virgins in his time and had found it wasn't all it was cracked up to be. Hard work, actually, to rupture the hymen, and often too tight for his cock. Also, the maidens concerned hadn't known what to do, alarmed by the blood and the pain. No, virginity was over-rated and he could understand why an ivory lingam was used by the Romans to do the deed for the bridegroom. They had adopted the custom from the Hindus.

She sighed and yawned and Greg rocked her, hoping she'd fall asleep. He was wrong. 'Carry me into the bedroom,' she murmured, and he could read her like a book: she was imagining herself as the heroine of a TV drama.

He set her from him resolutely. 'No, Nicole. It's my duty to look out for you and it wouldn't be right for me to take advantage of your parents' trust,' he said, thinking what a prat he sounded, like a character in a 1940s war film, all stiff upper lip and BBC accent, talking as if he had a plum in his mouth.

She gave him a starry-eyed look and smiled. 'Oh, dear. I wish you weren't quite such a nice man. Why can't you be a teeny bit rotten? But I know you're right.'

'It will be all the sweeter for waiting, and we'll spend our honeymoon in bed,' he promised, and now that this was settled, he could be patient and even offer her a drink before ringing for a taxi.

She clung to him till the last possible moment as he escorted her down in the lift to the entrance and put her in the cab, then he spoke to Piers on his mobile.

'OK, I'll see you there in half an hour. Order drinks

and nobble Scarlett, if she's about. God save me from clinging vines.'

'A surfeit of Nicole?'

'Too right.'

'I thought I'd drop by,' Ed said, leaning against the jamb as Jody opened her front door.

That was the moment she capitulated. There would be a lot of talk, argument, debate on the subject, but the result was a forgone conclusion. They went through the motions, however.

'You could have let me know,' she said, in token protest.

'I had a few hours off and it was an impulse thing,' he replied, as he walked past her into the hall.

'Don't mind me,' she retorted sarcastically. 'Make yourself at home.'

'I intend to.'

Greg, too, had invaded her privacy, but this was different. Apart from Clarissa – and she doubted there was much of a bond between them – there was nothing to stop her shagging Ed if she wanted to, and she did.

'Finished filming?' she asked, and he followed her into the kitchen where, automatically, she switched on the kettle.

'The London sequences. We're setting up in Bath tomorrow. These Regency pieces provide a lot of work for the extras. Clarissa's been in several now. The parts of snotty, stuck-up society tarts suit her. She going over her lines ready for the next shoot. So I kind of played hooky and came to see you.'

'No stunts to perform?'

'A duel on a green outside some place called The Circus. In the morning.'

'Better get a good night's sleep, then.'

She was standing by the work top, spooning Instant into mugs when he suddenly came up behind her, twirled her round and put his hands either side of her head to hold her still as he kissed her. She resisted for a second, then thought, what the fuck, and parted her lips. It was lovely to be kissed by someone new and handsome and dashing, someone, moreover, who had a film star eating out of his hand, and yet he wanted *her* – Jody.

He moved in closer and wound his arms round her and she closed her eyes and wallowed in enjoyment. Katrina and Bobby were at ante-natal class, and the stillness of the house, the fact that she and Ed were entirely alone in it, acted as a powerful aphrodisiac. She had been wary of him before, but now she was on her own turf. She called the shots. Or she thought she did until he suddenly pushed her down on the kitchen table (thank God, there were no dirty crocks on it), and then he parted her legs and leaned over her, and put his lips to her throat and sucked. I shall have love-bites, she thought, feeling herself dissolving into helplessness. The girls will tease me – Miriam and Katrina – but what the hell's it got to do with them?

He took his hand from her back and fought his way into her dungarees, unbuttoning the braces and bib, flipping it down to reveal her breasts. The nipples were sharply pointed under her white vest. He took them in his mouth, one by one, his saliva making round wet patches, and arousal darted from her breasts to her clitoris, and she helped him unzip her fly front and wriggled out of the restrictive garment. Her panties consisted of a black string with a triangle that covered her mons. All she had on was the vest and her toe-post sandals and these dropped off, leaving her feet bare.

'I've been thinking of this since we swam together,'

Ed grated. His face was still and his eyes burned. There was nothing else for it. She removed her panties.

He looked at her naked sex and placed a kiss on the rounded curve of her stomach, then he caressed the damp, pink flesh of her labia and she moaned, 'Oh – ooh . . .'

This sound fired him and he lost it, coming on strong and rubbing her clit hard. It was painful but exquisite and his harshness thrilled her. It expressed his need, that raging desire so flattering if one was the recipient. They struggled like protagonists, sliding across the slippery pine surface, and a scene from an old movie blazed across her memory, where the guilty, adulterous lovers did it on the table.

Ed pushed up her vest and pinched her nipples while, with his other hand, he squeezed her sex. She moaned again and arched her spine and he thrust two fingers inside her, muttering, 'God, you're so wet.'

She tensed and clamped her muscles round his fingers, and he drove them in and out, but it wasn't the right place. She tried to squirm round to include her clit, and Ed sensed this and cooled down. He scooped her juice from inside her and spread it over her cleft, using an amazingly gentle frottage on her bud, and urging her towards that pleasure plateau from which there was only one return – orgasm. But it wasn't quite right – she needed perfection in this, their first mating.

'Not yet,' she gasped. 'Not here.'

He released her, frowning in disappointment, but following her when she took him by the hand and led him into her studio. The rain pattered on the skylight, but the sun was there, behind the clouds, soon to break out again.

'This is where you work? You've produced all these?'

And he went round admiring the blow-up photographs of her sculptures, and shook his head in wonderment.

'Yes, and this is my latest. It is three-quarters finished,' she said, pointing to the Abbotson pyramid, and there seemed nothing odd in standing there with him, naked except for her vest.

She wanted it this way, wanted this to be the setting – this place where her essence was most strongly felt – where she was inspired and creative. The place where she had witnessed Katrina and Bobby expressing their love through the bodies they had chosen to inhabit this time round.

Slowly, she gripped the hem of her vest and pulled it off over her head. She turned to him and her hands went to his zipper, her fingers delighting at the soft texture of his skin. It was slightly slicked with sweat. She inhaled the personal body odour of him, and for a moment he struggled to assist her, kicking off his trainers and getting out of his jeans, then peeling away his T-shirt. They were naked together for the first time, really naked, not like at the pool when there had been bits and pieces covering the vital parts.

They kissed, and she was walking backwards, till her knees met the edge of the couch, that place where she rested sometimes, and where she had seen Katrina and Bobby making love – not simply fucking, but taking responsibility for each other's pleasure, expressing something much, much deeper and long-lasting. She sank down into its softness, pulling Ed with her.

'Oh, Jody, Jody,' he whispered, and lay beside her, his hands returning to weave their magic, his lips adding to the sharp sensations as he tongued her nipples.

She gripped his powerful cock, admiring its length and girth, fingering the ridge of skin that strained back from the helm. 'We should...' she murmured, too excited to think coherently, but aware of the need for protection.

'I'll see to it. Don't worry. Just enjoy,' he promised, and her hips jerked against his hand as she attained the blissful heights.

She cried out and he slowed his stroke, gentling her clit and bringing her slowly down. 'No wonder it's called "the little death",' she almost sobbed. 'My God, I've touched eternity. I've never experienced anything like it.'

He smiled, and the harsh facial lines were smoothed away, giving her a glimpse of how he must have appeared when he was eighteen. He was stunning now, with his tan and his sun-bleached hair, but then he must have resembled a god.

'I'm glad I pleased you, petal,' he said, adding jokingly to cover his emotion, 'That's my mission in life.'

He moved, turned, until he was lying beside her and searching her face with eyes that were a little anxious. She lifted her lids, as content as a cat when it had demolished a tin of tuna, and said, 'Ed – oh, Ed...'

Even his name was perfect – not Edward, or Ned, or Eddie. Just a simple word that encapsulated the personality of the man. Ed.

He slipped a hand under her knee and lifted her leg over his thigh, then moved between hers and she felt the hard bough of his penis pressing against her entrance. He looked at her questioningly, as if asking her permission. She nodded and clasped him to her, lifting her pubis towards that very welcome probe. He thrust and the whole length of him slid inside her, touching her in all those internal spots that ached to be filled after her massive climax. She gasped and tugged at his buttocks, urging him on, and he started to move in slow, deep waves that stirred her to the core. He had been patient, waiting for his climax, and she helped him achieve it.

She looked up at him as he strained above her, taking his weight on his flat hands and his knees, his hips driving his cock in and out. Then the release overwhelmed him and she tightened her hands on his haunches and immersed herself in his possession, giving all that she could in return for the wealth of pleasure he had given her.

If this is love, she thought, as they rested together in the afterglow, then it could be truly said that I am in that state. Oh, dear, and it wasn't my intention to go there ever again.

9

'London's fun, but there's nothing like the country,' Nicole said through the length of straw held in her teeth. She was seated on a five-barred gate beside Ben.

'I thought you wouldn't want to come back,' he grunted, then shouted to his spaniel-collie-cross sheep-dog. 'Oi! Mandy! Get your arse over here and stop digging at that rabbit-hole. Give the poor buggers a break.'

Things don't alter, Nicole thought, and was glad. We sat like this ten years ago. There's a changeless quality about Heronswood. Miriam may refer to it as in a time warp, but I like it.

'I shall keep nagging on till Greg buys a house here,' she avowed, jeans stretched over her bottom that was angled outwards as she perched on the top bar. She hunched into her anorak, hood up. There had been a persistent drizzle all morning, the kind that appears with no warning on an August day, then clears up equally quickly.

The capricious climate was another reason why she wanted to live there. She was used to it, and it did wonders for the complexion. Jody and Miriam swore by it, and washed their faces in dew when in residence, that's if they got up early enough. She missed the routine of school, missed the hubbub and the kids with their eternal 'Miss! Miss! What do we do now, Miss? What's this mean, Miss?'

Once she'd had her fill of having a lie-in, then pottering round the shops and going over endless wedding arrangements and lists with Maggie, there wasn't much else to fill her time. She had sent thank-you letters in answer to messages and gifts from well-wishers who couldn't make the actual day but, this task behind her, she was heartsick for Greg. He appeared most week-ends. Unlike Jody and Miriam and even Nanette, who could laze for hours in the sun by a pool, Nicole wearied of this after a while and wanted to be up and doing, though what, she didn't know.

'Hopefully, when Greg does decide on a rural retreat, it may need redecorating and I'll be given the job of choosing wallpapers, paints and furnishings,' she said, while Mandy jumped up, muddying her jeans, and licking her face. This gesture of affection was all very well, but one never knew where her tongue had been, rather like that of a promiscuous lover.

'Don't be disappointed if it doesn't work out,' Ben remarked, screwing up his eyes and staring into the middle distance as if he could snuff a predator's drop-pings on the breeze. 'That damned old fox was about again last night. Put my hens in a right two and eight. And they're trying to ban hunting? Bloody townies that don't know sweet FA when it comes to country matters.'

'That's as maybe, but you've got a funny idea about Greg,' she said crossly, tossing the straw away.

'Have I? And why's that?' he asked perversely.

'You think he orders me around.'

'Well, he does, as far as I can see.'

'You don't know him.'

He gave her a sideways glance, saying, 'And do you?'

'Of course,' she snapped, but did she?

The London visit had been fine, as far as it went. Greg had wined and dined her and booked tickets for the latest show but, at the end of the evening, had as always had her delivered to Jody's door, spotless and unsullied. It's only weeks now, she promised herself, and all that will be in the past.

She jumped down and tried to keep up with Ben's long stride as he made off towards the copse, Mandy rushing ahead, busy as only a farm dog can be. Creatures to be admired, she thought, who guard, herd sheep, catch rats and generally make themselves useful, as nature intended, unlike the sad, neurotic animals who were the child substitutes or fashion accessories for the rich and lonely.

'Why are you here, on my land?' Ben said suddenly, without looking at her.

'Because I love it,' she replied, surprised.

'But you could bring Greg on walks when he's down. I don't see that happening. So why are you hanging around with me?'

'We speak the same language,' she said, and it was true.

'Then why d'you want to go off and marry someone like Greg? He's not a countryman.'

'Neither is my Dad, but he's done all right. Fits in, doesn't he? He must or they wouldn't have elected him mayor.'

'That's different. My father respected him, but he wouldn't have had a good word to say about your fiancé.'

'That's not fair. Give him a chance. Just because he comes from town. Don't be so narrow-minded, Ben.'

He gave a bark of laughter that had Mandy running to him, head cocked. He leaned down to pat her reassuringly. 'Me? Narrow-minded? Ha! You're a fine one to talk. What were you doing with him in his luxury flat? Playing Scrabble?'

This angered her profoundly, especially as his suspicions were ungrounded. 'Nothing happened, more's the pity,' she shouted. 'Don't take the moral high ground with me. You've got it all wrong. Anyway, what about you and that farmer's wife?'

Ben's face darkened. She could have sworn he was blushing. 'That was years ago, and it meant nothing,' he mumbled. 'How did you know about it anyway?'

'Everyone knew about it, and she dumped you, didn't she?'

How can I be so cruel to a friend? she mourned. It seemed that she was changing lately, like a chameleon taking colour from Greg's opinions and manner of speech, and Jody's and Miriam's hip, flippant and sometimes downright unkind way of expressing themselves. She didn't like herself too much at the moment, but put it down to the stress of marriage preparations. She tried to think positively; everything will be all right when the day comes.

Ben had tramped into the copse, with Mandy ahead, rooting about in the undergrowth. The set of his shoulders beneath the lumber jacket shirt showed her that he was offended, embarrassed and upset. She felt dreadful, but was too involved with her own doubts and fears to pay much heed to his.

'Ben, wait for me,' she exclaimed, dragging at a bramble that was hooked into her sleeve. 'I'm sorry. I shouldn't have said that.'

'It doesn't matter,' he muttered. 'I made a fool of myself over her anyway.'

'You weren't to know that she wasn't sincere,' she said.

'I should have realised. What woman is going to fall for me?'

'Plenty,' she returned, keen now to boost his confidence.

'I don't see them queuing up.'

'There will be someone soon,' she insisted, and placed her hand on his arm.

'And supposing I've already found the girl I love, but she doesn't love me?'

'Then that's tough, and you'll have to try harder. You'll win her in the end.'

'I don't think so,' he said, and his eyes were sad.

'Courage, comrade,' she went on. 'I thought it would never happen to me, but it has.'

It began to rain harder, and blue-white lightning split the sky, followed by a roll of thunder. Mandy barked and fussed. The rods of rain were falling straight now, and they sheltered under a tree.

'We shouldn't be doing this,' Ben said. 'We might get struck.'

'At least we'll go out together,' she joked, and huddled against him, partly to feel more secure, but mostly to make up in some way for her nasty remarks.

There was another flash and a further thunderclap, and she was aware of his arm closing about her protectively and, looking up, saw something in his eyes that confused her. The dog was standing, waiting patiently. The trees were rustling and the country was showing a side of itself that all natives recognised – nature wasn't always smiling. The reverse of calm was chaos, and every so often it put on a display of its power and complete disregard for the laws of men. This was only a summer storm. God was merely spitting. But Ben respected it and so did Nicole, having seen savage gales and swollen rivers, thick snow and icy roads when the outside world was cut off. Not so much in Heronswood, perhaps, but here, at Northgate Farm. And this had toughened him and made him into what he was – a dedicated son of the soil.

Compared to this, what she had seen in London seemed paltry. The crowded streets where men and women, plugged into their cell phones, were rushing about like a colony of demented ants, concerned only with financial security. The smart clubs and cafés to which she had been taken by Jody, as well as Greg, had filled her with unease, the smart appearance of the occupants making her feel a real hick-from-the-sticks, though she was proud to be just that, longing to get back home.

And what did she do when she arrived? Be horrible to an old friend.

'I'm sorry for being beastly,' she said and stood on tiptoe and reached up to him. Ben bent his head and she felt the press of his chilly, wet lips. He tasted of rain. He stood very still, did not even put out his hands to hold her. It was as if he couldn't believe this was happening.

Nicole's reaction to the kiss was unexpected. She liked it, warmed to it, this demure salute with closed lips, and she glowed inside, not with lust, but with a sense of contentment, as if it was long overdue. She had experienced this when he had wiped chocolate from her mouth with his finger, and had often thought about the incident in the café, especially when feeling disheartened because of Greg's lack of communication.

She stopped kissing him and lowered her heels to the carpet of pine needles. They gave off a bittersweet odour, reminding her of Christmas trees and all the excitements of the Festive Season. This year would be an extra special one – her first as a married woman. She'd be able to send cards from 'Nicole and Greg', and buy gifts for them to give to friends and family. And greetings would come plopping through the letterbox, addressed to Mr and Mrs Crawford. How lovely to be 'us' and 'we', instead of plain old lonely 'me'.

Ben said nothing, simply bent and stroked Mandy whose tail was going round like a windmill. The thunder was moving away, and the lightning dying out. The rain was no longer a deluge, more of a sprinkle and Nicole said, 'I'd better be getting back before it pours down again.'

Ben stood up straight, towering over her like one of the spruces. 'Right. Mrs MacDonald has made some scones. Why not come back and sample them? I've got strawberry jam and clotted cream, too. Later, if you want, we can go and visit Josephine and her litter. She farrowed down last night and produced eight piglets.'

Nicole nodded, easier now they were back to prosaic subjects like scones and sows. 'You talk about your animals as if they were human,' she teased, as they left the copse and struck off across the sopping wet meadow to where the house could be glimpsed between the trees.

'They're more reliable. You can trust a pig,' he answered briefly, and opened the wicket gate leading into the vegetable garden.

Rehearsals were not going well. The atmosphere in the church hall was fraught. The amateurs were behaving like temperamental professionals. Aubrey was throwing a tantrum.

'My God, he's spitting his dummy out all over the place,' Nanette remarked to Stewart. 'We seem to be the only two who have the faintest idea of what's going on.'

'Nerves,' he pronounced solemnly. He was trying out the full-bottomed, curly black peruke worn by the Pirate King, though more modern versions deviated from tradition. A moustache twirled into waxed points had been fixed to his upper lip and he looked like Captain Hook.

Though not yet in costume (these were due to arrive from the theatrical suppliers next week), Nanette was impressed. Even in jeans and sweatshirt and without stage make-up, he was the embodiment of the archetypal sea-wolf – a swaggering, sword-flourishing rogue. She was interrupted in her admiration by an outraged shriek from Connie Barnes, doctor's wife and the opera's 'Mabel'.

'I can't possibly manage those coloratura trills at the end of my opening aria, *Poor Wandering One*, if the flautist doesn't keep up with me!'

Aubrey sank his head in his hands, and the females of the chorus, supposed to be Mabel's sisters, looked on, not sure who to side with. 'I'm trying, Connie. I really am,' he complained. 'No one else is creating such a fuss. It's supposed to be funny, not serious. Sullivan himself wrote, "now for farmyard noises," on the score. He was having a dig at the grand opera of the time, when all the sopranos performed vocal contortions, in the *belle canto* style.'

He walked across to where the orchestra were out front and just below the stage and said to Deirdre, 'Could you be an angel and go away somewhere and practise with Connie?'

'But what about me? I'm conducting,' protested Bernie Trent, flushing to the roots of his untidy, mad-professor hair. Now that the show was nearing its first night, he had taken up the baton of bandmaster.

'Look here. This is holding things up. Connie, I suggest that you, Bernie and Deirdre meet here tomorrow night and have another go – on your own, without the rest of us – and please get it right.'

'Oh, I don't know if I can,' Deirdre hesitated, and Nanette could see guilt and wedding preparations flashing across her face. It was as much as she could do to get away on Monday evenings. As luck would have it, the show went on a mere week before the nuptials. For Dierdre, all was rush and tear, worry and agitation and arguments.

Why on earth do people put themselves through this ordeal? Nanette wondered. I can remember my own wedding. The Manor House was an ideal setting. We had marquees on the lawn. So much trauma, and what good did it do me? Allan and I divorced in the end. You might as well have taken all the money it cost my father and flushed it down the loo, and he'd signed an insurance policy to cover it the day I was born.

'I'll give you a lift, if you like, and be around to help. I'll bring my oboe,' Derek jumped in promptly, diverting Nanette from her gloomy speculations and bringing a ray of sunshine into Deirdre's existence.

Oboe? Well, that's a new name for it, Nanette thought wryly. She had been pleased to see how well he and Deirdre got on. Playing in the orchestra had given her a new lease of life, or something had. Was it this old flame turning up out of the blue? Whatever, it had put a sparkle in her eyes and colour in her cheeks.

'I can drive here,' Deirdre responded, torn between duty and the novel idea of doing something to please herself. 'But, yes, support would be helpful. Thank you, Derek.'

No canoodling on the back seat of his car, then, Nanette conjectured. Their relationship is as chaste as ours. Stewart and I have done nothing but hold hands and kiss once or twice, though I've dropped massive hints and given him plenty of encouragement.

'Right, boys and girls. Take it from the top. Major-General Stanley, in you come,' Aubrey said bossily, and the head pharmacist from the local Boots chemist strutted about and acted competently as the doddery old fool of a Major-General. He got through the patter song without a flaw, even coping with its fast closing pace, and the chorus joined in and all was now proceeding swimmingly.

Act II, and Nanette was on stage with Stewart, singing about the paradox of Frederick being born in a leap-year, thus making him a little boy of five, instead of twenty-one and out of his piratical apprenticeship. It was typical Gilbertian nonsense, with twists and turns of fate that were sorted in the end, with boy getting girl and everyone happy. It had a feel-good factor, much needed in the troublesome climate of terrorism, rising taxes, blips in the education system and problems with the National Health Service.

'Coming back to mine?' Nanette asked Stewart when he had abandoned his wig and moustache and reverted to normality. He nodded.

Sometimes they went back to 'his', but her stereo was better and her video collection more comprehensive. They usually ended at the Manor House and she inevitably finished up alone, for he never stayed, making no attempt to seduce her. She didn't press it, behaving remarkably well, even cooling it with Shaun and Kevin. She wanted this one, whether or no, and even visualised becoming Mrs Stewart the Dentist's Wife in the Happy Families pack. She didn't know why this was so important.

She had met more attractive men – and men with more money. But the prospect of being alone as the years passed was not very appealing. She needed a companion as well as a lover, someone devoted who would cope with her losing her marbles or becoming crippled with arthritis or any of the hundred and one trials that accompany growing old. And she would be prepared to care for him in exchange.

Stewart and she were about the same age, liked the same things, and shared similar ambitions – nothing wild, simply a passion for Spain and Italy, enjoying the heat, the cuisine, the dancing and music. We could be content together, she had decided early on, and she knew that it only needed a nudge in the right direction to make two shy, wary and easily hurt people take the plunge. She was willing to wait – but not too long. When the show's launched, she promised herself. He'll be flushed with success and achieving critical acclaim. It will be wonderful. And if I don't bed him by the time of the Last Night Party, I'll eat my boots, laces and all.

'And where have you been, sonny boy?' Clarissa barked when Ed walked into her suite in the Empire Hotel in Bath's Royal Crescent.

'Running through the duel with Mark Lawson and the fight choreographer.'

'You didn't turn up last night. I had to leave without you.' She stared at him accusingly, wearing a thin dress and minimum of make-up, looking summery and attractive. 'Mark's a sweetie and gorgeous looking and such a notable actor, but he's bent as a corkscrew, no use to me at all. You almost missed me now. The car is waiting to take me to my caravan. We'll be shooting after lunch.'

'I shall be there,' he promised, but hung on to his bag, hoping to escape to his own room.

'And when did you get to Bath?'

'Early this morning. I came by train.'

'It was a woman who delayed you, I suppose,' she said flatly, and he did not bother to deny it. No doubt she had made up for his loss by sleeping with the bellboy or a convenient and obliging waiter.

The Empire was an old-fashioned establishment that

did not cater for the eccentricities of visiting film stars. Clarissa had been booked into the finest suite but this did not include a bedroom for her maid, or dresser, male companion, trainer or whatever. Ed was down the hall a little way, and this suited him. He was no longer at her beck and call, and had his personal landline, which meant he could contact Jody at any time without relying on his mobile being in credit.

They had spent an incredible night together. There was nothing they hadn't tried, doing it any which way, until he felt sure there wasn't the smallest drop of spunk left in him. He couldn't believe that, after all their snapping and snarling at each other, this fascinating woman wanted him, and not just for a one-nighter, though both hesitated to put a time on the affair. A week? A year? Forever? It was in the lap of the gods.

It was more than a crush he had, but he couldn't be sure Jody felt the same. Neither of them had dared mention it. It was going to be difficult to be together much. He had his career and she had hers. The simple logistics of the situation made it hard to plan ahead, even if they wanted to. He certainly did, but wasn't sure about her. He hadn't been seeking this, didn't want the pain involved in being apart, but it was there, that irrational emotion that he very much feared was love.

Now Clarissa had one thing on her mind, it seemed. Maybe she hadn't pulled last evening after all. 'Time for a quickie, Ed,' she murmured and lay back on the bed, pulling up her skirt inch by inch, displaying those long, honey-gold, carefully depilated legs that were insured for a king's ransom.

I can't, Ed thought. I'm drained and I don't want her. Not now, not after Jody. Even the fact that he could see her denuded pink mons didn't move him. Something remarkable had happened to him last night. It had been his epiphany, a Road to Damacus revelation and he didn't know why. There was nothing extraordinary about Jody. He had met scores of women with more going for them physically. It went deeper than that. Perhaps there was truth in the story about finding one's soul mate. Whatever it was, it had left him unable to make love to Clarissa.

'No can do,' he said, staring down at her and feeling nothing. Not the smallest sensation of desire moved in his loins. He simply wanted to get away, do his job, and meet up with Jody again as soon as possible.

'What d'you mean?' Clarissa's eyes sparked and her face was suddenly ugly. She wasn't used to being denied.

'I'm not interested any more,' he said bluntly. There was no way he could let her down gently.

'What? You lousy bastard! Are you trying to tell me that you don't want to fuck me?' She expressed all the venom and outrage of a woman who had always got her way.

Ed shrugged and backed towards the door. 'That's about the long and short of it,' he answered, and it was one of the hardest things he had ever had to do. Dangerous stunts were nothing compared to this.

She sat up and he thought she was about to fly at him, nails spread to rend and claw. Then he saw tears in her eyes and wished she'd attack him instead. He really didn't want to hurt her. Her pride had been dented by his refusal. All the insecurity of her addictive nature came to the fore. She looked like a child that has been smacked in the face.

'You can't do this to me,' she said, and her voice was trembling. 'I'll have you sacked. You'll never work again.'

Ed shook his head. He knew his own worth in the

industry and it was considerable. She might make waves, but it wouldn't affect him that much. 'Don't push it, Clarissa,' he advised. 'We've had a ball. Can't we still be friends?'

She got to her feet, tall and straight and controlled, retaining the charisma that had made her a household name. He admired her then and was glad that she hadn't broken down and grovelled. He wouldn't wish that on any woman, especially someone as proud as her.

'Friends?' she repeated in her perfect, Shakespearean-trained accent. 'Friends? How can you say this when we've been so much more?'

He wanted to go before things got any worse, but felt he couldn't leave her like this. 'It wasn't a love affair,' he reminded her.

'Wasn't it?' she replied with a sneer. 'What was it, then? A cheapskate muscle man getting into pictures on my back?'

This angered him. It was totally unfair, well, most of it anyway. Yes, he may have used her a little, but then, hadn't she used him, too? Getting her kicks when he spanked her, having her ego massaged by being seen out and about with a much younger man? It had been a fair exchange, but the time had come to end it.

'I'm sorry you feel this way,' he said, spreading his hands in an apologetic gesture. 'But you knew, surely, that it would be over one day. You don't want a permanent relationship. You've too much to give, too much to experience. It wouldn't be your style, shackling yourself to one man. Come on, Clarissa, admit that it's true.'

She glowered at him like a thwarted Lady Macbeth. 'How dare you speak to me that way? If it was to end, then I was the one to do it – not you. In my time and on my terms. I hope you rot in hell. Now get out of my sight.' She snatched up her wineglass and hurled it at him.

Ed's reaction was automatic. He dodged to one side. It smashed against the door and he didn't look at her again, simply opened it and let himself out.

Jody's protective goggles kept steaming up, and it was partly due to the sun in the studio, but more to do with her heated thoughts. She couldn't get Ed out of her mind. Standing on a stool, she chiselled away at the top section of the monolith. It was really coming together well, despite the fact that she had wakened with back ache, and was very tender between the legs.

Too much screwing! she admitted to herself, with a wide, silly grin. A wall mirror gave back her reflection and she was shocked. Jesus Christ, I look like I've been on the tiles all night. But this wasn't strictly accurate; she also looked like a woman in love. There was a softness in her eyes, a dewiness to her lips, and they looked fuller, redder, bruised with Ed's kisses.

They hadn't made a definite arrangement to meet again. He had taken a taxi to Paddington Station about seven that morning, leaving her to ruminate on what had happened, then to shower and dress and work. She was fired, inspired, tuned into her muse.

'Come to Bath with me,' he had urged, but no, she had a commission to complete.

She had the sort of day she liked best, uninterrupted, grabbing sandwiches and coffee when she felt like it. She guessed that the creative process was similar to pregnancy. Katrina was always eating, and so was Jody, when in the throes of inspiration. No one phoned her. No one called at the front door and she was blissfully unaware of the passage of time. The sun moved round and part of the studio was now in shade. The pyramid had taken shape, and she was adding the finishing touches. It shone like a beacon, sparkling with ceramic tiles, lumps of stone from deep in the earth, glittering with strands of fool's gold. It was barbaric, stunning, ageless yet entirely modern. She was sure that Aaron Abbotson would be over the moon.

He had rung her from California yesterday, sounding as close as if he was in the next room, saying, 'When are you coming over, honey?'

'At the end of September. I have a wedding to go to first. I'm a bridesmaid.'

'OK. How's the piece doing?'

'Looking impressive, and like the sketches I showed you.'

'That's great, babe. I'm having a grand opening ceremony and I want you to be there for the unveiling. Will you do that?'

'Wild horses wouldn't stop me,' she had said, and meant every word, but much water had flowed under the bridge since then. She had fucked Ed, and her perspectives had changed amazingly.

Go to America and leave him behind? It was unthinkable – painful – diabolical. No longer was she a free agent. He had promised that he would tell Clarissa about them, and she had believed him at the time. It was easy to believe when she was lying beneath him and his wonderful cock was buried to the hilt inside her. Then, blind and deaf to all save passion, she wouldn't have doubted anything he told her. She couldn't expect him to slow down in his career. It was important to him and therefore, by definition, important to her.

She stopped working, resting her backside on a high stool and putting down chisel, sander and the adhesive by which she attached the decorations to the concrete. Now that she had ceased, weariness flooded through her. Her arms ached, her legs ached, she had been on her feet all day. Who said that artists didn't work as hard as labourers? Whoever it was knew fuck all about it.

The doorbell buzzed and she swore, hesitated, wished the caller would go to hell, and then dragged herself along to answer it. Miriam stepped over the threshold, clad in shorts so skimpy it was a wonder she hadn't been arrested. Her brown legs shone with after-sun lotion, and her slim feet were thrust into thonged sandals. She took off her rimless shades and subjected Jody to a searching stare.

'Where were you last night? I rang and rang but you were engaged for hours,' she said sternly.

'I had the phone off the hook,' Jody replied, wiping stone dust and glue from her hands on a rag.

'Why?' Miriam sat down, slung one leg over the chair arm and lit up a cigarette.

'Because I was with Ed.'

'You were?'

'I was.'

'Yikes!' Miriam screamed. 'You really had a grope-fest with him?'

'More than that – I had a sex-fest.'

'That's my girl,' Miriam said, grinning. 'But I hope you were careful, and didn't fall in love with him.'

'I was careful, but as for love, it's too late. I am already there.'

'You muppet!' Miriam rejoined, pushing her sun-glasses up to her forehead. 'What have I told you about that? Screw them legless, but don't go all soft and squidgy and imagine a life of endless bliss with the dick-head concerned.'

'This is different,' Jody tried to say.

'Isn't it always, until they let you down? What about Clarissa? I thought she had first claim on him.'

'It's nothing serious. A casual thing between them.'

'That's what he told you.'

'Yes, and I think he's sincere.'

Miriam rolled her eyes towards the ceiling. 'Oh, God, what have I done to have a schmuck like you as a friend?' and she mashed her cigarette in the ashtray. 'Don't you ever listen to anything I say?'

'Not often,' Jody said, on the stool again, hugging her knees to her chest and beaming happily.

'Stop acting the giddy goat,' Miriam said crisply. 'On your head be it, girl. Ed's an adventurer, a loner, used to living off his wits and out of a suitcase. He'll love you and leave you when something else comes along that takes his fancy. If you can't recognise the type now, then you never will. And you'd better watch out for Clarissa. No matter what he says, "hell hath no fury like a woman scorned," and she'll have your guts for garters.'

'Oh, Miriam, don't be such a bloody killjoy. I know men. I'd recognise if he was pulling a fast one,' Jody protested, some of the rosy sparkle going out of the day. Why was it that there was always someone eager to point out facts that one didn't really want to know?

'No, you wouldn't. Not at this stage of the game, anyway. Love-struck. Cock-struck. It's my mission to point this out. Someone has to say it.'

'Why? Just leave me alone.' Jody was fast losing patience with her well meaning but pushy friend.

'OK, OK.' Miriam raised her hands. 'I'm a control freak. That's what I'm told at group therapy. I'm working on it. Honest, I am. Trying to mind my *own* business, not other people's. Sorry, Jody. It's just that I can't bear to see you hurt. You know what Australian men are like. They don't want to be tied down.'

'I know.' Contrite, Jody left the stool and put her arms round Miriam. 'I'm trying to handle Ed differently, and I really do believe that he's very fond of me.'

'And that's enough?' Miriam grabbed her hand and looked into her face searchingly.

'For the time being, yes.' And I mean it, Jody thought to herself. 'I'm not a passive person, but what else can I do anyway?'

'You're dead right. Forget him for the moment. How about we go to Janine's and get ourselves a sauna, then shower and socialise?'

'Not men,' Jody said quickly, shaking her head and holding her hands to her breasts as if warding off temptation.

'Did I mention men?' Miriam responded innocently. 'This is strictly for the girls.'

They booked in at Janine's and went for a workout. Dance music reverberated in the gym. It was early evening, but daylight still slanted through the plate-glass windows and was supplemented by spots. They gleamed on the rowing machines, exercise bikes, weight-lifting equipment and aerobic steps. The teacher, a statuesque woman with cropped blonde hair and wearing expensive soft grey gym clothes, flung her arms above her head and swung down to touch the toes of her thick-soled trainers.

A dozen other women of assorted sizes, wearing a similar uniform to hers, were attempting to copy her movements. There was a mixed rate of success, but one was outstanding. Her dark hair was confined by a bandeau, her lissom body as pliable as a dancer's, her long legs muscular yet feminine, and her eyes were flinty and critical as she watched herself in the mirror-covered wall.

'Isn't that the one called Scarlett?' Jody asked quietly, as they passed her on their way to the changing rooms.

'That's her. She patronises this place regularly. I'm on nodding terms with her. Maybe she'll have a drink with us later on,' Miriam replied, giving Scarlett an appraising glance. 'Dear me, but she's fit. Has to be so, I guess, considering her occupation. Got to keep those arm muscles in trim for whipping bad boys' backsides. She makes me feel like a tub of lard.'

They took off their clothes and wormed themselves into their gym gear. Miriam was wearing azure blue lycra, and began running on the spot in her silver Reeboks. Her breasts bounced under the oval-necked top.

'Ready?' she asked.

'As I'll ever be,' Jody responded, keeping one thought in mind: that of becoming fitter, more shapely and lovelier for Ed.

The instructress bore down on them, leaving the class to cope on their own, heaving and panting and sweating. 'Hello, Miriam,' she said. 'And this is...?'

'Jody, Jody Hamilton.'

'You've not been here before?'

'Only to have a massage.' Jody could feel her face growing hot as she remembered Kit. That incident seemed a world away now.

'My name's Denise,' said the blonde Amazon. She clapped her hands, had Jody and Miriam join the ranks, and proceeded to put them through the routine.

First, the warm-up, and this was almost as gruelling as what followed. Denise had little time for the feeble, looking down her nose at them. 'Reach as high as you can, and when you feel you can't go any further, then stretch that bit more. Come on. You can do it. Up, down. Legs apart. Heels on the floor. Bend. Bend. Take it from the waist. Don't lift with your back muscles. This may cause injury. Now, on, on, step, step.'

No time for the faint-hearted, Jody thought ten minutes later, her pulse racing, muscles screaming, face beaded with sweat. Lord, why did I let myself in for this torture? Even if I was to see Ed tonight I'd be unable to enter the sex Olympics with him. Too knackered!

'That's me done for,' she groaned when, class dismissed at last, she collapsed on one of the benches and sipped at a plastic cup filled with iced water.

'Till next time,' Miriam said cheerfully, a towel draped round her neck. She didn't seem as exhausted as Jody.

'Over my dead body,' Jody grumbled. 'I knew from the start that this wasn't for me.'

'Not even to keep up with the frightfully fit and manly Ed the Stuntman?'

'Oh, shut your face!' Jody snapped, really fed up now.

She wasn't looking forward to the next ordeal – a sojourn in the sauna. The cold plunge-pool would have been more tempting.

When they entered the steamy room, they found Scarlett already there, lying on the wooden slats, naked as Nature intended and beautiful with it. Jody was glad that the atmosphere was like a fog. She was feeling inadequate, out of sorts and just plain bushed. To curl up somewhere and sleep seemed a heavenly prospect at the moment.

Miriam had no such hang-ups, apparently. She sat with her legs apart, displaying her dark thatch. The lower angle of her mons was wide, a brown line dividing her fork, and Jody looked away, embarrassment adding to her body heat. Scarlett had no body hair: her mound of Venus was shaved, and both of them seemed so comfortable in their nudity, it made Jody feel like a prudish fool.

The ambience was somnolent, with the increasing warmth of water hissing over red-hot stones. Jody rested her head back against the pine-panelled walls, letting her towel slip away. The other two didn't seem to be bothering, so why should she? Her eyelids were heavy as if her body was carrying on the need for sleep that she had ignored while working, but was now catching up on her. I'd like to be in Ed's arms, she thought drowsily. Just to sleep and dream and wake to find him holding me. No sex, just that drowsy, comfortable sensation of him being with me.

Little rivers of sweat trickled from her hairline. They cruised down her face, and dripped from her chin, then continued their journey across her breasts to hang in heavy drops from her nipples. They tickled and she wanted to brush them away, but was too indolent, and they ran across her belly and dipped between her legs, finishing up amongst the matted, wet pubes that hid her slit.

When she opened her eyes again, she was surprised to see Miriam and Scarlett seated close together, and they were gazing at each other's bodies, as if assessing the enjoyment they might derive if they got it together. It was a sharp reminder that Miriam was bi. Presumably Scarlett dabbled in that direction, too. I hope they don't do it in here, Jody thought, though the idea was intriguing.

'You're awake, then?' Miriam said, smiling at her through the mist. 'Let me introduce you to Scarlett. We're going to have a drink when we've finished here and plunged into the cold bath.'

'Nice to meet you,' Scarlett said. 'I wanted to talk to

you about a girl who I understand is your friend. Her name is Nicole, and we met in the Jacuzzi. She said she is about to be married to a guy called Gregory Crawford. Seemed full of it and very excited.'

'That's right. Jody and I are to be bridesmaids. Is there more?'

Scarlett raised a hand and flicked a thumb across Miriam's right nipple, smiling mysteriously. 'That's what I want to talk to you about,' she said. 'Not here, but over drinks. You see, I know him – you might say *personally* – and it seems a crying shame that such a sweet girl is getting spliced to a wanker like him.'

10

'Come in,' Scarlett said, opening the door of her apartment.

Miriam had thought it would be palatial, given the address and outstanding architecture, but this far exceeded her expectations. Its spacious feel was exaggerated by the minimal décor. Everything was white, even the brickwork that had been exposed when the owner of this building, that had once been a warehouse, had decided to transform it into luxury flats. One room led to another, screened by sliding glass doors. It had a balcony but, more than this, there was a roof garden.

Miriam felt that she was in a detached house; there was no sound of neighbours, only the hum of the city as they stood overlooking it, and this was muted by distance. The lights twinkled, reflected by water, and the yellow streets shone like an amber necklace round the throat of a black giantess.

'You like it?' Scarlett asked, and they returned inside and she fixed drinks and lit up the first spliff of the evening.

'I'm impressed,' Miriam answered, taking a seat beside her on the red leather settee, the only concession to colour in the room. 'It's yours?'

'Not yet, but I'm working on it,' Scarlett said, smiling. Her eyes cut to Jody and she continued, 'So you're to be a bridesmaid, too. Where do you figure in the scheme of things?'

Jody blushed, and glanced at Miriam for support.

'Seems like Greg has set his sights on me, and I'm not the smallest degree interested.'

'And if you were?' Scarlett asked with a musing smile, smoke rings coiling from her nostrils.

'Nicole's my friend, and one of the golden rules is never do the dirty on a sister.'

'Too right,' Miriam agreed, hoping that Scarlett embraced this principle. 'We called ourselves the Three Musketeers when we were at school.'

'There's no way we'd screw each other's blokes,' Jody averred earnestly, seated opposite in a deep chair that resembled a wide white bucket. Then her eyes sharpened and she asked, 'What do you know about Greg?'

'It would be quicker to say what don't I know,' said Scarlett, and stretched like a sinuous cat and laid her slim thighs across Miriam's lap. Her skirt slid up and her fragrance brushed Miriam's senses, a combination of female musk and the perfumeries of France.

Miriam stroked her calves and Scarlett twiddled her toes, indicating that she wanted her to unlace and remove her stilt-heeled ankle boots. Miriam complied. Jody seemed impatient with this foreplay, leaning forward and saying quickly, 'Won't you tell us about him?'

Scarlett was playing with Miriam's tousled hair, but answered, 'It's not my policy to betray a confidence, particularly one that was imparted during pillow talk, but I don't much like what's going on here. He told me that he's getting married, and made fun of his bride-to-be, making her out to be some sort of dim-wit.'

'He doesn't love her,' Jody said with conviction. 'She thinks he does, but we had our doubts, didn't we, Miriam? Particularly when he started to come on to me.'

'He doesn't love anyone, only himself,' Scarlett replied, resting against the feather-filled cushions, and

Miriam was entranced by her, scarcely heeding the conversation, even though it was important.

'And what is he to you?' Jody went on, stern as a judge.

'He's a client, though he was beginning to mean more till I chanced on Nicole. He's very persuasive and credible. He'll make a first-class politician, have the voters eating out of his hand, I shouldn't wonder. He could even end up in the Cabinet.' Scarlett stopped relaxing and sat up, her eyes stormy. 'I'm his dominatrix. He likes me to control him as a change from him controlling everyone else, but his charm was starting to bewitch even me, and I thought I was blind and deaf to any man's wiles. He'll pay for this. I don't like being conned into letting my guard down.'

'Nicole will never believe it. Every word he utters is like the Sermon on the Mount,' Miriam put in, missing the warmth and ease she had been sharing with Scarlett.

'And how about you? Do you think I'm telling the truth? He's perverted, decadent, certainly not the squeaky-clean person he pretends to be,' Scarlett went on. 'Of course, it's none of my business, but I'd like to see him exposed. He's done nothing against the law, as yet, and is only a small fish in the big pool of politics, but he should be prevented from marrying Nicole.'

'I believe you,' Miriam said. 'Why should you bother to make this up? If you'd have wanted to, you could already have alerted the gutter press.'

'I don't think so. That could open up a can of worms and put me at a disadvantage. Don't forget I do well out of these men, and never inquire into their business. Greg, however, is a different kettle of fish. I almost fell for him, then learned about his fiancée and why he was getting married. Such callous selfishness sickened me, and I'm a tough cookie, remember? When I met Nicole, I was even more sorry for her. She reminded me of myself when I was as innocent, and in love for the first time.'

'So you'll help us?'

'Maybe.'

'Nicole won't listen,' Jody put in sadly.

'We can but try,' Miriam said.

'It's hard to believe he's such a sod,' Jody added. 'I felt it in my water, but Nicole won't want to hear, and we'll probably end up falling out with her. What is it he does that's such a no-no?'

'Apart from deceiving her and pretending that he loves her and intends to be a faithful husband? As to how he gets his kicks? Why don't you visit his favourite club, Willards, in Mayfair?' Scarlett suggested.

'How could we get in?' Miriam asked, and tingled when she felt Scarlett touch her right nipple with the long oval nail of her index finger, scratching across its hard tip. Miriam could hardly suppress a moan.

'I'm a member. I use my lover's card,' Scarlett said carelessly.

'Which one?' Miriam asked, speared by a sudden spasm of jealousy.

'The nice old guy who keeps me, of course,' Scarlett said unrepentantly, spreading her arms to embrace her surroundings. 'He pays the rent, but will buy it for me soon.'

'And he doesn't know about the others?'

'He likes me to humiliate him – even gets off on being watched by strange men,' Scarlett said airily. 'I must show you my toys. I've a walk-in wardrobe full of them. He gets his money's worth. So, I use his club, and if there's any question about me bringing you along, then I'm sure another of my submissives, Birdy Sutherland, would be only too happy to help.'

'What about it, Jody?' Miriam asked, feeling Scarlett's arms twining round her. She was more in the mood for love than playing private eye and tailing Greg.

'A sex club? I'm not sure,' Jody said, and Miriam could tell by her tone that she was finding their pleasure in one another awkward to accept.

'A very respectable gentlemen's club, on the surface,' Scarlett replied, a rich laugh bubbling up in her throat.

'And Greg will be there?'

'Probably, and his buddy, Piers.'

'So he *does* know all about it. The lying, shit-eating little toad,' Miriam exclaimed forcefully, really annoyed with him.

'A mate of yours?' Scarlett asked, bending closer and giving her a tongue-kiss in the ear.

'Could be. I was hoping he would grass on Greg.'

'I think not. They gee each other up. Piers likes his ladies to be hard on him.'

'I know,' Miriam said. 'That's what I've been working on.'

'What are you going to do about putting a spanner in the works?' Scarlett wanted to know.

'It depends on the state of play and from what you've already told us, the whole matter of the marriage and Greg's rise to glory helped by Nicole's father appears to be decidedly dodgy.'

Jody got up and started pacing around. 'It's as plain as the nose on your face. It's got to be stopped. I want to go now. There's a lot to think about, not the least of which is how we're going to broach Nicole about this. You keep the car, Miriam, and I'll ring for a cab. It's pretty obvious that you're not ready to leave yet.'

'We'll talk about it in the morning, maybe even go to Willards,' Miriam agreed, knowing herself all too well and her inability to concentrate when sex was in the offing. Delicious, Sapphic love with Scarlett. The wedding had faded into insignificance against this urge.

Nicole sat near the window in her bedroom. The warm breeze was heavy with fragrance, and the garden was looking truly magnificent, filled with an abundance of blossom – magnolia, sweet peas, jasmine and exotic plants that she couldn't name. It had cost her father a small fortune to achieve this Chelsea Flower Show excellence.

Maggie was behind it, naturally, having based the design on the gardens belonging to the Leigh Grove Hotel, the epitome of grace and grandeur in her opinion. She was looking forward to showing it off to various dignitaries from the council office, who would support their mayor at his daughter's wedding to a rising young politician.

Nicole sighed. It was humid and, though she had showered, she still felt overheated and listless. She got out her diary, re-read some of it, and decided to add more.

'"Wedding Day Countdown,"' she began. '"Gran has been on the case since just after the engagement. That's when she swung into action. Military campaigners have nothing on her. Once, it seemed there were months to go, but now it's only one! Right: here's what I have to do. (1) Arrange the hen night. (2) Have a session with the bridesmaids trying on everything to make sure it's all OK. (3) Have a practice run with the hairdresser. Gran's insisting on using hers and wants him to try out my headdress, and style hers and Jody's and Miriam's and Mum's. Sounds like a recipe for disaster. (4). Start getting my honeymoon luggage together. I've already bought my trousseau, gorgeous sexy underwear, pink, white, blue and lilac. I know Greg's going to love it."'

For a moment, she drifted off into a dream – herself and Greg in the bridal suite of a hotel in a fantastic location, and she was wearing a fragile white silk nightgown and negligée, with him sporting a foot-long boner.

'"Gran's done the seating plan for the reception, and Greg's organised the rehearsal in church and the certificate of licence from the registrar. We've been to see the vicar regularly, and he has explained the sanctity of marriage. I'm not religious in any shape or form, but I think it's all beautiful and can't wait to make my vows."'

She slammed the diary shut and thrust it into the bedside cabinet. She was restless and didn't know what to do with herself. There was still much to arrange, but not at that precise moment. Jody and Miriam were in London and there was no one to talk things over with – except Ben, of course. She decided to drive over to Northgate Farm and see if she could find him, though he'd probably be in the fields haymaking.

'There's a fancy-dress do at Willards,' Miriam informed Jody. 'What say we go along for a bit of snooping?'

'If Greg and Piers are there, they'll spot us,' Jody said, casting an eye round Top Table, half expecting to bump into him. This restaurant in the City Centre was a very 'now' venue, patronised by beautiful people: celebrities, television presenters, and those who sought notoriety in a different form, on the political stage.

'No, they won't. It's a Venetian Ball theme and everyone will be wearing masks.'

'So Scarlett says?'

'That's right, and she wants to help Nicole.'

'We're going home this weekend to try on our outfits and have our hair done by Maggie's pet bloke who owns UpperCut.'

'No one is touching mine, particularly an old queen who hasn't been on a refresher course for years. Maggie may be a fag-hag but I'm not,' Miriam stated flatly, sipping at her black coffee while scrutinising the crowd. She liked to be in the know – who was seen where and with whom.

'She'll get the knock,' Jody observed.

'And will probably say a bunch of stuff that will upset Nicole and Deirdre. Who cares?'

'I do. If there's a scene and Nicole gets involved with trying to keep the peace, she'll not be in a fit state to listen when we try to warn her about that scumbag,' Jody pointed out.

Miriam changed the subject, asking, 'Speaking of scumbags, have you seen Ed?'

Her question was like a knife-blow to the heart. 'No,' Jody answered. 'But we've spoken on the phone. He's still in Bath and can't get away and, from what I gather, Clarissa is being a bitch.'

Miriam wagged her head solemnly. 'I hate to say I told you so . . .'

'Then don't. Get off my case,' Jody snapped, more worried about the situation than she cared to admit.

'OK. Only wanting to help,' Miriam said, backing down. 'You're a big girl now.'

'That's right. I can handle it. When's this masked ball thingy?'

'On Saturday night of next week. We shall be back from Heronswood in good time. I want to get my costume sorted. Scarlett is going to take me to a shop in

Soho that deals in fetish gear, and much more besides. We'll go together, if you like.'

Jody wasn't sure, hoping against all hope that she would be able to make Nicole see reason, thus avoiding a trip to a club like Willards. Despite her sharpness with Miriam, she was worried on two counts: Nicole and Ed.

All went well, to begin with. They gathered in Nicole's bedroom and there was a party atmosphere. Even Maggie seemed relaxed. Fortunately, this was an adults-only try-out. The junior attendants would be coached on the wedding eve when the final rehearsal took place in church. Their outfits had been made and Nicole had seen them dressed up, had admired and approved and thought they looked sweet. No one had bouquets yet; these would be delivered on the day, and Greg had bought presents for all the attendants.

Her gown was perfect in every detail, and Jody and Miriam looked stunning in their aubergine dresses. Maggie clapped her hands and fiddled with Nicole's veil, while Deirdre looked on, no doubt admiring her daughter, but making little comment. No one could get a word in edgeways while Maggie was in full spate.

'That colour is better than I thought,' she said to Jody magnanimously. 'You look dignified and serene. So do you, Miriam, apart from the hair, of course, but Tony is going to fix that.'

'When?' Miriam said, and Nicole could almost see her hackles rising.

'As soon as we've finished here, dear. He's reserving a space for us early evening. Most conscientious and such a brilliant stylist. We'll take your veil and tiara with us, Nicole.'

The dresses were returned to their hangers and plastic shrouds, and Nicole was shunted into Maggie's car with Deirdre. Miriam opted to use hers, taking Jody with her. Nicole would have liked to have travelled with them, but it was almost as if Maggie was standing guard over her, keeping her in a glass case, uncorrupted by outside influences. She had grumbled when Nicole told her that she had been helping out with the harvest.

'But your hands, dear!' she had exclaimed, shocked to the core. 'You'll make them all rough and break your nails. What is Ben thinking about, encouraging you?'

Nicole had ignored her, slipping away to the farm whenever she could. Being there grounded her. It was real, earthy, a far cry from the ridiculous preparations for what should have been, after all, a solemn union between a man and a woman, not a circus.

UpperCut was in the High Street, and Maggie swept in dramatically with the rest tagging along behind her. 'Ah, there you are, Tony,' she cried, and rushed up, kissing him on both cheeks.

'Maggie, darling, as radiant as ever,' he carolled, waving a hand at one of his juniors and indicating that she should fetch fresh towels. 'You get younger every time I see you. I wish you'd tell me your secret. I'm getting broken veins again. Look,' and he pushed his face close to hers, a handsome face with chiselled features, a straight nose and hazel eyes. His figure was boyish, his hair curly.

'You're wearing terribly well, Tony, and you know it,' Maggie cooed. 'I can't see any broken veins.'

'Well, I can, and I'm off to have them treated. There's this wonderful woman who gets rid of them with the use of electrolysis. I've had it done before, and it hurts horribly and my face is red as a beetroot for days after, but it's worth it.'

Garrulous and bustling, he placed them in chairs as he talked, and the junior wrapped gowns round them, tied at the back. Tony concentrated on Nicole first, dampening her hair and winding the strands round fat rollers, then sitting her under the dryer.

'Maggie?' he said. 'Do you want something different, or your usual?'

'I'm wearing a large hat,' she confessed. 'Tulle, you know, rather like those worn by the Royals lately.'

'I know the ones. They look like meringues. Ah, in that case, we won't alter your hair. What about you, Mrs Carpenter?' he asked, turning to Deirdre.

'My hat is smaller and plainer,' she replied shyly.

'I think a pageboy bob would suit you, then your hat can perch on top. Let's try it, shall we?' he said kindly.

Nicole, incarcerated under the hood of the dryer, caught the drift of the conversation. She had known Tony for years and liked him a lot. It wasn't him who was tedious, but the foolish women who hung around him jealously. Married or not, they became obsessed with him, each imagining that she could change his sexuality, show him what it was like to have a *real* woman, make him fall in love with them.

'I think you're cooked,' he cried gaily, lifting back the hood and testing her hair. 'Over here, please,' he continued and sat her facing yet another mirror. The rollers were carefully unwound, and her pale hair started looking thicker, more alive as he backcombed it.

'Don't forget the tiara,' prompted Maggie.

'Would I?' he quipped. 'Better let me have the veil, too.'

There was no doubting his capabilities. He made a beautiful job of her hair, sweeping it up, leaving little tendrils trailing down by her cheeks and at the nape of her neck, fixing the veil, and holding it in place with the sparkling tiara.

He stood back, examining his handiwork reflected in

the glass. 'That's it, I think,' he said seriously, a master in his field. Everyone murmured congratulations, and he picked on Miriam next. 'Let's see if I can work the old magic on your ragged-looking locks. What have you been using on it? The garden rake?'

'Andrew Charles of Kensington does my hair,' she answered crabbily.

'Does he indeed?' Tony said with heavy irony. 'Well, dear, I can't say I'm impressed.' While he talked, he was brushing away the tangles, spraying her hair with water, combing and smoothing it till it resembled fiery satin. Then he began to create a coronet ornamented with a circle of small diamanté flowers. It was sleek and impressive, emphasising her high cheekbones, little ears and watchful feline eyes.

There was silence when he had finished, and Nicole could tell that Miriam was astonished, not to say impressed. 'You like?' he asked, and it was apparent that he was challenging her to find fault with a small-town operator like him.

'I like,' she answered, and prinked in the hand-mirror he gave her so that she could view the back. It was as skilfully done as the front, formed into a French pleat.

'I told you so,' Maggie snorted triumphantly. 'You next, Jody. Come along, girl. We haven't got all night.'

Jody's hair was treated in a similar fashion, though this time it was swept back into a high roll and secured with a pair of scintillating clips shaped like wings.

'Very sophisticated,' announced Miriam. 'It almost makes you look grown up.'

'Everyone happy? Then I'll turn up at seven on the wedding day and do you all,' promised Tony and, within a short time, they were back to normal again and heading for The Hollies.

They drove round to the front of the house and parked, then trundled into the lounge. Maggie appeared to be on a high, exalted by the success of the venture. 'It's going to be the wedding of the decade,' she pronounced. 'Did I tell you that *Hello* want an interview?'

'I'll ring for Helga to bring in tea,' Deirdre suggested, diffidently.

Just then there was a piercing scream and the au pair came running in, pale-faced and anxious. 'Oh, ma'am – Mrs Carpenter. Something awful has happened.'

'What? What? Speak up!' Maggie shouted.

'Look, madame. Look for yourself,' Helga sobbed, pointing towards the French windows. 'I saw them from the kitchen but couldn't do anything to stop them.'

Maggie darted for the terrace, then stopped dead, hand to her throat, face turning ashen as the enormity of what had taken place struck home. 'My God! The garden!' she gasped.

Nicole was there before anyone else, and she stared and stared, wanting to laugh, wanting to cry, not sure whether to be pleased or sorry. There, on the lawns and trampling the immaculate borders, were half a dozen russet-coloured cows, short-legged and long-coated, with wide-spaced horns. Ben's prize rare breed cattle were decimating the Carpenters' garden.

'Oh, shoo! Shoo! Get away from here, you stupid creatures,' Maggie shouted, running out and waving her arms frantically.

The rest followed, but Jody and Miriam could hardly move for laughing, leaning on one another and collapsing into shaking heaps. Helga ran about among the animals, flapping her apron. They ignored these interruptions, blissfully continuing their meal of expensive plants and doing what cattle do best – depositing cowpats on the once velvety lawn.

'I'll sue Ben Templeton,' Maggie stormed, like Boadicea intent on revenge. 'He must have left the farm gate open and they got out on the road, then wandered all the way down the lane and ended up in our garden.'

'I thought this estate was impregnable,' put in Miriam, wiping black streaks of mascara from her cheeks.

'It is. Well, almost, if careless farmers don't let their animals escape. I don't know what's the matter with Ben lately. He's walking around in a daze. Ring him up, Nicole, and tell him to come and collect his beasts at once. I shall expect him to pay for the damage. It's ruined, ruined, and it's unlikely that I can get it put right before the wedding.'

'Why don't you see what Daddy has to say?' Nicole ventured.

'Your father is a very busy man. He has left these matters to me, and I shan't let him down,' Maggie replied heroically. 'Deirdre, come with me, and see if we can salvage anything. Stop laughing, you two,' and she glared at Jody and Miriam. 'I can't see anything funny about it.'

It was as Jody had predicted. She managed to prise Nicole away from Maggie and co, getting her down to the Baker's Spinney cottage on the pretext of more discussions about the ceremony.

'Cup of tea?' she asked, as the three of them planted themselves round the kitchen table.

'Orange juice, please,' Nicole answered, and Jody thought how much better she was looking now that school had been let out. Sun-kissed, too, by hours spent among the corn stooks. She should be marrying Ben, not that other bastard. 'And how is Katrina?'

'Getting bigger. She and Bobby spend a lot of time and money shopping in Baby Gap.'

'How lovely,' Nicole said, misty-eyed. 'I can't wait.'

Sod it, Jody thought. This doesn't bode well.

She and Miriam had discussed at length how to break the news to Nicole. They felt rather helpless, having no shred of evidence and only Scarlett's word to go on. Jody fetched the juice from the fridge, and then sat down again. Miriam was chain-smoking. Jody decided that it wasn't going to get any better, so came right out with it. 'Nicole, there's something you ought to know. Maybe Greg has already told you about it.'

'About what?' Nicole said with a smile. 'About the honeymoon destination? It's a secret, from me anyway. I don't want to know. This will spoil the surprise.'

Jody tried another tack. 'Does he tell you what he gets up to when he's in London?' she asked, lamely, thinking: You devil, Greg! Leaving your dirty work to someone else. You haven't the guts to talk to her about your secret life. Or are you afraid of rocking the boat till your ring is well and truly welded to her finger?

'Of course.' Nicole replied loftily. 'He works extremely hard indeed, goes home, has something to eat, watches the news, then gets in an early night.'

'That's what he says, does he? And you believe it? You don't think he's lying?'

Nicole looked at her as if she had mouthed an obscenity. 'Absolutely not. Greg has said that one thing he never, ever does is lie. He's an honest, truthful person.'

'How do you know?' Miriam chimed in, not so patient as Jody.

Nicole began to show signs of distress. 'I trust him, and he's never given me any reason not to.'

'Supposing I were to say that he's been trying to get into my knickers since day one?' Jody brought out bluntly.

'I'd think you were winding me up. He wouldn't do anything like that. He's honourable, and doesn't even take advantage of the fact that I want to anticipate our wedding, and have offered to go to bed with him.'

'Oh, what a noble knight, Sir Galahad incarnate,' Miriam chipped in, topping up her coffee cup.

Nicole tried it shrug it off. 'He respects me, and there's no way he'd flirt with my friends.'

'He's done more than flirt,' Miriam retorted sternly. 'He wanted to shag Jody. She's had to fight him off.'

Jody was sorry to see the light go out of Nicole's face; her lips trembled but she stuck up for Greg loyally. 'You're joking. You must be. Where are you saying this happened?'

'At The Hollies, out riding, in the pool and at my house,' Jody answered levelly.

'He came to see you in London?'

'Didn't he tell you? He arrived with some feeble excuse about wanting to look at my work.'

'There you are, then. We had discussed commissioning a pyramid for our country retreat,' Nicole floundered, and Jody would have rather cut her own tongue out than be the purveyor of such bad news.

'They say love is blind, but I've never seen it working before. You need laser treatment,' quipped Miriam, but Jody knew that she was as heartsick as herself. 'That's not all,' Miriam went on, and Nicole looked towards her with huge, frightened eyes, like a deer expecting the hunter's bullet.

'What other nasty things have you to say about him?' she whispered.

It was a hot day outside the cottage, a day when they should have been enjoying a picnic, or swimming in the river, not giving their best friend the coup de grâce. Life is so unfair, Jody thought, and men are sent to bedevil us. Even Miriam and me, supposed to be independent, feisty, fearless New Age females, continue to be harassed by those bothersome creatures who can't hold more than one idea in their heads at a time. As for performing more than one task at a time? Forget it.

She looked at Miriam, seeking support, and Miriam nodded almost imperceptibly and put in her penny-worth. 'Did you know that he frequently uses a club called Willards?'

Nicole looked blank, then rallied. 'So what? I expect it's one of those gentlemen only establishments where he can meet members of Parliament and discuss affairs of the day.'

'Right, but wrong. OK, so the ground floor is respectable, but what about the basement? Are you aware that it's designed for those who get their jollies in, shall we say, *unusual* ways?'

'I don't know what you're talking about, and I don't want to hear you slandering Greg any more,' Nicole said, dashing away her tears and standing up resolutely. 'If you wish him so ill, then perhaps it would be better if I ask others to be my bridesmaids. It's late, but I'm sure a cousin or two would step in. '

'Don't be like that,' Jody pleaded, rising to put a hand on Jody's arm. 'We're only doing this because we love you, and can't bear the thought of you being taken in by a con artist and downright arsehole like Greg.'

'There you go again,' Nicole snapped and pulled herself free.

Miriam stepped in, saying, 'I've got it from source. I know one of the women who works in Willards dungeon. She's a dom. Men like her to tie them up and whip them, and Greg is one of her customers. So is Piers.'

'That's a wicked lie! Why should I listen to this? What proof have you?'

'No proof, only word of mouth, but she is concerned about you, Nicole.'

'She doesn't know me.'

'She met you in the Jacuzzi at Janine's beauty parlour. Her name is Scarlett. You told her you were marrying Gregory Crawford and she put two and two together and went out of her way to contact us, hoping that, as your friends, we could put a stop to the wedding.'

Nicole went white. The strength drained out of her and she leaned a hand on the table for support. 'She's a liar and so are you,' she hissed.

'We wouldn't upset you like this unless we thought she was telling the truth,' Jody said, while tears stung at the back of her eyes.

'Then she's taken you in,' Nicole persisted. 'Show me proof and I might consider believing you, but I won't listen to gossip, especially when it comes from a whore. She must be driven by spite and jealousy, if indeed she exists and isn't some fictional character invented by you in a vain effort to split up Greg and me. Why do you want to do this? Can't you bear to see me happy?'

'We wouldn't do that. Your happiness is all that matters,' Jody cried, vainly attempting to break down the barriers that Nicole was frantically throwing up between them. 'Just think it over, please. Speak to Greg about it. See if he can offer an explanation.'

'I wouldn't insult him by repeating filthy wicked

accusations,' Nicole replied frostily, and it seemed to Jody that she had aged. Even if she refused to believe that her fiancé was a villain, some of her certainties had been rocked.

'If we get proof, then will you believe us?' Jody insisted, thinking; that's it then. Venetian Ball, here we come, with a camera if possible, though I expect we'll be frisked at the door.

'I don't know,' Nicole replied, running her hands over her eyes in such a weary manner that Jody wanted to console her.

'I still want to be your bridesmaid, if you decide to go through with it,' she said.

'Me, too,' added Miriam.

'Of course I shall go through with it,' Nicole declared. 'When are you returning to London?'

'Monday,' they chorused.

'Good. I really don't want to have much to do with you any more,' Nicole said coldly. 'You can be my bridesmaids but I expect you to stop all the nonsense about Greg. There are such things as libel laws, you know. Slander carries strong penalties. So keep your vicious gobs shut.'

She went out of the door, head high and spine straight. 'Chah! She's an idiot,' Miriam said, as they heard her get in her car and drive off.

'There's nothing for it. We can't give up now, and let him win.'

'The Ball,' said Miriam.

'And if that doesn't work?'

'We'll have to dream up something truly spectacular, won't we?'

'We've a job on,' Jody sighed and sagged in one of the oak rush-seated chairs.

'Come on. Chin up, musketeer,' Miriam encouraged. 'As my Dad is fond of saying, "Faint heart never fucked a pig."'

'Are you sure Scarlett is right about Greg? You fancy her rotten, don't you?' Jody said dubiously, not quite able to cope with Miriam's dual sexuality.

'Darling, that has nothing to do with it. If she was a fraud, I'd know it. You may not approve of her way of making a living, but there are some things, many things, in fact, that she won't tolerate. Double-dealing pricks like Greg, for example,' Miriam averred, and Jody was certain that her shrewd friend wouldn't have been taken in.

'And now we've got Nicole against us, all holier-than-thou and "Stand by Your Man,"' she said, and her thoughts strayed to Ed, and she wondered if he would be able to escape. They were planning to drive to a picturesque village outside Bath so that they could spend a night together in an old pub.

'If we can pull this off, then she'll thank us for it,' Miriam declared, jolting her back to the here and now.

'Will she ever forgive us?' Jody hated falling out with anyone.

'Wait and see. First of all we've got to expose him, in public if possible,' and Miriam grinned at her across the table. 'Wouldn't it be a crack if we *could* pull it off?'

11

Jody was as excited as a teenager on her first date. It had been arranged that she should drive to the George at Norton St Mary, where Ed had booked a room. Midweek, and the inn wasn't busy, a respite from his work on location, an escape from the still furious Clarissa, and a merciful release from her own worries. She needed to see him desperately, girding her loins in anticipation of the Willards bash that she was not keen on attending.

She arrived first, and it gave her time to park her car and appreciate the pub's architecture, some of which dated back to the thirteenth century, or so the blurb on the brochure claimed. She picked up a copy in the public bar where she waited for Ed, and read it, seated on an oak settle by the monumentally large, log-heaped fireplace. It wasn't lit, for the evening was warm, but she wanted to return there in the depths of winter and enjoy the old-world scene.

According to the blurb, the George was famous on several counts. Not the least of which was its proud boast to have sheltered the Duke of Monmouth during the uprising of 1685, when this bastard son of King Charles II had tried to inherit his father's throne, claiming to be legitimate. He and his followers were beaten at the Battle of Sedgemoor and he was subsequently beheaded at the Tower of London. Opposite the George was another ancient alehouse, the White Hart, also noted for its part in the Monmouth Rebellion, and reported to have sheltered the duke's enemy, the notorious and brutal Judge Jeffreys.

The brochure went on to speak of the George's reputation for being haunted. Jody fervently hoped that wailing spirits would not interrupt her night of passion. It was difficult enough to rendezvous without having to cope with the supernatural.

Ed came in then, and her heart skipped a heat, a tremor of excitement like tiny shocks running under her skin. He was so good to look at, and she noticed how several women in the bar turned to stare. No wonder Clarissa was resentful. Jody could feel the green-eyed monster digging its talons into her own gut.

'I've missed you,' he said, not even pausing to get a beer. 'Do you want to eat? It's a five star restaurant.'

'No,' she replied. It wasn't food she craved. 'Unless you're hungry.'

'Straight to our room, then?'

'Yes.'

He got the keys and directions from the manageress. They went up a flight of broad wooden stairs, worn down in the middle by the countless feet of generations. It had elaborately turned oak balustrades, complete with acanthus leaves through which the Green Man leered. The scent of beeswax augmented the feeling of age, so did the uneven floorboards when Ed paused at their door, inserted the key and said, 'Maybe I should carry you over the threshold.'

'We're not newly-weds,' she said, pleased yet turning it into a joke lest the reality of a comedown hurt too much.

'Would you like us to be?' he asked, closing the door behind them and putting his arms round her.

What a question and how to answer sensibly with such a man holding her, and kissing her and pressing his strong body against hers? 'I don't know,' she whispered into his mouth.

He chuckled. 'Think about it, babe. You're the first sheila I've ever asked.'

'I will,' she promised, but could not begin to let on that she believed him. It would be just too devastating should he be using this as a chat-up line.

The four-poster was genuine Jacobean, with a carved headboard and tester, and the chintz curtains were more for effect than to keep it draught free. 'I made sure we had one like this,' he said, and suddenly swept her off her feet, an arm under her thighs, the other round her shoulders. 'If I can't carry you into the room, then I'll carry you to bed.'

Is he for real? she thought, as he laid her down.

He didn't hurry; they had all night, and he wooed her accordingly. First he switched off his mobile, kicked off his trainers, stretched out beside her and folded her in his arms. His hands roamed over her spine, a firm, friendly, massaging touch outside her clothes. Then he slipped under her blouse, finding the fastening of her bra and prising it apart. It fell open, the straps falling down, her breasts escaping.

'This isn't the first time you've sprung a back-loader,' she joked, so comfortable with him that it was as if they had been together for years. She slid her arms out of both straps and blouse, pressing her nipples against the cotton barrier he still wore.

He grunted and licked round the rim of her ear, and she moaned at the spasm of pleasure that made her womb clench. She cuddled up to him, and buried her face in the hollow of his throat, filling her senses with the smell of him, the smooth texture of his skin, the sprinkling of chest hair at the rounded neck of his T-shirt, and the steady beat of his heart.

'All right, baby?' he asked, and his voice was husky.

She looked up and saw the crooked nose and the scars that said, 'tough man with a soft centre,' and wanted him as she had never wanted anyone before. 'I'm as right as I'll ever be,' she said.

'Are you going to let me make love to you?' he asked, quite unnecessarily. Only a meteor hit would have stopped her. Why the hell did he think she'd come all that way, if it wasn't to be fucked?

'Yes,' she said simply, and wriggled her body suggestively up and down his groin, her skirt riding high, exposing her bare thighs. She slipped her hand round to caress his tight butt, then came back to the front and dived between his legs. They relaxed, and she felt the swelling inside his jeans, the ridged bar of flesh rising towards his waistband.

She recalled going to a girls' night out at a club that employed Chippendale copy-cat dancers, and how she had chanted, 'Get 'em off!' along with the rest of the screaming, overheated, liberated females who no longer had to stay shtoom while their men enjoyed strippers. She had the urge to shout this now but refrained, letting him set the pace.

Ed was undressing her slowly, revealing each part of her with evident relish, taking his time, winding her arousal to screaming pitch, caressing every inch of flesh as it was exposed to his admiring eyes. The man was a lover – plus, plus! He paused now and again, as if wanting to fill his memory with her, and then he kissed her, the slow, deep penetration of his tongue meeting hers. She caught hold of his still hidden erection, rubbing her palm over the denim, absorbing the heat and dampness.

She became more and more lost in him, all else forgotten. The setting was perfect, panelled walls and tapestries, and that marvellous bed. It was soft, but not too soft. It had a magenta duvet cover and black sheets and pillowcases. It seemed to embrace them, as it had undoubtedly embraced scores of rutting couples in its time. The whole milieu of the room was one of love, not lust: sweet, poetic, promising much, though Jody was wise enough to recognise that this might be an illusion. It was easy to take on the mantle of star-crossed lovers, and phrases tumbled into her mind: 'the world well lost for love', and 'all for love, and nothing for reward'. The Bard was full of them. And I'm losing the plot, my mind, my common sense and, if I don't watch out, my self-respect.

Useless to fight it. Might as well submit and hope she didn't regret it afterwards. Jody tugged at his jeans. He undid them, eased them over his buttocks and down his legs. He wasn't wearing anything on his feet, thus avoiding the ridiculous picture even the most charismatic of men present when naked but for socks. Jody admired him, so muscular and lean, his penis tenting the white fabric of his boxer shorts. His skin was almost shockingly brown in contrast, the tan so solid that it could only have been imparted by hours spent in the tropics or the West Coast of America, or exotic settings where he had gone to film.

The whole episode was magical, neither could put a foot, or a hand, wrong, it seemed. He unbuttoned her denim skirt and it fell away, blue against magenta. Her bra was gone and her blouse and mules and only her panties remained. Ed took them off, pausing to stare at her brown bush, with the pinkish slit showing through, and she closed her eyes as he leaned over her. She felt his lips brushing her nipples and the exquisite pleasure as they crimped. He took them into his mouth, one by one, and sucked strongly, drawing the tips out, making them bigger, harder, and tingling with desire. Her clitoris ached and she wanted him to go on sucking, but start rubbing her at the same time.

His erection was protruding through the gap in his boxers. Jody touched the tip. He shivered and looked down at it, and she pressed her fingertip into the weeping eye and wanted to have it inside her, but not until she had climaxed. Ed got rid of his underwear and rolled on a condom. She liked the look of his lean, wiry body, hard muscles and sinews. He obviously kept it in trim by riding, fencing, boxing and putting himself on the line, paid by the insurance companies to take risks instead of the stars.

He was still studying her ultimately, spreading her legs wide with his knee, his fingers on her thighs with a feather-light touch. She hoped he wouldn't want to penetrate her straight away, then remembered their first coupling and how he had brought her to a thunderous climax first. There was no chance that she would be disappointed. He lowered his head and his lips travelled up the inside of one leg and his fingers opened all her nooks and crannies, making way for that questing tongue.

He teased her a little, working down the length of her divide, pausing to caress the puckered moue of her anus, licking round it, embarrassing her because she was enjoying this so much but regretting she hadn't taken a shower first. Supposing he objected to the taste or smell? But he gave no indication of this, indeed it seemed to be spurring him on, his dick harder than ever. His tongue was firm and wet, licking up her slit and hovering over her clit. He breathed on it softly and she arched her spine and raised her hips, that whisper of air taking on such acute proportions that she nearly came.

Ed was reading her reactions like an open book. He held her steady with both hands, then poked his tongue inside her. It was penetration of the most gentle kind, and as he entered and withdrew and entered again, she yearned for something harder, larger – his forceful prick.

She squeezed it blindly, urged herself towards it, but Ed was not done with her yet. 'No, sweetheart, no,' he murmured, lifting his head from her crotch, smiling across her pubes and up the length of her body. 'I'm going to give you the best come you've ever had. Lie back and enjoy.'

She felt his fingers sliding each side of her slick-wet clit. He massaged the stem, moving it from side to side as well as up and down, but avoiding the head. She was racked by the most intense spasms, rising and rising but unable to reach perfection unless he stroked her vital place. She moved slightly, trying to get more stimulation there. Ed placed a firm hand on her belly and stretched her cleft upwards. Her clitoris protruded, inflamed and needy. He slicked more juice over it and rubbed fast. She was so close, so close – nearly there.

'I must have it! I must! I must!' she panted, then groaned loudly as her orgasm burst, too good to be true, mighty in its power.

Ed moved, on his knees between her thighs, impaling her on his hugeness, pumping through her contractions till he, too, reached his Nirvana.

When they had the strength to stir, they flipped back the duvet, settled on the black silk sheet and curled up in each other's arms. They lay together like two spoons in a cutlery drawer. His back was pressed against her spine, his lips at her nape, his arms round her shoulders and his hands holding each breast. His penis, limp for the moment, nestled between her bum cheeks, his thighs followed hers, and their feet touched.

I want to stay like this forever, she thought dreamily. There are hours till dawn. We shall get to know one another, and I don't mean in the Biblical sense. I shall tell him my life history, but won't involve him in the Greg/Nicole tangle – not yet – not till it has been resolved.

They slept, woke up to make love again, several times, and on the last occasion a greyish light was stealing through the diamond-paned casement and, out in a barnyard somewhere, a cockerel was stridently heralding the new day.

The shop was unusual, to say the least. Off Wardour Street, in the heartland of London's Soho, it had two bay windows displaying some of its stock, with a pur-ple-painted door between. It was colourful, and the pungent scent of incense wafted through the air as Scarlett led the way inside.

Oh, shite, Jody thought, why did I agree to this? Friday and she had parted from Ed the day before. He had rung her several times since, but it wasn't the same as being able to touch him and hold him. Her pity for Nicole increased. What a sorry state to be in if Nicole was as love-struck as herself, but with a man who, it appeared, was an unprincipled, lying cheat.

The shop had a lively ambience, and the music was as kinky as the wares on display. They hung on racks, were worn by dummies, just the torso, no limbs or head; they draped stands, they were lined up on shelves, they jostled for space on the walls. There was no getting away from sequinned bustiers, satin corsets, split-crotch panties, peep-hole bras and suspender belts. These were only the tip of the iceberg. Jody stared agog at rubber stays with restrictive lacing, vinyl cat suits with showy zips, and gowns that revealed more than they concealed. Black predominated throughout.

No one hassled them as they browsed, staring at the hats; toppers, wide-brimmed, feathered, cloche and skullcaps. There was a wide range of stockings; seamed, patterned, some deliberately laddered, and shoes, too – plain courts, mules, sling-backs, ankle-straps, platform soles and mile-high heels.

'Look at those!' Miriam exclaimed, as excited as a child in a candy store.

Jody looked, impressed by the provocative, thigh-reaching leather boots. Some had straps and buckles and spurs. All were tight, with stiletto heels. 'How could anyone possibly walk in them?' she asked.

'You get used to it,' Scarlet answered, and went to a cabinet where, locked behind a glass, various apparatus was on show.

'What on earth...?' Jody was puzzled, though advertisements she had seen in Alec's collection of top-shelf magazines came to mind.

She had never been able to understand why he wanted to lech over the sexually explicit photos when he had her. Now she was beginning to get a glimmer of understanding, the contrast between black rubber and pale flesh, the idea of leather whips and being held captive, unable to move a muscle, entirely at the mercy of a master or dominatrix. Her pussy warmed at the thought.

'Toys,' Scarlet murmured, lovingly. 'Harnesses and bondage gear. Snaffles and bits for exceptionally naughty boys who have dared to answer me back. Dog collars with spikes to make them behave. Reins to make them trot when I give the command. Muzzles to prevent them from gnashing their teeth at me. The dirty tykes.'

'You don't use them, surely?'

'I can assure you that I do,' Scarlett replied firmly, and nodded to an assistant who was standing near the till.

He, she or it stalked across, a multiply-pierced alien with spiked cerise hair and plastic extensions. The heaviest of heavy make-up made the face mask-like, an off-shoulder black vest with the shop's logo, Get It!, was emblazoned across her/his flat chest. A leather skirt, thick with metal studs, just about covered the person's crotch. Fishnets with holes in embraced the skinny legs and a cross between Hell's Angel's biking boots and trainers with soles six inches thick encased the feet.

'Hi, Dodi,' Scarlett said. 'Open up, will you? There's a couple of items I'd like to test.' She glanced at Jody and smiled. 'It's all right. You were wondering if Dodi is a transsexual? I can assure you she's a girl. I know. I've been there.'

Dodi had keys jangling on a chain from the hipster belt spanning her non child-bearing pelvis. Jody watched, fascinated, as Scarlett examined the flails and canes, taws and paddles, ball-gags and blindfolds, the use of which she explained as she handled them expertly. She knew precisely what they weighed and their expected impact and how far they would push the pain threshold. She ordered several, and Jody kept thinking: Is Greg really into this?

'Now for our outfits for the party,' Scarlett said at last, handing her purchases to Dodi to be packed; apparently she was a regular customer. 'See anything you fancy? In the back room, girls, and let's have a try. Better than Marks and Sparks or Debenhams. Much more fun.'

Jody followed suit, but more cautiously, feeling rather a fool as Scarlett helped her with an emerald satin bodice that laced over her breasts, so tight that they bulged out of the top. She shook her head.

'I can't see anything that I remotely like,' she said, holding up a slinky crêpe skirt, slit to the waist on either side and wondering if Ed would be turned on by it.

'There are masses to choose from,' Miriam averred, working her nipples through the open tips of a crimson lurex brassière.

'It's cheesy,' Jody declared. 'Jesus God, I've never seen such a collection of tat.'

'Try this,' Scarlett said, appearing in the doorway holding a shimmering black something in one hand. Jody took it reluctantly, wanting to get into her own clothes and go and have a coffee, abandoning the idea of the Venetian fling. Let Miriam and Scarlett do it if they wanted, but she was fed up with the whole shebang.

'Yes, go on. Give it a whirl,' Miriam encouraged.

Jody looked at the dress, held it this way and that, and Scarlett helped her to put it on. With it came a tanga, no more than a triangle in front and a string that crossed her cleft and entered her bottom crease. The dress scintillated as if coated with diamond dust. It had two tiny cups that held her breasts and were supported by spaghetti straps. There was a long skirt that covered her decently enough in front, but when she turned to view herself, she was shocked to see that the back was non-existent. Her thighs were exposed, as were the full globes of her buttocks, her sex protected only by the thong.

'I can't go out in public in this!' she protested.

'Of course, you can. Wear it with an air,' advised Miriam, who was already sold on the idea of a crimson plastic cat suit that embraced her body like a second skin. Slinky and gleaming, it clung to her breasts and waist and hips, and had a zipper that started at her sternum and, when the tag was pulled, slid down effortlessly, all the way, then between the legs and up the arse crease.

'Help! I'll have to be careful not to catch it in my bush!' Miriam yelped, having just done so.

'Get it waxed. A smooth quim is so attractive,' Scarlett advised.

She had chosen a severe outfit, consisting of a tailored pinstriped jacket with lapels that barely covered her breasts, leaving a deep cleavage. The matching skirt was knee-length, the stockings thick and supported by garters and she had added black lace-up shoes with medium heels. She looked the part of a severe schoolmarm, strutting around and rapping the palm of her left hand with the flexible cane held in her right, ready to deliver six of the best. Sometimes she lifted her skirt, displaying stocking tops and no knickers and her denuded mons.

'That's us sorted,' she announced and, when they were dressed in their ordinary clothes, took the purchases to Dodi and selected masks. The choice was large; strips of velvet with eye-holes, weird monster-looking ones, or elaborate designs suitable for the Mardi Gras, trimmed with peacock feathers and hiding the entire face.

They picked the ones they wanted, hefted up their black carrier bags bearing the words Get It! in gold, and went to see and be seen at Top Table.

Rehearsals were in full flood. Nanette was putting everything else on hold. This was to be her best performance yet. She had roped in a couple of horse-mad

teenagers to muck-out and take the riding-school juniors through their paces and had put Kevin in charge.
Doris, general factotum and live-in housekeeper, would
see that everyone was fed, clothed and watered. Shaun
would carry on as per usual, though his rewards were
thin on the ground these days.

As for herself? She was going for gold, learning her
lines and mastering her moves with the aid of a prompt
copy, dated 1893, when it had cost two and sixpence. It
was rare and valuable and she had picked it up for a
song (very apt, she thought) at a car boot sale. Aubrey
lusted after it, but she refused to let it out of her sight,
only allowing him to borrow it for rehearsals. There
was something comforting about it, assuring Nanette
that life was a circle that went on and on, and the
Wheel of Rebirth a strong possibility.

When she held it, this small clothbound book with
the libretto on the right hand side and blank pages for
stage instructions on the other, she thought about the
person who had written in the details in a tiny, crabbed,
copperplate hand. A minion working for the D'Oyly
Carte Opera Company based at the Savoy Theatre had
most likely done it. Provincial productions had to follow
the London ones to the letter, and these rules had
applied till way into the twentieth century, protected
by stringent copyright laws.

I'm supposed to be learning my part, Nanette
reflected, lying by the pool in the full blaze of noon, but
I can't help thinking about those who had played Ruth
in the past. They must have been women just like me,
maybe slightly over the hill, having romantic thoughts
(don't be daft; what you mean is sexy) about other
members of the cast, just as she was doing now. They
could have been adulteresses, secret drinkers, bigamists,
incestuous, off the wall – anything. The more she

learned about history, the more she realised that people hadn't altered. They were still the same, and yet the young held the view that sex had been invented purely for their gratification and delight. No way.

Her mobile was handy and she paused with her fingers over the buttons, considering ringing Stewart and inviting him over to lunch with the excuse of a practice. But if she did this, she'd miss out on an uninterrupted afternoon spent soaking up the sun and cooling off in the water. Nothing, but *nothing*, was important enough to disturb this routine. Instead she played the whole of *The Pirates of Penzance* on her portable stereo. There wasn't much nicer than doing this, three passions satisfied at once – sunbathing, swimming and filling her ears with her favourite music.

By mid-afternoon, the CD had finished and Nanette was dozing. She woke fully and sat up to apply a further layer of screening lotion and, as she did so, she recalled a certain, worrying frigidity that had suddenly sprung into existence between Nicole and Jody and Miriam. What had gone wrong? They had been such close friends until the last visit when they had tried on their frocks and had Tony do their hair. The thought popped into her mind that Greg was at the bottom of it.

An untrustworthy young man, and she'd never really taken to him. He was too sure of himself, convinced that his cock would get him everywhere. He had even tried it on with Clarissa, flirting with her outrageously and she, silly conceited apology for a woman, had been flattered. Nanette hadn't missed the chemistry that had sparked between Jody and Clarissa's lover, Ed. What was going on, and why was it that weddings seemed to bring out the worst in the participants?

Damn it, she'd be forced to see Allan and Patricia on

the bloody day. She had asked Stewart if he would come and he had accepted. At least she'd have him as her escort and rub Allan's nose in it. Adam and Sinclair would be there, too, but it was hardly fair on them to show her animosity towards their stepmother. Life was an absolute bitch, wasn't it? Greg and Nicole? She was uneasy and wondered whether to chew it over with Deirdre, then decided not. Deirdre was so much happier these days, thanks to Derek. What would happen when the show was over? Why, they could continue meeting, practising for the pantomime, *Mother Goose*, programmed for January.

She narrowed her eyes against the strong light, caressing her limbs, breasts and belly as she applied the milky fluid and wondered if she might summons Shaun. A fuck in the pool house would be just what the doctor ordered. As for the dentist? She'd given him ample opportunity, getting impatient with his tepidity. If he didn't come up with the goods at the Last Night Party, then she'd give him up as a bad job.

Willards had a most discreet frontage, but Scarlett used the side entrance. A big, shaven-headed bruiser in an evening suit barred the door. She showed her card and vouched for Jody and Miriam. He let them in.

Music swelled from below and a staircase wound down into gloom. Jody, uncomfortable in a gilded mask (it was too tight and messed up her hair), followed her and Miriam, stepping carefully in her excruciatingly high heels. All three were shrouded in dominoes, those long hooded capes of billowing black silk that were traditionally worn for masked balls. So far, the whole episode had cost a lot; the purchase of attire, the cab there, the entrance tickets. Jody considered it a shocking waste on clothes she was unlikely to wear again, but agreed that it would be money well spent if they succeeded in exposing Greg.

They retained their cloaks at the start, and there was something exciting about being anonymous. The bar was filling up, and most were in disguise. Scarlett recognised one, however. 'Hello, Birdy,' she said in a low, seductive voice. 'How are your parts?'

'Springing to attention at seeing you, mistress,' he lisped.

'How did you know it was me?'

'I could smell your unmistakable perfume, goddess. Isn't this fun? Will you introduce me to your friends? I can't see them, but I'm sure they are delightful.'

'Oh, they are,' Scarlett replied, diving a gloved hand down between his legs and squeezing his balls. He gave a smothered yelp, but seemed thrilled by her harsh handling. She had let her cloak slide off and her head-mistress outfit was causing a storm.

She strutted and posed with legs astride, and the men circled round her like a collection of honey-crazed wasps. She treated them appallingly, lashing them with her tongue. 'What do you want, imbeciles?' she snarled icily. 'Shall I order you to my study after school? You there, Johnson Major! Get your pants down and let me swipe at your bare bum.'

He couldn't wait to drop them and bend over, while the others cheered and got excited simply by watching, flies open, cocks in their hands. Jody watched, disgusted but not a little aroused, and Miriam thought it highly amusing.

Birdy cheered Scarlett on, and clamoured for his turn. He hadn't bothered to dress up, apart from a tuxedo, and he was not wearing a mask. Jody found him a most unattractive person, feeling quite sick when she thought of what Scarlett probably did to him. His smooth cheeks were fat and his mouth was flabby. It jutted out, with a pendulous underlip.

'I won't ask your names, ladies,' he said archly, bowing to herself and Miriam, but with his eyes glued to his mistress's arm, rising and falling with asperity, the sound of rattan on bare flesh heard above the music. 'What would you like to drink?'

And this set the tenor of the evening; canings, drinks, cloaks cast aside, masks retained, and Jody wishing she were anywhere else but there. She had told Ed where she was going but not why, and he had expressed amusement and arousal. What is it about men? she brooded over her third Screwball. Why does this kind of event stir their dicks? Is it something tribal? Rivalry between them? The need to come out top dog? But no one is going to win or lose tonight, except perhaps Greg, if he turns up.

The basement was crowded now, and it was mostly the women who had made an effort, though there were a few devils, monks and cardinals. Still masked till midnight, their cloaks had been discarded and there were a number of harem girls in diaphanous trousers and veils and little jewelled boleros. A lot of them wore leather; short-shorts that barely disguised their clefts, bodices made from strips of material that fell open over the bosom, flimsy night-gowns that displayed bottoms reddened by a master who had already given them a thorough spanking. They were queuing up at the curtained alcove behind which he was administering punishment.

They giggled endlessly, stoned or inebriated or just plain randy, and Jody was struck by their upper-echelon accents. Scarlett was right. This was no venue for working-class scrubbers. The pace was hotting up. A lap dancer appeared, winding her long, coffee-coloured limbs round the seated males, moving from table to table, her actions imitating copulation as she straddled them, thrusting her naked breasts into their faces. The men fumbled and undid their trousers and she, with graceful cynicism, rubbed their cocks, while they tucked bank notes into her minute thong. That's all she permitted. They could squeeze her tits, but no one was allowed to kiss her or dip a finger into her pussy.

Jody admired her, while despising the Sloanes. The dancer was a working girl, doing it for money and honest about it, whereas the others were also into it for gain, but pretending to be enjoying the hands, cocks and mouths of the men there, going for those who had the most standing, wealth and clout. This acted on them like a love-potion, and even Birdy got his share of attention, though he seemed to be hankering after Scarlett.

Miriam was well away, flaunting and flirting, but Jody sat on a barstool, swathed in her cloak and hidden by her mask. Men approached her, but she turned away. She was here for one reason only. None of it excited her, not even the contortions of the lap dancer who, legs wide, showed the darkest recesses of her body, but forbade touching.

A film followed the dancer, shown on the large television screen. It was a pornographic DVD. Not the kind of thing Jody found stimulating, but even she had to admit that it was well done and the male lead had a huge, magnificent member.

'He's famous for it,' Miriam supplied, breaking off from winding her legs round a man dressed as Count Dracula; his hair was long and lank, his eyes red-rimmed and he wore fangs and mock blood that smeared his wide mouth. 'This is Archie, by the way.

He's a real count, and is trying to convince me that he's a real vampire. I may never return, my dear, away with the Undead. Regrets to Nicole. I shall miss her wedding.'

Jody lost her among the crowd which was becoming more abandoned, fired by the antics of the couple on the screen where there were no holds barred; arse-fucking, golden rain, the heroine suspended on a cross-piece and whipped by her master, the hulking young man with the outsized dick. Even Jody couldn't stop staring at it, and the camera seemed fixated by its hugeness, taking it from every angle. He wasn't circumcised, and his helm jutted out aggressively from the collar of rolled-down foreskin. His stem was so thick that Jody winced at the thought of taking it inside her. As he pulled in and out of the actress, it was slippery and red and knotted with veins.

Jody sat there alone, getting hot in spite of herself. Birdy came over and knelt at her feet, looking up and saying, 'Won't you let me see your face? I'm sure you're a princess in disguise,' and he started to caresses her shoes, adoring the high heels, and the way the straps clasped her insteps. 'I'm a lord, you know,' he added persuasively. 'I'll give you anything you want if you let me fuck you. Name it, and it's yours.'

She wanted to move, finding his fawning approach sickening, but then she stopped, holding her breath and remaining still. The porn film, the lustful crowd, Birdy holding her feet, all faded into insignificance as Greg and Piers walked in. It was twelve and mask-removing time, but she kept hers on and, having now seen him there confirming her worst fears, she longed to leave.

She couldn't get out for a while, but said to Birdy, 'Go and fetch my friend.'

'The one with the big boobs, snogging Dracula?'

'That's it.'

Miriam came over, dragging the count with her. She was pie-eyed and ratty with it. 'What is it, Jody?' she snapped. 'I suppose you want to go home. You always do, when I'm having a ball. I can't count the times I've seen you glancing at your watch, bored out of your skull and ready to leave.'

'It's not that, though I've had enough. Greg and Piers are here.'

'Where? Oh, my God, so they are. You're not kidding.'

'Keep your mask on.'

'What are we going to do?'

'Nothing. Just watch what he does.'

He went across and kissed Scarlett, and Piers put an arm round a tinsel-trimmed girl who looked like an ill-natured fairy. Both men seemed to be thoroughly at home, and a little gaggle of women gathered round Greg, caressing him and vying for his attention.

'The smarmy sod,' Miriam commented, disengaging herself from Dracula with a brisk, 'Not now, darling. I've business to see to.' She had sobered up and so had Jody. It was as if a bucket of icy water had been flung over them.

All they could think about was Nicole who, in her ignorance, was counting the days to her wedding to this slime-ball. Scarlett would help, and she arrived at that moment, their mentor and guide, demanding, 'What's the matter?'

'Greg's here.'

'I told you he would be.'

'What are we going to do about it? Even now, Nicole won't believe me,' Jody said, fumbling for a cigarette. Birdy leapt forward with his lighter.

'Go away,' Scarlett said, coldly dismissing him. 'This is girls' talk.'

'She's hardly spoken two words to us since we tried to warn her about her bridegroom.'

'Photos?' suggested Miriam.

'They're banned here. Too many famous people in compromising positions,' Scarlett rejoined.

'Blackmail?' Jody was desperate. 'I could threaten to tell her father.'

'Old man Carpenter is probably in it up to his neck,' put in Miriam, trusting no one, least of all a mayor.

'It needs to be spectacular and totally damning. I'll think of something,' Scarlett promised while, behind her, the Ball was degenerating into an orgy and one of the leading participants was Greg.

'Oh, for a camcorder,' Jody wailed. 'That's all it would take to make her see sense.'

'He'd lie his way out of it,' Scarlett said. 'What we need is something that he can't deny.'

'A former wife and child?' Jody was floundering desperately.

'He'd spin a yarn that would convince Nicole he was the innocent party.'

'What about producing a boyfriend? Say he's gay.'

'Unlikely to be convincing,' cut in Miriam, then smacked a hand across her brow, exclaiming, 'I know. Silly me. Go get him, Jody. Make the ultimate sacrifice. Let him screw you and come back with a piece of evidence. I don't know what. Anything that she'd recognise.'

Jody shrivelled inside. 'I can't do that. Even at the start, I didn't want to, and now – there's Ed.'

'Oh, bloody hell,' Miriam groaned, glancing at Scarlett with a despairing lift of her eyebrows. 'Trust you to get besotted at a time like this. Can't you waive a principle to help a friend?'

'No,' Jody replied, refusing to budge. 'I'm going now. If you can come up with a solution, get in touch in the morning. Good night,' and she whisked her cloak about her like a royal robe and headed for the street.

It was late but she got a cab, huddling into the darkness, feeling shabby and soiled. If this was Greg's chosen venue than he certainly had nothing in common with either Nicole or Heronswood. She was tired and dispirited and wished Ed was waiting for her at home. She wanted to be with him all the time. This had become more apparent since Katrina and Bobby had become a twosome, soon to be a threesome.

She gave herself a mental shake. You have your work, she lectured inwardly. You're off to the States again soon. You don't need to be shackled to a partner.

But, oh, I do – I do, cried the lonely person within.

12

'"This time next week it will all be over. I shall be Mrs Gregory Crawford,"' Nicole scribbled, the bedside lamp throwing a glow over her diary. '"We shall be on our honeymoon, leaving our guests to carry on with the reception. I can't wait to get away. I haven't heard from Jody and Miriam since they were so unpleasant about Greg. Whatever got into them? I'm sure there's not a word of truth in their allegations. Too cruel and horrid. They are down this weekend, staying in the cottage. I never want to go there again, after what they said."'

She sat quietly for a moment, mulling over that unpleasant conversation. A pack of lies, of course. And yet? She had never known them be untruthful before. The Three Musketeers, faithful until death. One for all and all for one. Now she had only one real friend – Ben – and even he seemed mopey of late. Then she brightened and held her diary close to her breasts, rocking with the joy of thinking: But I have a real friend now, the only one that matters, my love and husband for life – Greg! He'll be here tomorrow. We have a final meeting with the vicar on Sunday. I think I'll take to going to church more often. There must be a god somewhere, surely? Whatever else but divine intervention could have brought Greg and me together?

She meant to write these observations down, but snuggled among the pillows, book laid aside as she dwelt on tomorrow. Her father, grandmother, Greg, Piers and herself, were going along to see the final performance of *The Pirates of Penzance*. It had been running since Wednesday evening and hailed as a great success. The local press representative had written a glowing review. He dared do no other. His wife was in it, a small part it was true, but vital to the plot. He could hardly damn the production. Others had said it was worth seeing, and Nicole was looking forward to it, but then, even the most prosaic event assumed a radiance if Greg was with her.

She sighed and curled up in a ball. Only eight days and she would be sharing a bed with her bridegroom.

It had arrived – The Last Night, to be followed by the all-important party. Nanette had rarely enjoyed herself more. The show had opened to a packed house and, even though the dress rehearsal had been shambolic, when it came to the crunch everyone pulled out all the stops and gave very professional performances. They did the same on Thursday and Friday, and the Saturday matinée, just concluded.

Nanette was in the dressing room, a cramped area behind the stage that she shared with the other women. It wasn't worth going home or changing out of costume. They'd be on again in a couple of hours. It was hot and noisy, every female there wishing it wasn't over, but anticipating the shindig to come. Listening to their conversation, all girls together and exchanging confidences, barriers removed by mutual success, she gathered that some of them hoped to be able to carry on liaisons started during the weeks of rehearsal. They were aroused, hormones on the rampage, fired by their satisfaction in appearing in public and giving pleasure. Not only to the audience, apparently, but to the fellow players they had serviced, and intended to go on servicing, come hell or high water.

'Oh, Danny's so clever. He's been a wonderful Frederick,' simpered Connie Barnes. 'I doubted it at first, but he's come up trumps. Lovely tenor voice, too.'

Nanette, determined to keep her cat well and truly in the bag, listened and watched. Connie and Danny, eh? She must be all of thirty, married to the chief honcho in the Chancery Surgery, and Danny was in his mid-twenties. Good on you, girl, Nanette thought.

She brooded on what the ladies would say if they knew she was after Stewart. She had been very careful not to arouse suspicion. Of what? she thought peevishly. Nothing has happened. We're as chaste as novices in a nunnery. Probably more so. What on earth is wrong with him?

She kept remembering a line from the finale of the last Act when Frederick sings, though not apropos of sex, '"Beautiful Mabel, I would if I could but I am not able."'

Heaven forfend! Nanette thought. Could this be Stewart's problem? Does he need a dose of Viagra?

She pursued this idea as she touched up her 'Ruth' disguise. Some enterprising person had rigged lights round the dressing table mirror, giving it a reasonably authentic look. These bare bulbs threw a harsh, uncompromising reflection, fine for putting on make-up, but merciless if one was worried about ageing. The table's surface was littered with cotton-buds and tissues, and presided over by her Mickey Mouse mascot, a soft toy she had had since childhood. There was also a wooden cigar box, containing grease paint, wet-white and other paraphernalia needed if one was a thespian, albeit part-time. She called it her lucky box and always brought it with her, no matter what. The show must go on.

Could Stewart be impotent? she brooded darkly. She'd never yet had a man who couldn't get it up. What a cruel twist of fate if it should happened with someone for whom she felt more than just lust. I won't allow it, she resolved, and added another layer of mascara. Her costume was dashing, that of a 'piratical maid-of-all-work', with a crimson velvet jacket and breeches, sea-boots, and a fringed waist sash with a pistol tucked in it. She wore her three-cornered hat canted over one eye, and never, ever, upstaged the Pirate King.

The ladies of the chorus were high as kites, not on drugs but on adrenaline. She was high on it, too, but more so on Stewart. He was in the room next door, with Danny dressed as Frederick and the Major-General still in uniform and looking nothing like a pharmacist who dispensed prescriptions. They were surrounded by a motley collection of policemen and pirates. Nanette could hear them talking loudly, and guffawing. She hoped they hadn't been at the beer, reserving their thirst for the party, and not getting too drunk even then, with classic cases of brewer's droop.

Deirdre joined her from the kitchen, bringing two cups of tea. 'It's going so well,' she enthused. 'I really didn't think an amateur show would be so good.'

'Aubrey knows his stuff,' Nanette commented.

'I know. I'm most impressed, and Bernie's a first-rate conductor.'

'So you've enjoyed it?' Nanette asked, helping herself to a piece of Deirdre's homemade shortbread.

'Tremendously,' Deirdre said, and she looked as if she had shed at least five years.

'Are you going to sign up again?' Nanette was genuinely interested, but her immediate thought was: Will Stewart?'

'I'd like to, and there will be much more time when Nicole's married and life settles back to normal. I'm thinking of having flute lessons again.'

You probably need a refresher course in fucking, Nanette mused. I'll bet Ronald hasn't brought you to climax in ages.

It was 6.30. Only another hour and Bernie would lift his baton and the orchestra would strike up. 'I don't think I'd ever get used to the stress of acting,' Nanette said, refusing a second cup of tea. As it was, she kept on dashing to the toilet. She wasn't the only one. There was always a queue. What was it bullfighters called it, when they waited behind the *barrera* about to face several tons of hoofs and horns and bad temper? *The release of fear!*

The clock ticked on. 'Overture and beginners, please,' announced Aubrey's son who had been press-ganged into being the callboy. Deirdre shot off like a startled hare.

Standing in the wings, listening to the music, and getting ready to join the pirates before the curtain went up on them doing what sailors do best, in this case singing, Nanette felt a presence behind her. An arm came round her waist and Stewart's deep voice murmured, 'Here we go, then, Ruth.' He, too, was in this opening scene.

'Break a leg,' she whispered, leaning against him, while his powerful arms (dentists had to have strong wrists when it came to extractions) held her tightly, and it wasn't his sword prodding her arse.

That moment encapsulated heaven for her – a show to do – songs to sing – and a man to seduce at the Last Night Party.

Ed had promised to be there, but he arrived late, causing much shuffling and hushing among the already seated audience. The farcical romp on stage was keeping everyone amused. Jody had booked a seat for him and was glad that she had had the foresight to do so, for now it was standing room only.

She was with Miriam in the third row from the orchestral pit. Ronald had captured the first two, using mayoral privilege. With him were his colleagues in business and on the council, also Greg, Piers, Nicole and Maggie, who had been press-ganged into coming along to support Deirdre. The hall was well equipped for shows, concerts, bingo, parish meetings, and any other form of entertainment that might cause a minor flutter amidst the general apathy of Heronswood.

Jody was pleasantly surprised. Money had been spent on it recently and the lighting was up to professional standard, with spots and floats and dimmers under the firm control of a group of local electricians. There were sound effects, too – the hiss of waves, and the cry of sea gulls, directed by the engineers in charge of the audio and computer system. A group of enthusiastic volunteers had painted the scenery, and the rocks down which the maidens minced were realistic. One could almost imagine that one was visiting the Cornish coast.

'Sorry I'm late,' Ed whispered, reaching for Jody's hand.

'That's all right,' she answered. Heads turned and a couple of old dears glared. She ignored them, swamped with relief because he had made it.

He was on the end of the row, his legs stretched out in the aisle, and she had Miriam on her other side. From that moment on, she literally lost the plot, unable to concentrate on anything. The auditorium was dark and everyone's attention on the action. Jody felt Ed's shoulder pressing against her, and the length of his thigh following the shape of hers. His hand, still holding hers, came to rest in her lap. She was wearing a thin cotton skirt and, to her surprise and disbelief, felt his finger flicking open one of the buttons that fastened it all the way down. His prize was what lay beneath the silk triangle that covered her mons.

'Ed!' she hissed warningly, but didn't move. How could she when the finger was now tracing the damp groove that divided her like a split fig?

He didn't answer; simply increased the pressure. He was looking straight ahead at the stage, and he was smiling. Jody, as if mesmerised, opened her thighs a little, giving him greater access to her secrets. She sat up, pretending to be absorbed in the burgeoning love between Frederick and Mabel and the antics of the Major-General, but inside she quivered. Ed's fingertip passed along the hem of her briefs and touched her bush and combed through the curls.

Dear God! I shall come in a minute, she panicked, but would have died had he stopped.

Motionless, she felt his long, skilled finger exploring her, diving deeper between her lips, wetting itself and withdrawing to where her bud swelled and throbbed. She had the presence of mind to hold her handbag on her knee, rather like a pensioner waiting for a bus. It formed a cover of sorts, but not to an observant eye and she prayed that Miriam wouldn't get wind of what was going on.

She tried to control her ragged breathing and stared at the stage as if being vouchsafed a holy vision, while Ed continued his leisurely, Oscar-winning duet with her clitoris. Now all that bothered her was climaxing before Act 1 ended, the curtains came down and the house lights went up. She concentrated like a thing possessed, straining against his finger without appearing to move, trying to stop herself from collapsing in the aisle and lying there, legs spread, in complete, wanton abandonment for all to see.

'Please,' she whispered, asking for it or begging him not to?

'It's all right. Do it, babe, do it for me,' he breathed in her ear.

The finger was insistent. The scene was drawing to its close with a hymn to poetry. The pirates were kneeling, the girls were looking upwards with angelic expressions, and Jody reached such a tumultuous orgasm that she blacked out for a second.

'You're bad,' she scolded when the applause had petered out, and people were getting up and going to the bar, everyone chattering about the performance. And what about mine? she thought, ashamed yet triumphant at having achieved such a monumental come under those circumstances.

'Not at all,' Ed replied, grinning in a way that reminded her of his native kangaroos.

'Hi, Ed,' Miriam said, and Jody knew at once that she had seen what they had been doing. Trust her not to miss a trick. He nodded, stood up and escorted them to the refreshment room, stolidly organised by the WI's finest.

Jody and Miriam could not avoid the Carpenters, and neither of them tried. It was Nicole who had taken objection to what they had told her. As far as they knew, no one had mentioned it to Maggie, or Ronald or Deirdre. Greg was his usual debonair self, insisting on ordering the drinks, while Maggie, immaculate in navy-blue and white, cast a piercing glance at Ed.

'Where's Clarissa?' she demanded.

'In Bath,' he answered promptly, not in the least fazed.

'I suppose she would hardly enjoy this kind of show, used as she is to the very highest quality performances,' Maggie countered, staring suspiciously at Jody who turned to Nicole, wanting to make amends.

'Hello. Wasn't it good?' she began. 'I didn't realise that your mother was such a talented flautist.'

'Thank you,' Nicole said stiffly, and slipped her hand into the crook of Greg's elbow.

Jody tried again. 'Not long now,' she observed brightly. 'Next weekend, unless anything happens to rock the boat.'

Greg's brows winged down, and he snapped, 'What are you talking about? Nothing is going to spoil our day.'

'Of course not,' Nicole stated firmly, and Jody could tell by the way she hung on to his arm that she would be the most loyal of wives if the deed was done, cleaving to him through thick and thin.

It hardly seemed possible that the last time Jody had seen him he had been indulging his taste for unbridled passion in Willards dungeon. He was like one of those Regency rakes, the type who had belonged to secret societies like the Hellfire Club, practising obscenities and blasphemy, and calling themselves devotees of Satan. They, too, had been well educated and well born, using their positions of power to get whatever they wanted.

Jody was leaving the arrangements for the dénouement to Miriam and Scarlett, merely following their instructions. What they planned to do was drastic but, if it worked and there was no reason to think otherwise, it would prove devastatingly effective. Now Piers had gyrated towards Miriam, blissfully unaware that his cover had been blown. And she, that provocative temptress, was as nice as pie to him. Jody had the impression that she was not going to let this one go. Even if Greg was foiled, Piers could probably be guided by a strong woman, making his mark with the help of the power behind the throne.

All around them was the hubbub of a crowd who had come to see their own; proud parents, husband, wives or partners. A carnival atmosphere reigned, and when the bell rang for them to return to their seats for the Second Act, everyone moved off happily, eager to see the rest.

'No more mucking about,' Jody warned Ed, fanning herself with her programme as they sat down.

'*Would I?*' he asked, a picture of injured innocence but, to torment her, he ran his finger under his nose, the very finger he had used to bring her off. He sniffed luxuriantly, and his eyes were wicked – wolf's eyes, gypsy's eyes. This was a man who would never be tamed.

Out of her costume, off with the grease paint, into her own dress – and she had spent time deliberating over the choice – and on with her usual make-up, a little heavier than normal but, say, why not? It was party time!

The cast had taken numerous curtain calls, the audience had gone wild, she had received a bouquet, so had Mabel, Bernie had been clapped, Aubrey had been cheered, and the Pirate King had gone down a storm, easily the most popular character. All in all, Nanette thought as she applied a new shade of plum-coloured lipstick, a very successful venture, in more ways than one. She was hopeful. Stewart had kept touching her, off stage and on, nothing serious, just little pats, but it seemed as if his body had its own particular bent towards her, like the leaning Tower of Pisa.

Would his cock behave the same way? Straight, listing to one side, tipped up cheekily, round-headed, dome-shaped, cut or uncut? The variety that existed among male appendages never ceased to amaze her. If all went according to plan, she would be familiar with his before tomorrow dawned.

Helpers had been busy in the hall. The interlocking chairs were now ranged along the walls. A space had been cleared for dancing and the DJ had arrived, complete with assistants. His head was shaved bald as an egg, and tattooed with a big, black spider. Various piercings adorned his person, and he wore jeans and a string vest. His team set up on the stage, and were immediately besieged by a flock of teenage girls with bored faces and a disdainful air, cool cats who ogled the men on the decks.

There was a series of sound checks – weird honking and squealings and electronic distortion, but soon a cacophony rattled the plasterboard ceiling as they wound up the levels. The DJ bellowed through the mike, extolling his audience to 'Big it up for Heronswood.'

Nanette was greeted by Maggie, who shook her hand in an icy grip and offered totally insincere congratulations. Deirdre, too, was treated to a similarly patronising speech that damned her with faint praise.

'Well done, darling,' boomed Ronald, stealing the limelight. 'I told you to take up the flute again, didn't I?'

His friends who had stayed for a drink après show nodded and agreed, while Greg swept Nicole on to the dance floor where Piers waggled his pelvis and stomped around in an uncouth parody of rave dance moves. Miriam partnered him. A number of party-goers were sitting at little round tables, eating and drinking and discussing the production, but the younger ones were dancing. Nanette stared into the crush, getting more irritated by the minute as she failed to locate Stewart.

Aubrey was there, monopolised by Peggy Watts. There was no wife in evidence; rumour had it that he was divorced, had been so for years. Peggy was his staunch ally, dancing instructress supreme. He was in his element, praised and adored. What more could a man with a soul trapped in the body of a bank manager want in life, except for the courage to break the chains and head for freedom?

Every time she worked with him, Nanette hoped this would happen, but it never did. Next week he would be behind his desk in his office, meeting customers and advising them how to get the best out of their money. It was a crying shame.

'Nice one, Mum,' Jody said, coming over and kissing her. 'You should have been an actress. Wasted among horses.'

'I know my limitations,' she said, then looked at her keenly, intuition saying that all was not as it should be. 'Ready for the wedding?'

'I'm staying at the cottage this week. Miriam has to go back to London.'

'Good. Then you and me can catch up. It's all been such a rush – the show, preparations for the bridal bash, getting ready to see Adam and Sinclair,' Nanette answered vaguely. She knew that she should be paying attention to her daughter, but couldn't.

'To say nothing of Daddy and Patricia.'

'That's right. I'll breathe a sigh of relief when Sunday comes.'

But shall I? Nanette wondered and escaped as soon as she could, perambulating the hall in search of Stewart. He wasn't there and her heart was like a stone.

People stopped her on the way, wanting to talk about the production, laughing and joking, while she longed to fight her way out of the well-meaning crowd.

She hadn't had much to drink, although what she now wryly termed as her 'fans' wanted to buy them for her. 'I'll be back later. There's something I must do,' she said, and extricated herself.

She needed air. It was all getting too much. The door to the entrance was open. A few smokers were standing outside enjoying what almost amounted to an illicit drug nowadays. Nanette could remember a time when holding a cigarette between ones fingers was considered the acme of sophistication.

She leaned against the wall, enjoying the breeze on her brow. It was a perfect night with a full, round harvest moon. Nanette sighed, trying to accept that Stewart had gone home and wasn't really interested in her. Then she heard a door creak open close by, and felt a hand grab her arm and pull her inside.

The corridor was dimly lit, and connected back-stage, leading to the dressing rooms and the property room that now housed wicker dress-baskets. These contained the costumes and stage props that the HOS had hired. Now everything had been folded, labelled and packed, ready for transport. Nanette was rendered speechless by the speed with which she was hustled inside.

Then Stewart pushed her against the wall and said, his voice low, 'Nanette, I've decided that this is ridiculous. I care about you. I want to be with you. How do you feel?'

She started to say gob-smacked, but restrained herself. Then it began to bubble up within her – a sort of mad, glad happiness. 'I feel wonderful,' she answered, battling with the tears thickening her throat.

'You mean you'd like to go out with me?' he said, using that endearing term thirty years out of date among adults and now only used by pre-teens.

'Yes. That's exactly what I mean,' she said promptly, and flung her arms round his neck, pulling his face down to hers. 'I thought you'd never ask.'

'And I thought I wouldn't stand a chance. You are so popular and beautiful and have so many admirers,' he replied, hugging her.

'I *wish*,' she mocked, and then they were kissing and she opened her lips and welcomed him in and, of course, there wasn't the smallest trace of halitosis or gum disorders.

She slipped into his embrace as easily as if she had always been there. He was bulky but gentle, feeling his way very carefully, not wanting to do anything wrong in this, their first serious encounter. Nanette respected him for it and her confidence soared. So did her temperature. This mating was long overdue, and she kicked the door shut.

Now she was entirely alone with him among the dress-baskets, lit by a 40-watt bulb. It was dim and warm in there, the baskets giving off the faint odour of mothballs and canework, dust and leather straps. Stewart lifted her easily and sat her on top of one of them. It creaked even more, and she thought how much noise it would make when they got down to bonking.

'We can't, can we? Not here. Not like this. Supposing someone comes in?' she said hurriedly, but she was already opening his flies and taking out a long penis that thickened and grew as she touched it.

'Then they can go straight out again,' he answered, and held her breasts in his warm palms, and took his tongue to hers again, exploring and sucking, licking and tasting till she thought she couldn't stand any more. He just had to enter her soon.

He stood between her legs. The basket was crotch level. She lay back, taking her weight on her elbows, and he pushed up her skirt and she pulled down her knickers and cast them aside. His shirt was undone over a heavily furred chest, and she foraged among the hair till she found his wine-red nipples and tweaked and circled them, making him groan. He sought hers, baring her breasts of bodice and bra, and she was proud of their largeness, knowing that he had seen them before, when she was sunbathing. This was the first time he had touched them. It was deliciously exciting. Nanette could feel that ache inside her that heralded her headlong plunge into surrender. She had imagined she would seduce him. Now the boot was on the other foot. It didn't matter one way or another, just as long as it happened – and quickly.

'God, God . . .' Stewart muttered, and worshipped her breasts with his mouth.

This made her grit her teeth in extreme delight, but it wasn't what she wanted. She gripped him by the shoulders and pulled him towards her, easing her hips upwards. The heat of his helm pressed against her sex lips, and she reached down and guided him. He slid inside her in one fluid motion and she closed her legs round his buttocks and pulled him closer till she could feel his balls tapping her anus. It was then that she remembered that neither of them had mentioned protection; possibly he hadn't even thought about it. She was tempted to imagine that his professional status would make him aware and careful. She wanted to ask him, but it wasn't the time or place. What should she do? Go for it, or take a risk?

She slid back on the basket, his cock springing out of her. He looked down, frowning and asking, 'What's wrong?'

For answer, she reached for her bag and found a condom in the side pocket. 'Nothing. Just a precaution,' and she undid the packet and leaned over to roll it down his engorged prick, working it carefully towards his tight, updrawn testicles, their weight promising as they brushed the back of her hand.

'Now you can pleasure me,' she murmured, watching him as he dropped to his knees and moved up between her parted thighs.

Tentatively, he licked the whole length of her crack, then flicked his tongue-tip over her bud, side to side but not on the tip, till she was on the point of screaming, 'Lick me there. There!'

She didn't have to beg, however. He understood, lapping at her clit with firm strokes, lifting her higher and higher, till the feeling inside her was almost unbearable and she cried out. It started at the tips of her toes and rippled up her legs and into her loins, hot as a dragon's breath. It *was* just that. Kundalini, serpent power, roaring up her spine and soaring into her brain, bringing her wave after wave of pleasure.

'Now, now. Put it in me, Stewart,' she gasped as she climaxed.

He grunted as he took her and she loved every powerful thrust, and then he gave a sharp bark and threw back his head and bared his teeth as his whole body shuddered with the force of his ejaculation.

'Wow!' Nanette exclaimed, hugging him tightly as he collapsed on her. ' "Hurrah for our Pirate King!" '

Outside, another couple were standing looking at the moon and finding love again. 'I wish it wasn't over,' sighed Deirdre, and she wanted to be with this good-natured, self-effacing man for always. Not that they had said or done anything,

'It need not be,' answered Derek.

'How can it not?' she sighed wistfully, and did not draw away when he twined his fingers in hers.

'All it takes is courage and a leap into the void,' he answered quietly.

'There's so much involved,' she said.

'Is there? Your children are grown up, and you no longer love Ronald, do you?'

'That's true. He would miss me, perhaps, in that his routine might be disrupted.'

'But he'll always have his mother. She'd be delighted to jump into the breach,' and he put an arm round her waist and Deirdre dared to lean against him and dream of a happy future.

'I want you to see Ben. You know him better than me. Tell him everything that has gone on and get him to help,' ordered Miriam before she left for London on Monday morning.

'I'll do my best,' Jody promised, putting away the breakfast things. 'But do you think anyone else should know about this? Supposing he tells Nicole?'

'He won't. Not if he's keen on her. It's up to you to put it properly. I'll be back on Friday for the last rehearsal in church.'

Jody was pleased to have the cottage to herself. It was off the beaten track, but this didn't worry her. She had a lot to think about – her career – Ed. He had said he would call her, and nip over from location if possible. He'd definitely be there for the wedding, but in his capacity as Clarissa's escort. This was galling. Jody wasn't convinced that he had made the position clear.

She wanted to be able to stand by him at the reception and for all to know that his affair with the actress was finished and that Jody was now his chosen one.

She walked through the cottage, its tranquility enhanced by the bird-song outside, and the brightness of the day and the smell of new-mown hay from Ben's fields that lay towards the moor. She picked up the phone and dialled his number. He wasn't there and his housekeeper answered. Jody left a message to say that she'd call again later.

Odd to have time to herself, and she was sure she'd soon find it boring. Usually there was work to be finished, people to see, correspondence to catch up on, but now she could do as she pleased. Towards the end of the week she would be joined by Katrina and Bobby. Nicole had taken a great fancy to them, made broody by the ever-increasing bump, and had invited them to the wedding. Jody almost wished she hadn't. The day was going to be fraught enough without additional people to witness Nicole's humiliation. It didn't matter about Greg's exposure. The more the merrier, and Miriam was poised to alert the press.

But now she really must do something to help ease Nicole's pain. She was unsettled, and didn't ring Ben again but got in her car and drove to North Farm. He was incinerating toast in the kitchen, and looked at her and said, 'Mrs MacDonald gave me your message. What's up?'

That was the thing about Ben. He was very much to the point. A man of few words and Jody was unsure of how to say what she had come to say. As before, she found him attractive and damned Nicole for her blindness. Why even consider a wide City boy when she could have the salt of the earth?

'I have to talk to you about something serious, concerning Nicole,' she began, and sat at the table.

He scraped the carbon from his toast into the sink, then buttered it, thick, golden gobbets dripping on the plate. 'Want a cup of tea?' he asked, already munching.

'Thank you. Shall I do it?'

'No. You're all right,' and he switched on the kettle and spooned tealeaves into a big brown earthenware pot. He added the boiling water and let it stand. 'Milk and sugar?' he asked.

She nodded and he handed her a mug, the contents of which resembled tomato soup. It was so strong that the spoon almost stood up in it. 'Thank you,' she said again and took a sip. It very nearly skinned her tongue. 'You like it strong?' she spluttered.

'Got to have some body in it. I often stand the pot on the Aga. It's better when it's stewed.'

Jody gave a mental shudder and was glad when he pushed a tin of biscuits in her direction. At least she could dunk them and hide the taste. They sat there in silence, and she looked him over and didn't find him wanting. His broad, tanned shoulders and muscular arms were displayed in a top without sleeves. His torso tapered to a firm waist. There was wasn't an ounce of superfluous fat anywhere: his belly was flat, his hips taut, and the length of his Levi-covered legs made her think of him rushing to her rescue – saving her from what? A fate worse than death? Lucky Nicole if he came to her aid, but would he?

'What can I do for you, Jody?' he asked in his direct way.

'It's not for me. It's for Nicole. I'll cut to the chase. Do you love her?'

His expression did not change, and she admired his

cool. His had arresting eyes but now his dark, curly lashes were lowered. 'I've known her since we were nippers,' he said at last.

'That's right. We all grew up together. That's not what I'm asking. I want to know if you love her and how much, and is it sincere and would you go through fire for her?'

He pondered on this, never one for impetuosity, then, 'I suppose I do love her like that, but she doesn't want me. Got this London chap, and is marrying him on Saturday. She wants me to go. Must think I'm made of stone or something. She hasn't a clue how I feel.'

'Would you stop her making a fool of herself if you could?'

'Of course, but she won't listen to anything I've got to say.'

'You don't have to. Leave it to us – that's me, Miriam and a friend. All we want you to do is be there, at the back of the church with your Range Rover. Will you do that?

'Not in the church, then?'

'No, and wear your ordinary gear. Don't tell anyone, but be prepared to stay away for at least a night.'

'What about my animals and the harvest supper?'

'Leave someone else in charge.' She heaved an exasperated sigh, adding, 'Do you love her or not?'

He glowered down at his hands and said, 'I love her, all right. But can't you tell me what's going on?'

'No,' Jody said. 'You'll have to take my word for it. This isn't a hoax and we aren't pulling your leg. Are you on?'

He looked up at her, and it was as if a cloud had been lifted from his face. 'You mean we might prevent the wedding and she'll come round to loving me after all?'

Jody nodded vigorously. 'That's the scheme. Can I count you in?'

'You certainly can. Just tell me what to do,' Ben replied.

'You're not to breathe a word to any one. Not Nicole. Nobody. I'll keep in touch, and tell you where to be and what time.'

'OK, ma'am!' and Ben saluted smartly.

Jody left shortly after, popped into Heronswood to gather together ingredients for a meal, then went back to the cottage and started to prepare it. She was expecting Ed. One thing all this had taught her was that she wasn't going to ignore the window of opportunity, determined that her life should be full on.

13

'I'll never forgive Ben Templeton for letting his cows loose. They ruined the lawns and borders,' Maggie fumed, standing at Nicole's window and glaring down. The emergency team of gardeners hired at great expense had done their best, but it wasn't the same.

'I'm sure it was an accident. He wouldn't have deliberately done anything that might have harmed his girls, like letting them out on the road on their own,' Nicole said, wrapped in a bath-towel, having just stepped out of the shower. It was six o'clock in the morning and Tony would be arriving with his cohorts at seven.

He would fix the bride's hair first, and this would take ages, and then one of his assistants would see to her make-up. She wouldn't put on her dress till later and he would be there to arrange her veil and tiara. Jody and Miriam were due to arrive at nine and last of all, Deirdre and Maggie in wedding array, including hats, which meant that Tony's handiwork would be hidden from view. The ceremony was at noon, but the preparations had to be started early, in case of hold-ups.

Everything was ready, planned to the last detail, the groom's gifts to the bridesmaids and pages already distributed, the presents on display at The Hollies, the limousines booked for 11.20, the photographers primed, and the bouquets due to be delivered from the florists. Leigh Grove was bedecked and garlanded and the caterers were already slaving away in the kitchens. The cake was a triumph, festooned with icing sugar roses and topped by a miniature bride and groom.

The small attendants were with their parents who would convey them to the church, for which Nicole was relieved. The run-through last evening had been a nightmare, for they were tired, over-excited and fractious. Their mothers, grim-faced and flustered but incapable of uttering the magic word 'no', or administering a sharp slap, had sworn that they would behave on the morrow. Nicole wasn't so sure.

'Let it go,' Jody had whispered to her, in her supportive role of bridesmaid. Miriam was there, too, but Nicole was ill at ease with them now, poised to defend Greg should they start.

The hen-party had been modest and sober, forty-eight hours before the wedding. Nicole had feared that someone would order a kissogram, some handsome, semi-nude stud hired to embrace her in public. This hadn't happened, and the event had fallen rather flat with Nicole leaving early. The spontaneity had gone, everything spoilt between her and those who had once been her dearest friends. Greg had stayed in London for his stag do, and Nicole deplored these silly customs that might once have been apt, but were now a waste of effort and money.

Time was all over the place. It dragged, yet seemed to fly by. She slipped into her new white silk underwear, adding an antique necklace, a frilly azure garter loaned by Clarissa, and a bracelet that had been her mother's, following the tradition of 'something old, something new, something borrowed and something blue'.

Her stomach felt hollow, but she couldn't eat. What an ordeal, she thought. Does Greg feel as nervous? Will Piers have the rings? Oh, God, there's a hundred and one things that can go wrong. Not with Gran at the helm, she comforted herself, at least I can rely on her. But even she was jittery because her divorced husband would be at the church. He was eighty and molly-coddled by his two sisters who thought the sun shone out of his backside and blamed Maggie for the break-up of the marriage.

Nicole's brother, Jeffrey, had flown in yesterday, made much of by their father. She had so little in common with him that it was as if they had sprung from different wombs. He was a chip off the old block, a dead-ringer for his father and grandfather. Nicole found him intimidating, though Greg and he got on like a house on fire, having met last year. He was staying at The Hollies and had brought an anaemic-looking girl friend with him. Apparently she was most frightfully clever and a partner in his business. Nicole wondered if she had crept into Jeffrey's bed after everyone was asleep, having been circumspectly placed in one of the guestrooms. Maggie disapproved of pre-nuptial hanky-panky. No chance of that for Nicole. Greg had spent the night at the Yew Tree, chaperoned by Piers.

It's me that can't communicate with Jeffrey, Nicole sighed, and I just don't have the knack of putting people at ease. Lack of confidence, I suppose. I hope this will improve when I'm married, and she stared at the barely recognisable image of herself in the mirror. Dress on, train adjusted, veil in place, bouquet in her hands, dripping with stephanotis, carnations, roses and a deli-cate fern called Baby's Breath, and she stood there like a waxen doll. It was hard to believe it was herself.

Katrina and Bobby had only just got up. They were lounging around in the kitchen, while Jody and Miriam prepared to depart for the appointment with Tony.

'Enjoy yourselves, you two,' Miriam said. 'And don't be put off if anything unusual happens.'

'Didn't you say something about Scarlett coming?' Katrina asked, a much softer version now impending motherhood had sandpapered the spiky edges.

'I did, but you're not to breathe a word. She stayed in Bath last night,' Miriam said.

'Didn't know she knew Nicole. You, yes. You've a thing going between you. But why is she here?' Katrina asked, avoiding coffee or cigarettes and drinking orange juice.

Jody smiled across at her, having changed her mind and happy to have this friend around on what was going to prove a traumatic time. 'Don't worry. We know what we're doing.'

'Then it's a first,' grinned Bobby. 'You're shot away, you two. It's like you're on the wacky baccy twenty-four hours a day.'

'You'll be glad of us as your birthing partners,' Jody said firmly. 'Me and Miriam, medicine women and midwives – it'll be tribal. See you at the church. Caio.'

'OK. Your back-up will be there.'

'I hope Scarlett comes,' Jody said, in the passenger seat of Miriam's runabout.

'Everything is cool,' Miriam assured her, adjusting the wing-mirror.

'Oh, fuck, why can't this be a regular wedding, where we could have enjoyed ourselves and been happy for Nicole?' Jody exclaimed, not looking forward to the next few hours.

'It's the Fickle Finger of Fate,' Miriam declared in sepulchral tones. 'You know what this means, don't you?'

'What?'

'My plans for seducing the ushers, the sidesmen and

every other loose bachelor there have gone down the tube. We'll have to make ourselves scarce after the balloon goes up. The lynch mob will be after us.'

The scene was dazzling. Like something out of a happy-ending feel-good movie. It almost took Jody's breath away and she had kidded herself that she was an urban sophisticate, cynically immune to churches and bells and well-wishers armed with confetti.

She stood with the other attendants outside the ancient place of worship, waiting for the arrival of the bride. The shadowy entrance was busy. There was a lively atmosphere of anticipation. Greg and Piers were already inside. Ushers in morning suits, white carnations in their buttonholes, were coping with new arrivals, checking the guest list, making sure that the Carpenters' friends sat on one side of the aisle and the Crawfords' on the other. There weren't so many of his, and Jody assumed that he'd been reluctant to invite his London cronies. They probably knew too much about him. His relatives were thin on the ground, too.

It hurt to see Ed escorting Clarissa, though he had warned Jody of this. She was glamorous in wild silk and the paparazzi were circling like predators. Ed's words kept ringing in Jody's head from his phone call last night: 'It's over. I've told her. It's you and me from now on, kiddo.'

Music drifted under the Norman porch, the organist filling in till the given signal. Jody edged forward and peered inside. The congregation fidgeted and whispered, and the ladies had striven to out-do one another. Their heads, in large hats, kept craning round occasionally to see if there was any sign of the bride. Jody caught a glimpse of Nanette, wearing a flowing caftan in defiance of bridal ensembles. She was arm in arm with the dentist, and cocking a snook at Allan and his wife, and her sons were supporting her, too. Deirdre's friend, the oboist, was in the pew beside them. And there, sitting by Bobby and giving her a little wave, was Katrina in her customary hip gear, the short skirt stretched round her belly that was the shape of a Christmas pudding.

Jody heard the purr of an engine and then saw the sleek white limousine pull up, the chauffeur leap out and open the rear door. The crowd that had gathered in the road that skirted the churchyard clapped and exclaimed as Nicole stepped out, accompanied by her father. The music changed to the Bridal March from *Lohengrin*, and Jody couldn't stop repeating the parody under her breath.

'"Here comes the bride, fair, fat and wide. There is no room at the bridegroom's side."'

Now they were ready, Nicole a vision in white gauze and satin, carrying a cascade of flowers and wearing a full train that brushed the ground for yards behind her. The bridesmaids took their places, the little girls carrying posies and crowned with floral wreaths, the boys manly in tuxedos, with bow ties. Miriam and Jody walked together, ready to hold Nicole's bouquet when she took her vows and the ring was slipped on her finger, though they prayed it would never get that far.

The rest waited, poised for action under the warm sun. It couldn't have been more perfect weather, and Jody's wayward brain kept repeating, '"Happy the bride the sun shines on today."' If only!

Then the procession started to move. The guests rose. A sigh rippled round the nave, coming from the breasts of women who saw themselves as brides, either in the past or future. The smell of the church filled Jody's nostrils: flowers, must, age, and the strong aroma of piety. It was always the same, be it weddings, christenings or funerals, anathema to her, raising goosebumps on her skin. She looked past Nicole and saw the group at the altar through a blur of light flooding from the stained glass windows. Her attention sharpened, then centred on Greg, suave in a black morning suit, with a damask waistcoat and cravat.

Nicole came to rest beside him at last, leaning on her father's arm. There was the rustle of silk as her train was arranged (Jody's and Miriam's duty) and then the vicar, resplendent in his robes, began the service.

The acoustics were marvellous, though designed long before the invention of the microphone so that the priest could be heard in that vast space. Hymns, selected by Maggie mostly, words, prayers, more words. Where the hell was Scarlett?

'This man and woman, united in holy wedlock.'

Holy deadlock, Jody thought, if something doesn't happen soon.

Now he came to the passage where anyone was advised to speak if they knew of a reason why the marriage should not take place. The church seemed to be suspended in a time/space capsule. The congregation held its breath, though convinced nothing would happen. It was an impossibility in their closely structured circles, besides which, the bride was the mayor's daughter!

Then the main door crashed open, light pouring through and silhouetting the figure that stood there like an avenging angel. Everyone turned and looked. The vicar appeared to be dumbstruck. Jody knew a moment's heady triumph, and Miriam reached for her hand and squeezed it.

'I know a reason why this marriage should be stopped,' shouted Scarlett, advancing on her high heels.

She wore a full-length black leather trench coat belted at the waist, and there was a girl on either side of her dressed in furs, and the entrance was crowded with the reporters, photographers and cameramen from HTV's *News West*. They had been on duty anyway, but this was a heaven-sent bonus for them. Just for a fraction of time, Jody's eyes met Ed's and he gave her the thumbs up.

A horrified gasp arose, and all eyes remained glued to Scarlett and her companions as they marched up the aisle, passing the attendants, ignoring Piers and the bride and bearing down on Greg.

He turned a muddy shade of grey as she stood in front of him, unbuckled her coat and shrugged her arms out of it. Beneath it she wore a black bustier, black briefs with zips in appropriate places, suspenders, net stockings and thigh boots.

Her companions took off their coats and appeared in their pole dancer's gear, braless, with minute thongs cupping their sex, and the highest of high stilettos. They were blond and brassy and bold, posing before the altar. One carried a red album and a whip, and the other a laptop.

'What the hell are you doing here?' Greg croaked.

'Will someone tell me what's going on?' bellowed Ronald.

'What is the meaning of this?' thundered the vicar, as the congregation erupted into gasps and whispers.

'It means that you, Gregory Crawford, are a fraud and a liar,' Scarlett announced clearly, then turned to Nicole, asking, 'Did he tell you that he frequents S and M clubs and that I am his dominatrix? Did he say that he likes to be whipped – like this?' and she snatched the implement from her colleague's hand and cracked it with a force and violence that echoed beneath the fan-vaulted roof. 'Did he confess that he'll bed anything under the sun, man, woman or dog? He's not fussy where he puts it if it will aid his advancement.'

The congregation had been thrown into pandemonium. 'Please, ladies and gentlemen, keep calm,' pleaded the vicar, then he addressed the bride, the groom and Scarlett's posse, saying, 'I think it would be better if we discussed this in the vestry.'

'What are you inferring?' Ronald demanded, scowling at Scarlett.

'How dare you interrupt the wedding, you trollop!' Maggie shouted, descending on her like a Fury.

'Wait till you hear what I have to say,' Scarlett retorted, calm in the circumstances.

'Oh, Nicole, my poor darling,' said Deirdre, trying to hug her, but she was as if turned to stone, ashen-faced and mute.

'Into the vestry,' urged the vicar, then addressed the confused audience. 'Stay in your seats, please. I'm sure this is some silly prank,' and he signalled frantically to the organist who started to play soothing music.

Greg strode ahead, a muscle twitching at the side of his mouth, and Piers shuffled after him, head and eyes cast down. Jody was afraid that she and Miriam were going to be excluded but Nicole turned to them at the vestry door and spoke for the first time.

'I want them here,' she said.

Inside the vestry, the pole dancer with the laptop fired it up on its batteries and launched a disc they had brought along. Soon, images the like of which had never been screened in Heronswood's centre of Anglican worship filled the screen. 'Sorry about the quality,' Scarlett observed. 'It was filmed in my flat, but you won't have any difficulty recognising Greg. That's him there ...

bollock naked and tied to my bed while I give him a taste of the lash.'

The vicar winced.

'You bitch!' Greg ground out.

'I know you, don't I?' Nicole said in that dead, flat voice.

'We met in the Jacuzzi,' Scarlett answered. 'You told me you were engaged to this creep and I was sorry for you. Jody, Miriam and me set this up. They tried to warn you about him.'

'I wouldn't listen,' Nicole replied.

'You were in love ... still may be, but I hope not.'

'Don't listen to her, Nicole,' Greg shouted.

'I don't have to. I can see. You could have told me, explained why you need this kind of thing,' she answered, and Jody admired her control. She had expected tears and recriminations, but Nicole was possessed of an unusual calm.

'It won't make any difference. I'll give it all up once we're married.' He was clutching at straws.

'You think I'll marry you now?'

'And do you imagine for one moment that I'd let her?' Ronald said, trying to put a protective arm round her. She moved aside.

'Oh, come on, mayor. Do you really expect me to believe that you don't have dirty habits that you keep secret?' Greg mocked, sneering as he glanced round at everyone and added, ' "Let he who is without sin cast the first stone." '

'But what are we going to do? The guests ... the reception ...' Maggie blurted out.

'That doesn't matter,' Deirdre exclaimed. 'It's Nicole's happiness that is at stake.'

'And what are you getting out of all this, Scarlett? A

fat wad of money? You're nothing but a mercenary whore!' Greg shouted, fists clenched, a vein throbbing in the centre of his forehead. If looks could have killed, she would have been dead at his feet.

'I've seen justice done,' she said, and pouted her poppy-red lips at him, giving the whip a flick. 'You're well on the ropes this time, Greg.'

Behind her, the disc still played and the real whip was joined by the sound of the recorded one, striking his bare flesh while he groaned in pain/pleasure.

'It's disgusting. Turn it off,' ordered the vicar. 'What do you want to do? Shall we return and complete the ceremony?'

'After this? And you call yourself a man of God,' Deirdre cried.

Jody had moved to the outer door of the vestry, and now she opened it to admit Ben. 'Nicole,' he said and went to her, taking her ice-cold hands in his. 'I've always been here for you. The Range Rover is outside. Come with me. Stay in Heronswood, where you belong, not where that decadent rabble hang out.'

'Nicole, don't!' said her grandmother. 'He let his cows run amok in the garden.'

'You'd rather see me married to *that*?' Nicole retorted, pointing at Greg.

'It would be much better. Think of the scandal, and in front of my ex and his bitch sisters, too. We can say that there was a misunderstanding, but that it's all right now. The wedding and reception can go ahead,' Maggie gabbled, wanting to cover it up, to hide and lie, anything to prevent people knowing that the wedding of the year was a fiasco.

'Over my dead body,' Deirdre averred stoutly. 'Tell her, Ronald, tell her it's off.'

Nicole looked towards Ben and the door and freedom,

threw her bouquet on the floor, picked up her train and said, 'What are we waiting for? Let's go.'

Nicole was beyond tears. She sat in front of the Range Rover beside Ben, high above the road, as he drove from the church, the crowds, the guests, her parents – and Greg.

Her veil was still in place, her satin skirts hitched up, and those beautiful shoes of which she had been so proud were already muddied and totally unsuitable for such a vehicle. She had left the church without a ring, and still unwedded. There was the engagement one, of course, that glittering circle of diamonds and sapphires. She wanted to drag it off and toss it out of the window.

'Keep it. He owes you something. Sell it, and I'll buy you another. I got your cases from the hotel,' Ben said, staring straight ahead.

'Who put you up to this?' she demanded.

'Jody came and saw me about it. She didn't say why, just told me to get your things and be there, at the vestry.'

'Is that all?' There was a numbness within Nicole's chest, an appalling pain in her heart, and she felt physically sick.

'No. Not quite all. First of all she asked me if . . .' He hesitated.

'If what?'

'If I love you,' he said sullenly, as if the words were being torn out of him with red-hot pincers.

This gave her pause for thought, and clarified something that she had always known but rigorously denied. 'And do you?' she asked, as they left Heronswood behind and hit the open road.

He said nothing for a while, and she looked at his hands on the wheel, relaxed, easy and in control. He was dressed in blue jeans and a white T-shirt, and his tan was deep and coppery, his sinewy arms strong, his neck ridged with tendons. He smelled fresh and clean, his brown hair slicked back and damp from a recent shower. A musky male scent breathed out from his pores, stirring her senses.

'Well? Do you?' she insisted, and rested a hand on his knee. She felt him start, and was amazed at his reaction and the power this gave her. She had never felt powerful with Greg.

He still refused to look at her or answer, concentrating on the secondary road they now took. She had no idea what was happening or where he was taking her. She hoped her mobile, handbag and personal effects were in the cases.

'I should be married by now, enjoying the reception and looking forward to my honeymoon!' she suddenly burst out, and the tears started, running down her cheeks and dripping on to the gorgeous lace corsage of a dress that had cost thousands of pounds.

'I know,' Ben said, as village after village flashed by, and now they were heading West, having joined the motorway that led to Cornwall. 'Look here – no pressure, but I've got a mate near Redruth who'll put us up for a couple of days, just till the uproar dies down. I've rung him and he say's it's OK.'

She was throbbing with hurt inside; the whole thing was like some horrible dream and yet the signs had been there, but she had been too stupid to see them or to listen to the advice of her friends. 'I can't believe that I've been such a prat,' she said huskily.

Ben handed her a tissue, his very silence acting like balm on her bruised spirit. Her head ached and both shoes and dress were uncomfortably restrictive. She wanted to get out of them and dragged off her veil and headdress. 'Can't we stop somewhere?' she asked.

'Not yet,' he said, and drove on, steadily, carefully and without a trace of road rage.

Nicole wasn't aware of the passage of time. All was a blur, shot through with stabbing pain when she re-ran the scene in the church; Scarlett and those two dancers, and Greg recognising her and unable to deny her accusations. She looked back over the months and it was as if a blindfold had been taken from her eyes, revealing his fabric of lies.

They had turned on to a minor road, and fields lay on either side between scatterings of houses and hayricks. She supposed she must have fallen asleep for a while for her neck was stiff and she had pins and needles from being too long in one position. The FWD left the tarmac and bumped over ruts as it traversed rough ground and came to rest outside a barn.

'Oh, thank goodness!' she sighed as he came round and helped her out. 'I need to pee. It this your friend's place?'

'Not quite. Not his house anyway, but the land belongs to him. I'd thought we'd hole up here and have something to eat. Mrs MacDonald packed a picnic.'

'Oh, so she knew all about this, did she?' Nicole said indignantly. 'Seems like everyone knew, except me.'

'She didn't know, only that I was driving down to see Pete. Come inside.'

She shook her head, lifted her skirt high and trudged round to the back. There was no one about for miles, or so it seemed, and she squatted in the lee of the barn, muttering as she passed water, 'My God, that's worth a thousand pounds!'

She returned to the entrance, wondering if she could get out of this now ridiculous bridal wear and into her own clothes. Ben was inside, and had already opened the picnic basket and spread the contents on a straw bale. 'I'd like to change,' she said. 'Can you fetch out my bags?'

'Have something to eat first,' he insisted, holding out a packet of sandwiches. She realised how hungry she was.

'These are delicious,' she said, munching hard boiled egg and mayonnaise crammed between slices of crusty white bread.

He unscrewed the top off a vacuum flask and poured tea into plastic mugs, adding milk and sugar. 'I didn't bring wine, as I'm driving.'

'That's cool,' and she accepted a slice of pork pie, and was suddenly glad that she wasn't sitting in the banqueting room of Leigh Grove, facing the guests and listening to Piers give a fatuous speech, followed by one from her father. It hurt like hell, but she was beginning to realise that she had had a lucky escape.

'Greg's rotten,' she said quietly.

Ben kept his peace, and she was pleased that he did not take this opportunity to traduce his rival, if that's how he saw him. He still hadn't voiced his feelings for her. More tea, and then they lay back against the straw that was bound into mighty stacks in the barn, with smaller ones that made comfortable couches. The sun was sinking, casting long shadows through the doors, and the air was hay sweet and the sounds those of the country.

'I don't think you'd have been happy in London,' Ben remarked, and she suddenly quivered in response to the timbre of his voice.

'Maybe you're right,' she replied, and wanted him to hug and comfort her, but he still hadn't said it. 'Ben,' she went on, and eased a little closer to him. 'When Jody asked you if you loved me, what did you say?'

'I said yes, I do love her, but she's not in love with me,' he muttered, avoiding her eyes.

'Not true. I've always loved you. You're my friend,' she protested.

'Not like you loved him. Not in that way, not like you want to go to bed with me,' he growled, and this made her want to prove to him, and herself, that it wasn't so.

The isolation of the barn, the sunset glow of evening, the adventure on which she had embarked with him, the heartbreak she was sustaining, all combined to rouse her into a sort of desperate need to show that Greg wasn't the be all and end all. 'Come here,' she whispered and opened her arms to him. 'Come to me, friend, and soon, I think, lover.'

'Will you marry me, Nicole?' he asked.

'One step at a time, darling,' she answered. 'But yes, most likely I will.'

She didn't bother about protection as Ben, unable to believe his luck, unwrapped her from the intricacies of the wedding gown, laying her naked before him, adoring her, kissing, stroking and familiarising himself with her breasts, nipples and those folds between her thighs. And when the moment came for him to possess her, pressing his solid organ into her virgin passage, condoms were far from her mind.

Anyway, it was high time North Farm was filled with babies, the sooner the better.

'Bloody hell! What a to-do!' Jody said, blowing out her cheeks as she collapsed on the settee in the cottage and took off her shoes.

'I thought it was a hoot,' Ed chuckled, and sprawled beside her, full-length with his head on her lap.

'You're creasing my frock,' she complained, but not meaning it. What did she care for aubergine bridesmaid's dresses? The whole thing had been a farce.

'Take it off, then,' he said, and began to do just that, getting her out of the offending garment that she had never wanted to wear in the first place. He laid it carefully over a chair, adding, 'You never know when you might need it again.'

'It'll go to the nearest charity shop. I'm not getting involved in this kind of carry-on again.'

'Quite right,' he agreed solemnly, furling his tongue tip over a nipple that he had released from its strapless brassière. 'Where's Miriam?'

'Keeping tabs on Piers, I guess. Greg rushed off in high dudgeon after Nicole's brother planted one on him.'

'I saw that. The whole thing was so bloody funny. Clarissa was furious because the press didn't give her a second glance once they'd got wind of it. Does this mean we've got the place to ourselves?' And he ran a hand up her leg, found the stocking top and eased round it, his fingers brushing her bush. Little electric shocks darted along her nerves.

They had been drinking champagne. There had been a real muddle when Nicole decamped with Ben. The reception had been paid for and there seemed no point in wasting it, so those guests who wanted to, and that meant the majority, trolled off to the Leigh Grove Hotel and started to wade into the food and drink. The wedding party, with the exception of the bride and groom, joined them, and no one blamed Jody and Miriam. By this time, Jeffrey and Greg had exchanged hot words and Greg had sustained a black eye. He and Piers has taken themselves off.

Scarlett and her troupe had left, after giving detailed interviews to the press. It would be tomorrow's headlines and next day's chip-paper. It seemed that Greg's career had been nipped in the bud. 'But, he's not the type to give up,' Jody said, opening Ed's shirt and fondling his chest. 'He'll let it die down, then be up to his tricks again, conning some other poor woman into thinking that he loves her.'

'It will only last so long,' Ed said, grabbing her hand and tucking it down the front of his chinos. 'He won't always be the charming playboy.'

Jody no longer cared what happened to Greg, just as long as he kept out of her way. Miriam intended to associate with Piers, but she was following her own agenda. She was made of sterner stuff than Nicole, and Piers would be very much under the thumb. But now she had her own future to plan, and, with Ed's trousers undone and his cock in her hand, she rather wanted this situation to go on – and on.

'I'm going to Los Angeles at the end of the month,' she said, leaning over him and breathing on his swollen helm. 'Work, you know.'

'I'll come with you,' he murmured, under the spell of her clever fingers and busy mouth.

She relinquished his cock long enough to ask, 'How so?'

'I've finished filming here. Clarissa can go screw herself, which she probably will until she finds another man. I have contacts in Hollywood, but how long are you staying?'

'Not long,' she admitted. 'Then it's back to England. And you?'

'Who knows? I lead a nomadic existence, but maybe it's time to settle down,' he answered, then sat up and hauled her to her feet. 'We'll work something out, but now, I want to screw you legless. The sight of you looking all prissy and holier-than-thou in the church made me horny as a billy-goat. Let's take advantage of this peaceful old cottage and go to bed.'

Why not? she thought as, with his arm around her waist, she climbed the oak stairs. I have a good feeling about this. Ed and me? Yes, it could work, and if it doesn't? Well, I'm solid enough to take care of that, too.

Visit the Black Lace website at
www.blacklace-books.co.uk

LOOK OUT FOR THE ALL-NEW BLACK LACE BOOKS – AVAILABLE NOW!

All books priced £6.99 in the UK. Please note publication dates apply to the UK only. For other territories, please contact your retailer.

HARD BLUE MIDNIGHT
Alaine Hood
ISBN 0 352 33851 2

Lori owns an antique clothes shop in a seaside town in New England, devoting all her energies to the business at the expense of her sex life. When she meets handsome Gavin MacLellan, a transformation begins. Gavin is writing a book about Lori's great-aunt, an erotic photographer who disappeared during World War II. Lori gets so wrapped up in solving the mystery that she accompanies Gavin to Paris to trace her ancestor's past. A growing fascination with bondage and discipline leads her into a world of secrecy and danger. **A contemporary story of erotic delights that explores the sexual underground of wartime Paris.**

DOCTOR'S ORDERS
Deanna Ashford
ISBN 0 352 33453 3

Helen Dawson is a dedicated doctor who has taken a short-term assignment at an exclusive private hospital that caters for the every need of its rich and famous clientele. The matron, Sandra Pope, ensures this includes their most curious sexual fantasies. When Helen risks an affair with a famous actor, she is drawn deeper into the hedonistic lifestyle of the clinic. **Naughty nurses get busy behind the screens!**

WICKED WORDS 9
Various
ISBN 0352 33860 1

Wicked Words collections are the hottest anthologies of women's erotic writing to be found anywhere in the world. With settings and scenarios to suit all tastes, this is fun erotica at the cutting edge from the UK and USA. The diversity of themes and styles reflects the multi-faceted nature of the female sexual imagination. Combining humour, warmth and attitude with imaginative writing, these stories sizzle with horny action. **Another scorching collection of wild fantasies.**

THE AMULET
Lisette Allen
ISBN 0 352 33019 8

Roman Britain, near the end of the second century. Catarina, an orphan adopted by the pagan Celts, has grown into a beautiful young woman with the gift of second sight. When her tribe captures a Roman garrison, she falls in love with their hunky leader, Alexius. Yet he betrays her, stealing her precious amulet. Vowing revenge, Catarina follows Alexius to Rome, but the salacious pagan rituals and endless orgies prove to be a formidable distraction. **Wonderfully decadent fiction from a pioneer of female erotica.**

Black Lace Booklist

Information is correct at time of printing. To avoid disappointment
check availability before ordering. Go to www.blacklace-books.co.uk.
All books are priced £6.99 unless another price is given.

BLACK LACE BOOKS WITH A CONTEMPORARY SETTING

☐ ARIA APPASSIONATA Juliet Hastings	ISBN O 352 33056 2
☐ THE RELUCTANT PRINCESS Patty Glenn	ISBN O 352 33809 1
☐ WILD IN THE COUNTRY Monica Belle	ISBN O 352 33824 5
☐ THE TUTOR Portia Da Costa	ISBN O 352 32946 7
☐ SEXUAL STRATEGY Felice de Vere	ISBN O 352 33843 1
☐ HARD BLUE MIDNIGHT Alaine Hood	ISBN O 352 33851 2

BLACK LACE BOOKS WITH AN HISTORICAL SETTING

☐ PRIMAL SKIN Leona Benkt Rhys	ISBN O 352 33500 9	£5.99
☐ DEVIL'S FIRE Melissa MacNeal	ISBN O 352 33527 0	£5.99
☐ DARKER THAN LOVE Kristina Lloyd	ISBN O 352 33279 4	
☐ THE CAPTIVATION Natasha Rostova	ISBN O 352 33234 4	
☐ MINX Megan Blythe	ISBN O 352 33638 2	
☐ JULIET RISING Cleo Cordell	ISBN O 352 32938 6	
☐ DEMON'S DARE Melissa MacNeal	ISBN O 352 33683 8	
☐ DIVINE TORMENT Janine Ashbless	ISBN O 352 33719 2	
☐ SATAN'S ANGEL Melissa MacNeal	ISBN O 352 33726 5	
☐ THE INTIMATE EYE Georgia Angelis	ISBN O 352 33004 X	
☐ OPAL DARKNESS Cleo Cordell	ISBN O 352 33033 3	
☐ SILKEN CHAINS Jodi Nicol	ISBN O 352 33143 7	
☐ EVIL'S NIECE Melissa MacNeal	ISBN O 352 33781 8	
☐ ACE OF HEARTS Lisette Allen	ISBN O 352 33059 7	
☐ A GENTLEMAN'S WAGER Madelynne Ellis	ISBN O 352 33800 8	
☐ THE LION LOVER Mercedes Kelly	ISBN O 352 33162 3	
☐ ARTISTIC LICENCE Vivienne La Fay	ISBN O 352 33210 7	

BLACK LACE ANTHOLOGIES

☐ WICKED WORDS 6 Various	ISBN O 352 33590 0
☐ WICKED WORDS 8 Various	ISBN O 352 33787 7
☐ THE BEST OF BLACK LACE 2 Various	ISBN O 352 33718 4

BLACK LACE NON-FICTION

☐ THE BLACK LACE BOOK OF WOMEN'S SEXUAL FANTASIES Ed. Kerri Sharp	ISBN O 352 33793 1	£6.99

To find out the latest information about Black Lace titles, check out the website: www.blacklace-books.co.uk or send for a booklist with complete synopses by writing to:

Black Lace Booklist, Virgin Books Ltd
Thames Wharf Studios
Rainville Road
London W6 9HA

Please include an SAE of decent size. Please note only British stamps are valid.

Our privacy policy
We will not disclose information you supply us to any other parties. We will not disclose any information which identifies you personally to any person without your express consent.

From time to time we may send out information about Black Lace books and special offers. Please tick here if you do <u>not</u> wish to receive Black Lace information. ❏

Please send me the books I have ticked above.

Name ....

Address ....

....

....

....

Post Code ....

Send to: Cash Sales, Black Lace Books, Thames Wharf Studios, Rainville Road, London W6 9HA.

US customers: for prices and details of how to order books for delivery by mail, call 1-800-343-4499.

Please enclose a cheque or postal order, made payable to Virgin Books Ltd, to the value of the books you have ordered plus postage and packing costs as follows:

UK and BFPO – £1.00 for the first book, 50p for each subsequent book.

Overseas (including Republic of Ireland) – £2.00 for the first book, £1.00 for each subsequent book.

If you would prefer to pay by VISA, ACCESS/MASTERCARD, DINERS CLUB, AMEX or SWITCH, please write your card number and expiry date here:

....

Signature ....

Please allow up to 28 days for delivery.